WOLF IN SHEEP'S CLOTHING

Ellis began to make his way down the corridor, moving quietly while Crell Moset spoke.

"Hello, Sekaya. I'm flattered that you recognized me. I must have made quite an impression. No, no, dear, don't struggle, you'll hurt yourself and I'll have to sedate you."

"And that just wouldn't be any fun at all, would it, Chakotay?" Ellis said, stepping inside. He couldn't help grinning as he saw Chakotay's dark eyes dart from his face to that of the real Andrew Ellis, stuck in a stasis chamber.

"It wouldn't be any fun at all." And this was the moment he had been waiting for, the moment when Chakotay, after so many years, would finally understand. He let his features shift, blur, rearrange themselves into a face Chakotay had known well, so long ago.

"Arak Katal," breathed Chakotay.

STAR TREK VOYAGER®
ENEMY OF MY ENEMY

SPIRIT WALK, BOOK TWO

CHRISTIE GOLDEN

Based upon STAR TREK®
created by Gene Roddenberry
and STAR TREK: VOYAGER
created by Rick Berman &
Michael Piller & Jeri Taylor

POCKET BOOKS
New York   London   Toronto   Sydney

This book is a work of fiction. Names, characters, places and incidents are products of the author's imagination or are used fictitiously. Any resemblance to actual events or locales or persons, living or dead, is entirely coincidental.

An *Original* Publication of POCKET BOOKS

POCKET BOOKS, a division of Simon & Schuster, Inc.
1230 Avenue of the Americas, New York, NY 10020

STAR TREK is a Registered Trademark of Paramount Pictures.

This book is published by Pocket Books, a division of Simon & Schuster, Inc., under exclusive license from Paramount Pictures.
All rights reserved, including the right to reproduce this book or portions thereof in any form whatsoever. For information address Pocket Books, 1230 Avenue of the Americas, New York, NY 10020
ISBN 978-1-4516-2333-8

First Pocket Books printing December 2004

10   9   8   7   6   5   4   3   2   1

POCKET and colophon are registered trademarks of Simon & Schuster, Inc.
Manufactured in the United States of America

For information regarding special discounts for bulk purchases, please contact Simon & Schuster Special Sales at 1-800-456-6798 or business@simonandschuster.com
Cover design by John Vairo Jr.

*This book is dedicated
to those who have done battle with darkness,
of any sort,
and emerged whole.*

Many blessings.

Chapter 1

COMMANDER ANDREW ELLIS LIFTED HIS THUMB off the small button concealed in the soil. He regarded Captain Chakotay and his sister, Sekaya, as they lay sprawled on the chalk image his partner had drawn. Unconscious, both of them. Excellent. He pressed a second button, then rose from his kneeling position and dusted off his hands.

It took only a few minutes for his . . . servants . . . to arrive. They were largely silent as they approached, their presence revealed only by the soft swishing of their massive legs through the long grasses. He surveyed them with approval.

It could be said they were humanoid in shape, but only vaguely so. Standing well over two meters tall, they had grossly overdeveloped chests and arms, and

CHRISTIE GOLDEN

their mouths were crammed full of sharp teeth. Rusty orange fur covered their bodies, crowned by a ridge of spines that crested along their backs. Small, bright black eyes peered out at their master through thick falls of hair. One of them began to salivate in anticipation; a long rope of drool hung from its lower lip. Their scent was musky and rank, all the stronger for their present state of excitement.

"You," Ellis said, selecting two at random, "take these two to the center." He indicated the fallen bodies of Chakotay and Sekaya. "The rest of you, pay attention to me."

He raised his hand and pointed his third and index fingers to his eyes, as he might with a dog he was trying to train. Their eyes fastened on his obediently.

"You will find four people in uniforms like this one wandering about. You will attack them."

One of the creatures roared its approval and began to jump about happily. "Silence!" Ellis cried, irritated. The creature quieted.

"You are not to kill them. Understand?"

They looked disappointed. One of them whimpered.

Ellis continued. "You are to chase them, frighten them, hurt them *if you must,* but I will be very, very angry if any of them dies. I will find the one who did it and kill him or her. Understand?"

They grunted.

"Good. Now. Go and have fun."

The creatures scattered, chittering and hooting,

eager to perform so pleasant a duty. The two chosen to bear Chakotay and Sekaya lumbered forward, easily picking up the limp bodies in their powerful arms.

Ellis watched them go. Delight was warm inside him. It was all going according to plan. There'd been a slight glitch when Chakotay had unexpectedly decided to follow regulations regarding the away team, but Ellis had recovered. After some quick thinking, he'd been able to lure not only the human captain to the planet, but his sister as well. His Cardassian ally would be so pleased.

He followed his creatures as they walked to a seemingly solid boulder and passed easily through. It had been difficult to convince them they could safely walk through something their eyes told them was solid. Eventually, though, they became familiar with the holographic illusion. Now Ellis followed them down the rough stairs carved into the rock. He couldn't wait until Chakotay awoke.

Lieutenant Devi Patel loved the sciences. She practically romanced them, sometimes to the exclusion of less intellectual attachments. The only pain her passion for science had ever caused her was at the Academy, when she had been forced to choose a field of specialty. She wished there were such a thing as a "generalist." Even after choosing biology, she had taken a staggering number of extra courses in other fields to the point where she was practically an expert in all of the sciences.

She had decided, reluctantly, to let medicine be one

3

of the fields she could bear to part with. She'd never felt drawn to be a healer, but rather an explorer. She had an insatiable curiosity that had gotten her into trouble more than once, and a peculiar blend of cheery optimism and logical intellect that had gotten her out of most of the tight spots in which she'd found herself. During her first assignment, aboard the *U.S.S. Victory,* she had been given the nickname "Fearless." She wasn't sure if it was appropriate. Patel had always associated "fearless" with "heroic," and she certainly never felt heroic. She just was almost always, in any situation, more curious than afraid. The universe was full of scientific wonders and marvels, and her brain automatically snapped into that mode rather than *get me out of here.*

This planet, actually, was rather boring from a scientific viewpoint. She'd spent her free time on the trip here analyzing the data Marius Fortier and the other colonists had collected, and it was pretty standard Class-M stuff. While as always there were interesting variations on things, such as a new strain of orchid or arachnid, there was nothing startling or amazing or wondrous. Still, she had her tricorder out and was analyzing it intently. Who knew but that something exciting and unusual might register and she would be the one to—

Patel took a swift breath and her eyes widened as she stared at the tricorder.

They were enormous, mammalian, bipedal—

And heading right for her.

*　*　*

This was such a beautiful planet, Lieutenant Harry Kim thought as he strode toward the center of the colony, which had been designated as the rendezvous point. No wonder Fortier and the others wanted to return. He wondered if they would indeed still want to resume colonization of the place, now that they knew there were no survivors among the colonists who had chosen to stay behind.

He wished that hadn't been the case, and hoped at least that they would be able to find the colonists' bodies and give them a proper burial.

He crested a slight ridge and looked down at the group of buildings nestled in the valley. What was the word he was looking for? Pastoral? Bucolic? Either would do. It wasn't quite a rustic farmland of the eighteenth century or anything like that—Fortier and his friends certainly didn't eschew the benefits of technology—but the little town that lay before him had an aura of simplicity about it that made him want to walk its streets and sit and watch sunsets by its lakes.

Kim made his way down the hill, stepping sideways now and then to avoid stumbling on grass still slick from the recent rain. He looked again at the little square and suddenly saw something that made the scene look decidedly less bucolic—the fallen bodies of security officers Brendan Niemann and Kathryn Kaylar.

He had put away his phaser while he descended the slope. Now he pulled it out again and started running down the hill, his eyes glancing around for whoever or whatever might have done this.

Kim never saw the enemy that had stalked him silently and now launched itself at him from behind.

Patel had two instruments in her hands—her phaser and her tricorder. She thumbed a button on the latter and lifted the former, but she had underestimated the creature's speed. It sprang on her even as she fired and her shot went wild. Her small body fell beneath the creature's weight, and the tricorder flew from her hand.

The beast weighed several hundred kilos, and she felt her ribs crack. Ignoring the pain, her arms pinned, she squirmed stubbornly beneath it, staring up at its small dark eyes and muzzle crammed with teeth.

Carnivore, she thought in a detached part of her mind. She felt hot breath on her face and smelled rotting meat. *Yes, definitely carnivore.*

Patel braced herself for the crunching of those sharp teeth on her unprotected throat, but it didn't come. She and the creature locked gazes for the span of a few heartbeats. Saliva dripped onto her cheek.

Then, as suddenly as it had attacked, it was gone. Patel gasped for breath and wished she hadn't as the pain redoubled. Through the agony of each inhalation, she wondered: *Why didn't that thing kill me?*

"Sekky, are you all right?"

Oh, good, thought Ellis. *They're awake. That should*

make this more fun. He looked over at his companion, grinned, and inclined his head in the direction of the lab. His companion nodded and stepped briskly down the corridor toward their captives. Ellis waited, timing the moment.

"What happened?" Sekaya still sounded groggy.

"An excellent question, and one we'll be happy to answer."

Ellis smiled at Sekaya's gasp as she recognized the Cardassian. He wanted to see her reaction himself but knew that the moment would be sweeter if he prolonged it.

"You! You son of a *bitch!*"

Ellis raised an eyebrow in surprise. *Do you kiss your brother with that mouth?* he thought, amused. He began to make his own way down the corridor, moving quietly while Crell Moset spoke.

"Hello, Sekaya. I'm flattered that you recognized me. I must have made quite an impression. No, no, dear, don't struggle, you'll hurt yourself and I'll have to sedate you."

Now.

"And that just wouldn't be any fun at all, would it, Chakotay?" Ellis said, stepping inside. He couldn't help grinning as he saw Chakotay's dark eyes dart from his face to that of the real Andrew Ellis, stuck in a stasis chamber.

"It wouldn't be any fun at all." And this was the moment he had been waiting for, the moment when Chakotay, after so many years, would finally understand. He

7

let his features shift, blur, rearrange themselves into a face Chakotay had known well, so long ago.

"Arak Katal," breathed Chakotay.

The shape-shifter who wore the face of a Bajoran freedom fighter shrugged. Its earring danced with the movement. "Among others," he said.

"Suddenly it all makes perfect sense," said Chakotay. "I never could figure out why a Bajoran would want to betray the Maquis."

"That's been bothering you for a while, I know," said Katal/Ellis. "Glad I could solve that little mystery. But I didn't bring you down here just to reminisce. I've been looking for you for quite some time, Chakotay."

With each second that passed, Chakotay's thoughts grew clearer. He remembered now that it had been Katal who had sent him on his last mission as a Maquis—the mission that had forced him to hide in the Badlands, where his ship had been snatched by the Caretaker. Chakotay had operated from Tevlik's moon. As he had told Admiral Janeway, had he not headed for the Badlands in an attempt to evade the clutches of Gul Evek, he knew that he would have died at the massacre along with so many others. Being lost in the Delta Quadrant had probably saved his life.

"You sent me away," he said to the shape-shifter. "Into the Badlands. Did you know about the Caretaker somehow?"

"Of course not," Katal responded. "That would have

defeated the whole point. I just wanted you captured, Chakotay. Not dead, not abducted by some super-being and whisked seventy thousand light-years away—just safely captured by a Cardassian Gul."

Without appearing to, Chakotay subtly tested the restraints. They were solid. Next to him Sekaya had fallen silent. Out of the corner of his eye he saw her staring, wide-eyed, totally in shock at what she beheld.

Stay quiet, Sekky, he thought. *Let me handle this.*

"Safely captured by a Cardassian," he repeated, "and then turned over to the tender ministrations of one Dr. Crell Moset." *Better known as the Butcher of Bajor,* he thought.

"Exactly," said Moset. "I understand that you are what your people call a contrary. That made this quite difficult for me. Did you know that you were the only inhabitant of Dorvan V who ever left the planet? And I'm a completist."

"Sorry to have inconvenienced you," Chakotay said sarcastically. He was beginning to understand what was going on. For whatever reason, Crell Moset wanted to take samples from Chakotay, to finish his analysis of the colonists of Dorvan V.

What kind of sick mind would obsess about something so trivial when his people had been so thoroughly defeated? And why would Katal be assisting him? The whole thing was bizarre. Bizarre, and disturbing. Chakotay had no doubt but that if he and Sekaya couldn't manage to escape, they would be joining Blue Water Dreamer much sooner than either of them wanted.

"Just what is it you're trying to complete?" Chakotay asked, stalling for time. "You may not know this, Moset, but our Doctor on *Voyager* created a holographic version of you. Your expertise saved a crewman's life. A friend's life."

Moset managed to look both pleased and offended when he replied, "I am indeed aware of that, Captain. And I'm aware that despite my expertise, your doctor chose to delete my program permanently. Think of the lives I—excuse me, my hologram—could have saved! Think of the knowledge we would have gained! Wandering in the Delta Quadrant for seven years, all that new information—"

Chakotay kept his gaze on the Cardassian, but out of the corner of his eye he tried to take in everything else: the size of the room, the instruments, the tools, the type of rock that surrounded them, anything that could be used as a weapon. And of course he watched Katal— damn it—the shape-shifter. Probably a Changeling, given his easy way with the Cardassian.

Who was looking at him with an odd expression on his face at this very moment.

"He's playing you, Moset," the Changeling drawled. Chakotay's skin prickled and he felt a wave of anger and hatred wash over him at the sound of that familiar voice. The voice that he had thought belonged to a friend; the voice that had spoken lies that sounded so much like truths no one ever suspected what was really going on.

"Nonsense," said Moset, but he looked a little subdued.

"Come, my friend," the Changeling said, taking Moset by the arm and steering him away. "We have much to discuss."

They stepped down the corridor, speaking in low tones. Chakotay couldn't understand their words, but right now that wasn't his primary concern.

"Sekaya," he hissed, "are you all right?"

She didn't answer at once. Then she turned her head slowly on the bed to look at him. Her beautiful eyes were wet.

"He found us, Chakotay," she said, and her normally melodious voice was thick. "Great Spirit, he found us. I thought I'd left him behind. I thought he'd taken enough from me. First Blue Water Dreamer and then Father . . . and now he's going to murder us, too."

"No, he's not," said Chakotay. Yet even as he uttered the words, he looked around at their surroundings with dwindling hope, and wondered if he would prove to be as much a liar as Arak Katal.

Chapter 2

THE TRILL DOCTOR and the Huanni counselor bent their heads over the computer screen to see the results of the latest test. Dr. Jarem Kaz felt his heart leap a little as the information appeared.

"There, you see?" he said, pointing unnecessarily. "The isoboromine levels have increased substantially."

"But they're still not quite up to normal," Astall said. She gnawed her lower lip. "Jarem, I really don't know what I'm seeing here. I'm not as familiar with Trill physiology as you are."

"Believe me, it's good," he said. "I don't need to be relieved of duty."

"Truthfully," she said, looking up at him with large

eyes, "if this were someone else, would you say the same thing?"

He smiled and nodded. "Truthfully, yes," he replied, "although I'd want whoever this was monitored."

She smiled, obviously almost as relieved as he was. Impulsively she hugged him. He tensed in her embrace, then thought, *No one else is here, to hell with propriety,* and squeezed her back.

"Now, how about that lunch?" he asked.

The being who had worn the faces of the Bajoran Arak Katal and the human Starfleet officer, among dozens, perhaps hundreds, of others during his time in the Alpha Quadrant, herded Moset down the claustrophobic halls until he was certain they could not be overheard.

"Thanks for drawing the symbol," the Changeling said. "I couldn't have done it myself. We barely had enough time as it was."

"Think nothing of it," demurred Moset. "It was easy enough to do. And you've brought me exactly what I need. What *we* need," he corrected.

"I had to bring the girl, too," Katal said.

"Oh, that's a fortuitous happenstance," said Moset. "I can certainly use her as well. It's always helpful to have a genetically similar control subject. No, no, we're doing fine, just fine."

Katal turned to the scientist. Trying not to reveal his urgency, he asked, "So how are we doing? Really?"

Moset smiled happily. "The experiments are running

exactly as I predicted. No surprises. And now that I've got a fresh infusion with Chakotay and Sekaya, we should start to see some real progress very quickly. You'll soon be your old self again."

Katal clapped Moset on the back. "I can't tell you how pleased I am to hear that, my friend. What about our other project?"

Moset hesitated. "Well, it still needs a little bit of time and thought, but it, too, is progressing well. Come. Let's see what my latest effort will do."

The scientist turned and made as if to head back to the laboratory. Katal put a hand on his arm, stopping him.

"I'm not sure I want Chakotay to know what's going on," he said.

Moset smiled. "And where do you think he might run with the information?"

Katal laughed. "You have a point."

The two returned to the laboratory. Katal looked back over at Chakotay, who had clearly just seconds before been straining at his bonds. "You're not going to work yourself loose, Chakotay, so you might as well save your strength."

Chakotay looked at him with cold eyes. *By all the gods that are worshipped in this quadrant,* thought Katal, *I've never seen hatred like this.* A smile tugged at his lips.

"Trust me, you'll want your strength by the time Moset's done with you. You know a little something about that, don't you, Sekaya?"

The brother and sister had looked a great deal alike

to him when he first saw them side by side on *Voyager,* and now they both bore identical expressions of loathing. The only difference was that Chakotay's was cold and restrained and directed at him, whereas Sekaya's was as hot as a lava flow and focused with laser-sharp intensity on Moset. Any moment now he expected her to start growling like an animal.

While he observed the two siblings with amusement, Moset had been preparing a hypospray and humming something.

"Was that what you sang when you killed Blue Water Dreamer?" spat Sekaya.

Moset turned reproachful eyes on the woman. "No one was supposed to die, I assure you," he said. "My subjects are always more use to me alive than dead. I'm sorry for your loss."

"That's the biggest pile of—"

"Sekaya," said Chakotay, sharply. She looked at him, her breasts heaving with fury, and he shook his head slowly.

"Your brother's right," said Katal. "Moset doesn't particularly enjoy inflicting pain . . . usually. But if he's pushed far enough, well, I can't say for sure what he'd do."

"Oh, do stop frightening her," chided Moset. "Here. See how this feels."

He pressed the hypo to Katal's throat. It felt cool, and the Changeling could feel the misty contents of the hypo dissolving into him. He looked at his hands, con-

15

centrated. They shimmered, briefly, but then reformed into strong, five-fingered humanoid hands.

"Nothing," said Katal, his voice soft and angry.

"How disappointing," Moset said. He glared at the cylindrical hypospray, as if the failure were its fault and not his. "Hmmm. I'm not sure what went wrong. I'll have to go back over my notes. But don't worry, once I'm able to utilize these two, we'll make great strides, I'm certain of it."

Katal continued to stare at his hands, fighting down the red rage that threatened to boil up inside him. The Cardassian was so close. And he had proven his worth in the past. The fact that the Changeling stood before him wearing the face and body of a Bajoran Maquis was evidence of how much Moset had accomplished. But he was losing patience. He had been so patient for so long, for so very long. . . .

"You're right, of course," he said mildly, forcing a smile. "Once you start working on these two, I'm sure you'll make discoveries by leaps and bounds."

Moset cocked his head. "What an interesting expression."

"It's human. I picked it up from Ellis."

"Leaps and bounds. I like it. It sounds . . . fun. Vigorous. And very visual. Yes, I'll make discoveries by leaps and bounds."

"Now, if you'll excuse me," Katal said to Chakotay, Sekaya, and Moset, "I have some work to do."

Even as he said the words, he hesitated. He had

known Chakotay for so long, even though the human hadn't realized it. He enjoyed tricking the human. Chakotay was so terribly sincere. Noble. Easily led. The Changeling was reminded of an ancient Earth practice of piercing the noses of bulls and leading them around by the ring thus inserted. That's exactly what it was like with Chakotay; a large man, powerfully built, and, what made it more fun, not stupid. Just . . . trusting. A bull. He liked that image.

First as Katal, a "brother in arms," and then as stuffy, by-the-book "Priggy" Ellis, he had gulled Chakotay into trusting and even liking him. He knew that whatever Moset had in mind for the human, Chakotay would eventually be dead. Even if he and his sister survived the experiments Moset was certain to put them through, they'd have to die at the end of it all.

And then this game he'd played for more than eight years with Captain Chakotay would be at an end. Katal regretted that, but mentally shrugged.

One must make sacrifices.

He turned and left, moving purposefully down the narrow corridors phasered out of solid stone and into a large room. There were dozens of screens here, all of them active, all of them displaying something of import to Katal. He selected one and stood before it.

"Computer," he instructed, "activate holographic program A-4."

The gray-black stones of the cavern walls disappeared as the holographic background manifested. He fiddled with the color, deciding on a kind of slate blue with a bit of green. Thinking a bit, he put some art on the walls—nothing too distinctive—and added a soft, dark blue carpeting. There. Now the room looked like dozens of nondescript, neutrally decorated formal meeting or banquet halls scattered on planets throughout the Federation.

His setting thus appropriately adjusted, the Changeling now adjusted himself. His Bajoran features broadened. His mouth stretched wide, his skin tone turned a pale orange, and his hair went from dark brown to bright red. He watched his hands as his fingers grew longer and thicker, nodding approvingly as four fingers manifested where there had previously been five. He quickly checked the mirror, making sure that everything was as it should be, then put his message through.

Amar Merin Kol appeared on the viewscreen, her eyes lighting up with pleasure at seeing him. He inclined his head respectfully.

"Greetings, Amar," he said.

"Greetings, Alamys. You are a bit late in contacting me," she chided gently.

"My apologies, Amar." He frowned, trying to look both angry and unhappy at the same time. "I was embroiled in a . . . discussion."

"Oh, dear. I had hoped it would not come to unpleasantness."

That was Merin Kol, all right. She never liked to ruffle feathers, dreaded giving offense, and yet somehow managed to drive her platform forward just the same. The Changeling thought briefly that it would be a challenge to master that attitude. A hard act to imitate, certainly, especially as Kol was genuine.

Genuine, and like so many, easily gulled.

"I'm afraid there is a great deal of . . . unpleasantness . . . these days," he said, sighing. He rubbed his cheeks, where a cluster of nerves would be if he were truly a Kerovian, as if he were tired.

"You must be exhausted," she said sympathetically, picking up on the gesture at once. "You have served me well and loyally, Alamys—served Kerovi well. But clearly this is draining you."

She paused, looking thoughtful. "Perhaps I should recall you. There are others who can continue the discussions you have begun."

"No," he said instantly, and for a moment feared he had spoken too quickly. "No, Amar. I'd like to finish what I've begun. Some of the negotiations are tricky and a bit delicate. I have formed friendships. We have a better chance of succeeding if I stay and continue on."

"Very well. I admire your determination. But I confess I have missed your wise counsel, my friend."

"I hope I continue to give you wise counsel, wherever I am," he said obsequiously. "Now tell me, how are preparations going for the conference on Vaan?"

"As one might expect. I am looking forward to meeting Admiral Janeway."

The Changeling frowned. "I have heard she is a fine

19

diplomat, Amar. You must not let her change your mind."

Kol cocked her head. "I have not yet made a firm decision to secede from the Federation, Alamys. You know that. I will listen with an open mind and an open heart. I have no agenda, no point to prove. All I want is what is best for the people of Kerovi."

Damn it, he thought. The last time he had talked to her, she had been coming down quite firmly on the side of secession. Without the Federation hovering, he would be able to operate more freely on Kerovi. And he had many—oh, what was that human phrase—"irons in the fire" on that pretty little planet.

"Of course, Amar," he said soothingly. "I did not intend to imply otherwise. But I am somewhat confused. Do you wish me to cease discussions with these people until you have made up your mind?" It would be dangerous to return to Kerovi until everything was completed here, but it might be more dangerous not to go, if Kol was as undecided as she appeared to be.

"No." Her voice was firm, and he felt a little spurt of relief. "Continue as you have been doing. You are providing a valuable service. Much as I would like to have you by my side again, I know you're needed where you are."

She smiled a bit impishly. "And don't worry. I like Janeway a great deal, and I am looking forward to meeting her. I might even go so far as to consider her a friend. But the fate of my people is too important to be given away just to stay in a friend's good graces."

"As I have said before, you are as wise as you are beautiful, Amar." He put his hand on his chest and bowed to her.

"And you are a flatterer of the highest level, my old friend." She winked. "Kol out."

After the viewscreen went blank, he didn't immediately shift his shape. He went over the conversation in his mind. Perhaps he'd underestimated this Janeway. Knowing Chakotay as well as he did, he'd come to know Janeway vicariously. And of course, wearing the feathered face of the avian Captain Skhaa, he'd been able to download and read every one of *Voyager*'s logs, which was when he'd learned the important information about Chakotay.

At last he shook his head and with the gesture resumed the appearance of Commander Andrew Ellis. "Computer, end holographic program A-4."

He strode down the hall. Chakotay, still stalling for time, was trying to engage Moset in conversation. The Cardassian always had time to talk about himself, and Chakotay was smart enough to have picked up on it.

At any other time the Changeling would have been annoyed. But it didn't matter if Chakotay was to worm anything out of the scientist. As the Cardassian had said, he'd never be able to make any use of the information. Let Chakotay chat Moset up as much as he liked. He might inadvertently reveal something useful.

The conversation stopped as he entered, and Chako-

CHRISTIE GOLDEN

tay turned his full attention on the being who had masqueraded as an old friend and a new first officer.

He was glad; he wanted Chakotay to see this. Maybe it would shake him up a bit.

The Changeling wearing Andrew Ellis's face stepped next to the original encased in the stasis chamber. He locked gazes with Chakotay and smiled a little.

"I don't know that we'll have a chance to talk again, but I'm sure Dr. Moset will fill you in."

Before the horrified gazes of Chakotay and Sekaya, the Changeling's features bled and rearranged themselves. His skin went darker than Ellis's pale European-descended complexion; his eyes went from blue to brown. His hair changed from blond and thinning to black and short, and then finally, teasingly, the Changeling created a green pattern of lines on his temple.

Chakotay stared at himself.

The Changeling reached out to him, and Chakotay tensed. But all the Changeling wanted was Chakotay's combadge, which he fastened to his uniform with a slight wince. "So long, Chakotay," said the Changeling. He tapped a button, and he and the real Ellis disappeared.

Chapter 3

LIEUTENANT COMMANDER TOM PARIS FELT as if his brain had turned to oatmeal after his first set of briefings from Admiral Janeway and Commander Tuvok.

"Wow," he finally managed after they'd finished. "I think it would be easier for me to recite the entire contents of the Royal Protocol document." He paused. "Backward."

Janeway smiled and reached to squeeze his hand. "Don't worry. I don't expect you to remember everything, just to be a bit familiar with it. Here's a padd with all the information. You can peruse it at your leisure during the rest of the trip."

Paris glanced with longing up toward the bow of the

little vessel, where the stoic Vulcan sat at the *Delta Flyer*'s controls. "I'd rather be piloting."

"Of course you would," said Janeway, "and I'd rather be sitting where Captain Chakotay is now. But we must all make sacrifices, Tom."

Paris looked at her then. "Permission to speak freely, Admiral?"

"Of course."

"Do you miss it that much? Being a captain?"

Truth be told, he expected a quick, pat answer along the lines of "I serve at the pleasure of the Federation" or something like that. But she took his inquiry seriously, leaning back in the seat and regarding him thoughtfully.

"Actually, no," she replied. "I did at first, a great deal. But now I wonder if that was because I had to be captain for so long. Even on shore leave, over the last seven years I really never left the captain's chair. It was such an unusual situation that being captain became more ingrained in my self-identity than I think it would have otherwise. I like to consider myself well rounded, Tom. I like to think that if I hadn't been a starship captain, I still would have contributed to making my world—my quadrant, my galaxy—better, no matter what I chose to do with my life."

A little humbled by her honesty, Paris replied, gently, "I'm certain you would have."

She smiled and nodded, accepting the words. "But this is the path I chose, and it led to a very interesting seven years. So yes, when we made it home, it was a little hard to let that go. Especially considering the circumstances surrounding our return."

Paris couldn't help but grimace. That had been a bad, bad time.

"But once the dust settled, and I was able to move forward, I realized that I still have a lot to contribute to Starfleet and the Federation. I'm enjoying what I'm doing . . . and enjoying being able to pull some strings now and then to see that the right people get the right sort of opportunities."

Tom felt himself blushing.

"So," she continued, "do I envy Captain Chakotay? You bet your pips I do. I love that ship, and I loved being its captain. But you don't necessarily want to trade places with someone just because you envy them."

"I think I'm beginning to understand, Admiral."

"You will. It's one of those maturity things." She winked. "You know a tremendous amount about a great many things, Tom. And what you've undergone over the last seven years has catapulted you forward in the experience department. But a lot changed while we were gone, and we all need to make sure we're up on it."

Tom stared at the padd and sighed. "You're telling me."

Janeway continued to watch him intently. "How are you and B'Elanna doing?"

The question caught him by surprise. "We're doing great," he said, wondering where this was leading.

"How's life on Boreth?"

"It's . . . interesting. Cultural immersion."

Her lips curved in a grin. "That's one way of putting it, yes."

"It's been difficult, but if it's what B'Elanna wants, then I'm all for it. Recently we've been spending a lot of time trying to dig up some information on the scrolls that Kohlar referenced."

"About your little *Kuvah'Magh*?"

Tom grinned, slightly embarrassed. "I know it seems egotistical, but if you had a daughter who had possibly featured in another culture's savior prophecies, wouldn't you be curious?"

"Naturally. Find out anything?"

"I found out that I might want to become a vegetarian," Tom replied. "There's a little creature on Boreth called a *paagrat* that they eat *and* they use as parchment. It's pathetically adorable."

"Chakotay could give you some pointers. But honestly I can't see you settling for risotto while your pal Harry's devouring a steak."

"You're probably right."

She hesitated, then said, "You realize that if I can get you a first officer position, you're going to be away from your wife and child for long periods at a time?"

He nodded. "Of course. That's part of the job."

26

"And B'Elanna is all right with this?"

"Yes," said Tom firmly. "She's been very supportive."

Janeway smiled, gently. "Maybe because you've been so supportive of her and her needs. It's not every human male who could tolerate living on Boreth for six days, let alone six months."

Tom shrugged, a little uncomfortable with the intimate direction this conversation was taking. "She's my wife. I love her and I love Miral. Why wouldn't I do whatever she needed to make her happy?"

"That attitude is why she's willing to do the same for you," Janeway said. "Fortunately, with a little luck, you won't be gone for seven years if you are assigned to another starship."

"And thank God for that," Tom said, and meant every word.

The Changeling materialized on the surface of Loran II. Meticulous as ever, he had checked belowground, with equipment untroubled by the technology that so disturbed Starfleet's, to make sure there would be no troublesome Starfleet officers in the area to witness his appearance. He'd deal with them soon enough, but for now he needed solitude in order to complete his plans.

Lying on the ground beside him, eyes closed, pale face turned up to the sky, was the real Commander Andrew Ellis. The Starfleet officer was one of several humanoids that the Changeling kept in stasis, ready to be produced when needed at moments like this. His breathing was starting to deepen as he worked his way back to consciousness. Ellis had been in stasis for many years now; it would take him at least several seconds to revive.

Which would give the Changeling more than enough time to put his plan into action.

He hesitated as he looked down at the face that was so familiar to him. He had been impersonating Ellis for seven years now. It had been in this body that he had been—

The recollection of the lost years, of the agony of what he had been forced to endure, sent a shudder of rage and loathing through him. A second ago he had been thinking of Ellis with compassion, almost as a companion on a long, bitter journey. Now suddenly the Solid represented everything against which the Changeling had been struggling for so long, and his task, far from being a difficult one, suddenly seemed easy. Seemed enjoyable.

He had brought with him a long, sharp scalpel. It was something that was normally out of place in a high-tech science laboratory, but fortunately for the Changeling, Moset liked to utilize more "primitive" technology from time to time. And for the Changeling's purposes, a laser scalpel wouldn't quite do the job.

Ellis was coming out of stasis now. His breathing grew steady, and beneath the still-closed lids his pale blue eyes darted about. A hand twitched.

The Changeling struck. With more pleasure than he

thought he would experience, he leaned over the human and began to lacerate him with the knife. The first few cuts weren't deadly, and Ellis's eyes flew open at first shock of pain. He struggled, still groggy, still unable to coordinate the movements of his limbs in order to defend himself and save his life. He stared up into the face of a Starfleet captain, that utter shock costing him precious nanoseconds.

It was a lost battle from the beginning. The Changeling had had enough of the game and quickly darted in and slashed Ellis's throat. Scarlet fountained onto the ground as Ellis spasmed. Quickly the Changeling stepped back. He didn't want Ellis's blood on him; not yet, anyway.

It took longer than he expected for Ellis to die. Finally the human lay still. His eyes were wide open, staring at nothing.

"Good riddance," muttered the Changeling. "I was you for too long, Ellis. Now I'll never have to wear your pale, pinched face again." He was tempted to kick the body, but refrained. He had a job to do.

The Changeling imagined how he might look if he had been attacked by the creatures. Gashes on his face, certainly. On the throat, too, but not too deep. He wanted the look of a narrow escape. Nothing too extensive, nothing requiring Kaz's tender loving care upon immediate return. Just some cuts and slashes . . .

The wounds began to appear as he visualized them. Two claw marks raked his face and continued down his neck. Was Chakotay right- or left-handed? He realized he didn't know and cursed himself for not being more observant. To be safe, he created a few shallow scratches on both lower arms, as if he had held them up to protect himself.

Three across the abdomen; enough to tear the uniform and bleed a little, but nothing to arouse real worry.

Excellent.

He tapped his combadge. It was time to begin the performance.

"Chakotay to away team," he said, his voice tense but still calm, still in control. "Report."

Silence. The Changeling frowned. Perhaps his creatures had not obeyed his orders to frighten, not kill.

"Kim here." His breathing was ragged. "Captain, we've come under attack."

"I know, so have we. Any casualties?"

"Sir? Are you on the planet, too?"

That's right, thought the Changeling. "Ellis" never told them that Chakotay and Sekaya had also taken a shuttle down.

"Affirmative. I repeat, any casualties, Lieutenant?"

"Negative. Patel's been hurt pretty badly, but I think she'll make it. Niemann, Kaylar, and I were all knocked unconscious and we're scratched up. Are you all right?"

"We lost Ellis and Sekaya," the Changeling said, putting just the right amount of grief and stoicism in his voice.

"Sekaya? Oh, Captain, I'm sorry," said Kim, sincerity radiating in every word. The Changeling shook his head, grinning. They were so easy to manipulate, these Solids.

There'll be time for grief later. Where are you right now?"

"We're where Commander Ellis told us to report, at the main habitation area of the colony."

"I want everyone back to the shuttlecraft immediately. Prepare for liftoff the minute I join you. We'll have to—damn it!"

He pulled out his phaser and fired at a tree.

"Captain, what's going on?"

"I'm under attack!" It was difficult to keep the amusement out of his voice. This was simply too much fun. But he deserved a little fun, after the years of pain he'd suffered. After all the Solid nonsense he'd been forced to put up with.

"Do you need assistance?"

"Negative! Get back to the shuttle!" cried the Changeling, still firing. "Chakotay out!"

Smiling, he replaced his phaser and looked down at Ellis's body.

"Time for you to make your last journey, my friend," he said, lifting the body easily.

Brendan Niemann was treating Patel with the medikit when Kim trotted back to them. She was able to sit up now, though she looked very weak. She had obviously lost a lot of blood. Her eyes widened at the expression on Harry's face.

"The captain?" she asked.

"He's here, and he's under attack. He wants us to get back to the shuttle and he'll meet us there."

Kaylar didn't miss the fact that Kim had not mentioned anyone else. "Commander Ellis?" she asked, her voice catching slightly.

"Dead," said Kim bluntly. "And . . . and Sekaya, too. She came down with him."

"Poor Captain Chakotay," said Patel, her voice faint.

"Poor you if we don't get you to sickbay soon," said Niemann. "Can you walk?"

"I think so," Patel said, but the minute she got to her feet she went pale and her knees buckled. Fortunately, she was a small woman and Niemann was a large man. Gently he picked her up in both arms. She winced, but made no sound.

"All right, Patel?"

She nodded.

"Let's go," said Kim, and headed back toward the shuttlecraft. Inwardly he felt sorrowful and sick. He'd made fun of Ellis, along with everyone else, and now the man was dead. Killed on his first mission as first officer. And Sekaya—she wasn't even Starfleet. She'd just come along on the mission to help her brother. Kim thought bitterly that his second assignment on *Voyager* was shaping up to be at least as rough as his first.

He stayed on point. Niemann followed, carrying the injured Patel as carefully as he could and still move quickly. Kaylar brought up the rear. She and Kim both had their phasers out. Kim's nerves were strained and he tensed, ready to fire as they made their way back to the safety of the shuttlecraft, where they would await their captain and, perhaps, the bodies of their fallen comrades.

One thing Kim was certain of: the colonists' home-coming, once a joyfully anticipated occasion, had turned into a nightmare.

Chapter 4

THE MOMENTS TICKED BY, and still no sign of Chakotay.

Kim stood in the open doorway of the shuttle, phaser at the ready, scanning the area for any sign of his captain and friend. Kim was worried. The last he'd heard was that two people were dead and Chakotay was under direct attack, and the captain hadn't answered any subsequent attempts to contact him.

Two more minutes, Kim told himself. *Then we go after him. I'm not going to leave him here.*

Just as he turned, mouth open to issue the order to Kaylar to locate Chakotay's signal and start a rescue—or, he thought grimly, a recovery—attempt, he heard a sound from outside.

Whirling, his phaser in his hand, Kim saw the figure

of Chakotay hastening toward the shuttlecraft. Kim's relief at seeing his captain alive was mitigated by what Chakotay carried in his powerful arms: the limp body of First Officer Andrew Ellis.

Chakotay glanced over his shoulder as he ran toward the safety of the shuttle, indicating to Kim that the danger was still out there. He stepped aside as Chakotay hurried up the ramp into the shuttle and cried, "Kaylar, get us out of here! Now!"

"Aye, Captain," the young security officer replied. Her fingers flew over the controls and the shuttle lifted off quickly, if not exactly smoothly.

"There's no interference from the storm this time." Patel's voice drifted to Kim's ears. She sounded sleepy, and he saw how heavily she slumped against Niemann's broad chest. Kim was glad they were leaving. Patel needed more help than they could give her with the medikit.

It took a second for her words to register, and then he realized she was right. Trust Patel, possibly dying of her wounds, to be thinking about such things. There'd be time to analyze and ponder the whys and wherefores of the weather patterns on this planet later. Right now Kim was content to simply be grateful that they were able to leave so quickly.

He assisted Chakotay in placing Ellis's bloody body on the floor as gently and respectfully as possible. Chakotay looked at the face of his first officer for a moment, then reached down and closed the unseeing eyes.

"What happened?" asked Kim. He was aware that his voice was hushed.

"Probably the same thing that happened to you, from the looks of it," said Chakotay, eyeing Patel with concern. "We were attacked by several strange-looking creatures." He swallowed, then continued in a voice he obviously kept steady with an effort. "They . . . they got Sekaya first. Ellis was closest and he tried to defend her. I was the farthest away and I had the time to react, to fire on the creatures and drive them away. But by the time I reached Sekaya, she was dead and Ellis was fatally wounded."

"Captain, I'm so sorry. I don't know what to say."

"Nothing *to* say, Harry. But thank you."

Kim hesitated. "I'm glad you were able to recover Commander Ellis. But what about Sekaya?"

"I'm—I was—the closest relative she has in this area of space. According to our customs, I had the right to decide what to do with her body. I made the decision that the living were more important than the dead, that I should leave Sekaya behind in order to try to save Ellis. Unfortunately, he didn't live much longer after that."

"We can go back for your sister's body, too, if you would like. Give her a proper burial. I mean, if you want to. If that's what your tribe does." He realized he probably sounded like an idiot, but he didn't care. Chakotay knew him well enough to know the sincerity that lay behind the clumsy words.

"I know we could, but I don't think we should. We need to get Patel to sickbay. How badly injured is she?"

"I'm not a doctor, but she lost a lot of blood. We were able to close the wounds, but there's some internal damage and a few ribs are broken."

Chakotay smiled sadly. "Then once again, Harry, the living are more important than the dead."

"We could come back later," Kim insisted.

"No. I've got a lot of thinking to do before I decide whether anyone comes down here again. And those creatures . . . well, let's just say that I'm not sure what kind of shape my sister's body would be in by the time we found it."

Kim was confused. They could lock on to even a trace of Sekaya's DNA and transport whatever remains there were. Kim hadn't done much talking with Chakotay about his beliefs and tribal traditions, but he knew that the people of Dorvan V had taken their chances with Cardassian occupation rather than abandon the planet that had become their home. It made sense to him that if someone died, his or her wish would be to be taken home and buried in that place, that land that was obviously so sacred to Chakotay's people.

Maybe Chakotay was worried that it might look as if he was exploiting his position as captain. He'd recovered Ellis, but not Sekaya; granted the honor of a proper "burial at sea" for his first officer, but not for his blood sister. It was just the kind of noble gesture Chakotay would make.

But he didn't have to. It was an unnecessary sacrifice. Kim thought about arguing the point.

Chakotay touched Ellis's hand one last time, rose, and slipped into a seat beside Kaylar, taking over from her. Kim grabbed the medikit and followed.

Chakotay looked at him. "Put that away, Lieutenant," he said. "I'm fine. The wounds are superficial. Nothing that can't wait."

Kim made a little noise of amused exasperation. First Ellis, now Chakotay. There must be something about being first or second on the rungs of the command ladder that made you want to refuse medical treatment in all but obvious emergency situations.

He couldn't help but glance back at the mutilated body of Ellis. Strangely, Ellis's face seemed younger in death than in life to Kim.

A thought occurred to him. "Sir," he said to Chakotay, "what were you and Sekaya doing on the planet?"

"Ellis had found something he wanted us to see," Chakotay said. "Something he thought might be of archeological interest to us."

"What?"

Chakotay turned to Kim and there was anger and pain in his eyes. "Does it matter now?"

"No," said Kim, "I guess not. But I—"

Patel sighed softly and her head rolled onto Niemann's shoulder. The small motion grabbed Kim's attention instantly.

"She's unconscious," Niemann said in answer to Kim's unspoken question, after quickly placing two fingers on Patel's throat to check for a heartbeat.

"We've got to get her to sickbay," said Kim to Chakotay, who nodded acknowledgment.

"*Voyager* is in visual range," said Kaylar.

"Chakotay to *Voyager.*"

"Campbell here, Captain."

"Open shuttlebay doors in preparation for emergency docking. Notify Dr. Kaz that we've got wounded." He paused. "And dead."

"Aye, sir. Shuttlebay doors open."

Chakotay maneuvered the shuttle to a swift, smooth landing. The minute they touched the deck he said, "Everyone to sickbay. Let's go."

Kaz was nervous as he awaited the arrival of the injured and wondered as to the identity of the dead. He could feel Gradak just below the surface of his conscious mind; subdued for the moment, but seething, awaiting the time when he could shoot to the surface and share his torment.

You stay where you are, Kaz thought, and wondered if this was how people who were beginning to go insane felt. But no, this "multiple personality disorder" he had was not a manifestation of a traumatized brain, but a literal truth. Joined Trills *did* have multiple personalities inside them. They just didn't usually manifest quite so vigorously.

But once the sickbay doors hissed open and his eyes fell upon the limp form of Devi Patel, looking like a child as she was carried by the large Niemann, his mind snapped to attention. He needn't have worried; Gradak fell back before the medical emergency and Kaz quickly had Patel stabilized.

Once she was out of danger, Kaz turned to Chakotay. "You look like hell," he said, "all of you."

"Thanks," Kaylar said wryly.

Kaz gestured that they should all sit on the beds. Chakotay shook his head. "I'm fine."

Kaz raised an eyebrow, but a quick look at Chakotay revealed nothing dire. Chakotay could be treated last if he wanted.

"What happened?" Kaz asked as he began to examine Kaylar. "Who was . . . ?"

"We were attacked by several strange creatures on the planet," Chakotay said. "Kaz . . . they got Ellis. And Sekaya, too."

Kaz looked at Chakotay, deep sympathy flooding him. "Chakotay . . . damn. I'm so sorry." He also felt more than a twinge of guilt. *I'm sorry, Ellis. Sorry for everything.*

"I've ordered the body put in stasis," Chakotay continued. "When all this is over, we'll give him a burial with full honors."

"I assume you want Sekaya in stasis as well," Kaz said, thinking about the beautiful woman he'd met only briefly. She had all her brother's charm and charisma, and he'd hoped to get to know her better.

"I had to . . . to leave Sekaya on the planet." Chakotay rubbed his eyes and sighed.

"We can go back for her," said Kaz.

40

"Maybe later, after all this is taken care of," said Chakotay.

Kaz looked at him searchingly. Over the last six months he'd gotten to know the captain pretty well. Chakotay was under real strain right now.

"Captain," the doctor said, keeping his voice formal, "I think perhaps you ought to have a seat on one of the beds and let me examine you."

"I said I'm fine," Chakotay snapped. At once he softened. "Sorry. Treat them, Kaz. I'm going up to the bridge, and then I have to talk to Fortier and tell him his brother and the other colonists were probably killed by monsters and that I can't allow him to return to the home he and his people loved. I'm not looking forward to that."

"I understand," Kaz replied.

Chakotay started to leave, then turned. "By the way, I want you to delay the autopsy on Ellis."

Kaz frowned. "That's standard operating procedure, sir. I'm required to perform it."

"I said, delay it. We've got a lot going on right now, and there's no point in you wasting time on an autopsy. We know what killed him."

"With all due respect, Captain, we really don't know for certain what—"

"I saw it, Doctor." Chakotay's dark gaze was cold and angry. "I watched him die, firing a phaser in a futile attempt to try to save my sister and me. Sekaya was dead by the time I reached her, but Ellis—he died in

41

my arms as I tried to get him to safety. Like I said, Kaz. We know what killed him."

The door hissed closed behind him. For a moment Kaz stared at the door, then turned his attention back toward the patients.

"Hell of a first mission," Kaylar said bitterly.

Kaz nodded, slightly distracted. Gradak was stirring again, now that the emergency had passed. They shared emotions: shock at the senseless deaths mingling with anger. For Kaz, the dead were only slightly known, but for Gradak—

A wave of deep agony, of profound loss, washed over him and almost made him stumble.

"Stop it," he hissed, under his breath.

Kim looked at him. "Doctor?"

"Nothing," Kaz lied quickly, "this medical tricorder could use some readjusting." He retrieved another one to continue the pretense, although he knew there was nothing wrong with the first.

The silence was uncomfortable and heavy with sorrow. Kaz quickly treated Kim, Kaylar, and Niemann, all of whom had only minor injuries.

"What happened?" he asked.

"I'm not sure," said Kim. "It got me from behind."

"Us, too," said Niemann, and Kaylar nodded.

"Some kind of large predator, certainly," Kaz ventured. "With nice long, sharp claws." He looked at them. "You are all cleared to resume your duties." He wanted them out of here. He didn't want to risk them seeing what Astall had walked in on.

"How's Patel?" Kaylar asked, walking to the smaller woman's side and looking down at her with concern.

"I expect a full recovery in a day or two. She lost a lot of blood, and there are some internal injuries, but she'll be just fine."

The relief on all their faces was painfully obvious. They'd just lost two colleagues; they didn't want to lose another one.

"I suggest you return to your stations," Kaz said, trying to hurry them along. "Captain Chakotay will need everyone ready and alert."

"You're right, Doctor," Kim said. He gestured to the others. "Let's go, guys. You did a good job down there today."

Kaylar and Niemann exchanged glances. It was clear they disagreed with their superior, but neither said so.

Kaz exhaled and closed his eyes when the door hissed closed behind them. He wiped his forehead, feeling the skin warm and wet on his fingers.

The mission had taken a disastrous and tragic turn, and a previous host was all but taking up permanent residence inside his mind. He was more than ready for this to all be over.

Chapter 5

B'ELANNA TORRES HAD KNOWN she'd miss her husband when he left, but she hadn't anticipated missing him quite so much.

Without his jovial presence, she was forced to realize just how un-Klingon she really was. They'd banded together, the outsiders stubbornly insisting on staying in the monastery and perusing the scrolls, but now that he was gone, there was no one to share a joke with, no one to turn to when the whole Klingon thing just got old.

It wasn't that Tom had been a big help in transcribing the documents; he'd only just figured out how to write with the bone stylus, and Torres had picked it up after a couple of attempts. And, she had to admit, she was actually glad she didn't have to read everything she found aloud to him.

But she missed him, missed his warm, comforting, occasionally irritating presence. She missed having another pair of hands to hold their daughter and comfort her when the little girl squalled. She missed the physical expression of their love, passionate and sweet despite having to be performed on an animal hide on a cold stone floor.

More than anything else, she missed having someone to share her increasing suspicion that their daughter might, indeed, be the *Kuvah'Magh.*

The Scrolls of Ghargh, as Torres had discovered they were called, hadn't been touched by hands in decades, perhaps centuries. Perhaps Kohlar's ancestors, who had left this quadrant so long ago, had been the last ones to see them. They were certainly dusty enough.

She had had to specially request them, and Gura and Lakuur had made much of the fact that the mongrel was wasting their time. Although, since they were librarians, one might think they were supposed to spend their time pulling up scrolls for pilgrims to peruse. B'Elanna thought this, but said nothing.

The two had brought out a large, intricately carved, and dust-covered box. When the librarians lifted off the top, B'Elanna saw that the box was crammed full of scrolls.

"Ghargh was a heretic," Gura said. "He wanted to bring back the gods from the dead. The *Kuvah'Magh* was supposed to be the one who could do that."

45

CHRISTIE GOLDEN

Lakuur made a guttural sound in the back of his throat, and for a wild second Torres thought he was going to spit in contempt. But then, apparently, he realized where he was, and that spittle was not conducive to the preservation of old furniture and older tomes.

"Why do you wish to see these?" Gura asked. "Surely you do not truly believe your child to be a daughter of prophecy. Especially not *this* offensive, outlandish prophecy."

"Do you always interrogate pilgrims seeking knowledge in such a fashion?" B'Elanna had retorted. "Especially pilgrims who come with the blessing of Emperor Kahless?"

That had shut them up good and fast, and they mostly left her alone after that.

She'd held her breath as she touched the Scrolls of Ghargh, convinced they would crumble to dust themselves, but the *paagrat* hides upon which they were written were sturdier than they looked. The hand that had jotted down the words that had survived over the centuries had been an unsteady one, and the words were spidery and hard to read. But it was without a doubt the same author who had penned the scrolls Torres had read back on *Voyager,* and she realized she was trembling as she settled down to read.

Libby Webber materialized in her cabin and sat down heavily on the bed, trying to gather her thoughts. She was exhausted, so it was a more difficult task than usual. She got herself a cup of Vulcan mocha, extra sweet, from the replicator and sipped it slowly.

She was on the trail of a mole. A mole who was slippery, whose trails inevitably disappeared. He or she had accessed deeply personal information from a variety of sources, but there were no corresponding leaks.

Captain Skhaa, the avian who enjoyed the Vulcan lyre, had apparently been in two places at the same time: in attendance at a concert, and accessing *Voyager*'s logs from a site several light-years away. She'd spent the evening doing everything she could to corroborate Skhaa's presence at the concert, and was satisfied that he was indeed there.

Who, then, had accessed the information?

She jumped, startled, when her computer beeped. Composing herself, she touched a pad. Harry's face appeared on the screen.

A rush of pleasure rushed though her, followed immediately by worry. "Harry, what is it?"

His face was troubled, and though he managed a smile, she could sense its falseness. "Nothing I can really talk about yet. I just—I just wanted to see your face. Know you were all right."

Something bad had happened and Libby knew it. She also knew what he needed—light chitchat, giggles, warm smiles. A sense that no matter what was going on in Harry's life, she, Libby, was happy and carefree and safe. So Libby talked about the concert, about Montgomery sending flowers, about meeting her "fans." She realized that she could never tell Harry about her real life; he couldn't handle worrying about her and still do his job properly. He needed her safe and bubbly and in no danger whatsoever.

"Sounds like fun," Kim said. "You'd better make sure I'm in the front row for your next concert when . . . when I get back, okay?"

His voice cracked a little. How she ached for them to confide in each other! He was no raw recruit, not anymore. Something very bad must be going on.

"Of course, honey. I'll let you go. Love you."

When his face disappeared, so did her smile. She redoubled her efforts. A deep instinct told her that whatever was happening on *Voyager* was connected to the mole who had accessed that ship's logs.

She had to find him.

Marius Fortier sat with his head in his hands, his fingers tangled in his curly black hair.

"This world is hungry," he said in a hoarse voice. "It took my brother from me, and now it's taken your sister. Creatures, you said?" he asked, raising his eyes to look at Chakotay. "What kind of creatures?"

"We don't know, and we didn't get a chance to take any tricorder readings," the Changeling Chakotay replied. He wanted to get this over with, yet he knew that the real Chakotay would feel an empathy with this human and would take his time. He chafed at the forced kindness.

"It is likely that these . . . beasts . . . are what killed

those of us who stayed behind," Fortier continued, feeling his way to logic through his pain. "How strange this all is . . . we never saw any animals like them before. And now they have come like Death himself, out of nowhere, to take those we love. I am so sorry for your loss, Captain. Sekaya was a wonderful woman. We all felt so comfortable with her. She cared so much."

Yes, yes, we're all sorry for Chakotay and Sekaya, let's get on with this, the Changeling thought.

He stood, hoping Fortier would take the cue. "There's a saying among my people," he said, making one up on the spot. " 'Action heals the wounds.' I think it's time I took some action. We need to leave this planet and return you to Earth. Someone will help you find a new home."

Fortier shook his head. "I'm not sure that's a good idea, Captain. I understand that there are risks, but I would like to see if it's possible to recover the remains of our fallen friends and families. And see if we can't find a way to resettle and still protect ourselves from these creatures. The voices of our dead call to me."

I don't care if they're using communicators, "Chakotay" thought. He took care to conceal his irritation.

"I'll tell you what. We had to leave a shuttle on the surface. I'll be transporting down to retrieve it. I'll see what kind of readings I can get while I'm there and think about whether it's too risky to consider recolonizing. Will that be acceptable?"

Fortier considered the offer, then nodded. "I must tell you that we are still hopeful we can return to our home,

49

Captain. Despite the tragedies we have all endured." He rose and shook Chakotay's hand. "Again . . . please accept my deepest sympathies for your loss. I know what it is like to lose a beloved sibling."

"Thank you." The Changeling smiled tentatively. The smile evaporated as soon as the door closed behind Fortier. Damn the man and the typical human stubborn, "exploring" spirit. Well, it would probably be a good idea to have fake tricorder readings on hand anyway. It would silence any protest until he was able to complete his task.

He wished he could contact Moset, alert him as to his impending arrival. Probably he could contact him via Sekaya's combadge, but he couldn't risk either Campbell, the new ops officer, or Kim, the old one, detecting the transmission.

Speaking of which . . . "Chakotay to Kim."

"Kim here." The security officer was in command on the bridge while "Chakotay" talked to Fortier.

"We've got a shuttle on the surface that needs retrieving."

"Understood, sir. I'll send a security officer to pilot it back to *Voyager*."

"Negative. I'll go get it myself."

"Captain?"

"You heard me, Lieutenant. I don't want to put anyone else at risk."

A long pause. "If I may speak freely, Captain, I know that your sister's death has upset you, but surely—"

Thanks, Harry. Great idea. "Lieutenant Kim, I don't recall you arguing against my orders when I was first officer and you were ensign." It was a wild guess, but by the silence that followed, a good one. Kim had unwittingly just given the Changeling the perfect excuse for any "unusual" behavior Harry or anyone else might notice—distress and grief over the death of his poor, beloved Sekaya.

"As you wish, of course, sir. Do you want to inform Starfleet Command, or shall I do so while you're getting the shuttle?"

Damn. "Chakotay" hesitated. "Neither, Lieutenant. When I get back, we'll be returning directly to Earth." He hadn't told Fortier that, but who cared?

"Sir?" Kim's voice actually cracked on the word. "*Voyager* has just lost its first officer!"

"Mr. Kim, I'm getting tired of your insubordinate attitude." The real Chakotay hadn't exaggerated very much when he'd talked with "Ellis." He really had to have been a more casual leader than the Changeling had thought if Kim felt bold enough to protest so often. "We've all just been through a lot. I don't want to have to relieve you of duty. Is that clear?"

"Absolutely, sir. We'll maintain orbit and wait for your return, and make no contact with Starfleet Command or Admiral Janeway until you give the order."

"That's what I like to hear. Notify—" "Chakotay" paused. What the hell was the new transporter officer's name? Stefan? Stefaniak, that was it. He couldn't recall

51

the man's rank. "Notify Stefaniak that I'll be heading for the transporter room."

"Aye, sir. Kim out."

The Changeling sighed. This was much harder than playing "Priggy" Ellis. Nobody here knew Ellis, other than by reputation. And frankly, that reputation had been created by the Changeling himself. He'd been trapped in Ellis's body for so long, he'd practically invented who Andrew Ellis had become. This was much different. Chakotay was well known by a sizable portion of the crew, including several senior officers. The Sekaya excuse was handy, and he'd milk it for all it was worth. But he had to be careful, too. If he strayed too far away from the essence of Chakotay, the troublesome Kaz would relieve him of duty.

A wave of longing and nostalgia washed over him. Solid for so long . . . for too long . . . the memory of the Great Link, the sensations, the powerful feeling of union, was fading with each day. He wondered if he'd ever be able to return. He dismissed the wistful thought the instant it occurred. Even if Moset was able to completely solve his problem and he could contrive to get back to the Gamma Quadrant, he would not be permitted to partake in that union.

As humans would say, to hell with them.

If he could no longer be a part of something greater than a single entity, then he would embrace his uniqueness. There was no Changeling like him anywhere.

When he could, when this was all done, he'd design

a special shape to inhabit. He'd pick a name for himself. He'd have his own power instead of this borrowed kind; his own troops and servants and lackeys to carve out a niche in this quadrant that would be his and his alone.

Until then his goal, as it had been for nearly eight years, was to again become what he once had been.

He gathered his thoughts and headed for the transporter room.

Kaz was in his natural environment with a patient to treat and monitor, and for that he was selfishly grateful. Gradak had stepped back, for the moment, and Kaz's thoughts were clear and focused.

Patel had been pretty badly injured. She had several broken ribs, a bruised lung, and a ruptured spleen. Fortunately, no irreversible damage had been done, and he was able to successfully heal the injuries. Sleep was the best thing for her now. Since things were quiet in sickbay for the moment, Kaz had decided not to continue sedating Patel. She'd wake up on her own, and when she did, he'd send her off to her quarters for a few days to recover.

He watched her sleep, pleased to see the normal color returning to her round cheeks and the steady rise and fall of her chest. As he regarded her somewhat paternally—he couldn't help it; the Kaz symbiont always made him feel older than and protective of his friends and patients—his eye fell to the tricorder she still clutched in her small hand.

She'd let her phaser go, but not the tricorder. What was so important that she kept such a tight grip on it even when she was unconscious?

Gently, so as not to awaken her, he tried to maneuver her little fingers off of the instrument. She stirred at the movement and her eyelids fluttered open. A slow smile spread across her face.

"Hello, Dr. Kaz," she said drowsily.

"Hello yourself, Lieutenant," he replied, grinning back. "How do you feel?"

She didn't answer at once, but took a deep breath instead. "Decidedly less in agony."

He helped her sit up. She still held on to the tricorder. "Do you remember what happened?" he asked, reaching for his medical tricorder to take another scan.

"We took the shuttle down to the planet, and then we separated. I remember thinking that Loran II was going to be pretty boring. There was nothing about it that set it apart from other Class-M planets."

"Except for something large and furry and clawed, apparently," said Kaz. He nodded his head as he examined the tricorder readings. She was fine.

Her eyes brightened. "Oh, yes, they were quite intriguing!"

"They did a pretty good job squashing you and almost killing you, Patel," he said. "I'm not sure I'd call that intriguing."

"Oh, but they were!" A look of panic appeared fleetingly on her face, then she relaxed as she realized she still held the tricorder. "I got some good readings." She handed him the instrument. "You might be interested in taking a look yourself."

Patel looked so eager, so hopeful, that Kaz succumbed. "Certainly," he said. "Thank you."

"You're welcome. I'd be analyzing it myself first, of course, but somehow I've got a feeling that you're about to tell me to return to my quarters and not do any work for a while."

"Why, you didn't tell me you were a telepath, Lieutenant."

"Not at all. I just had several years of premed. I assure you it's not what I want to do, but I trust you'll notify me if you run across anything interesting."

"Indeed I will. Do you think you'll be able to rest, or shall I give you a sedative?"

"I'm still pretty tired," she confessed. "I'll be fine. I'll let you know if I need anything."

As she slipped off the table and walked out of sickbay, Kaz found himself wishing all of his patients were so willing to follow doctor's orders. He looked at the tricorder, smiled a little, carefully set it down, and returned to finishing his report on Patel's injuries.

She was tiny, fair-haired, with the biggest blue eyes he had ever seen. Eyes that he could easily drown in. When she had first joined his crew, he thought she wasn't even big enough to hold a phaser rifle. But she'd proven him wrong, time and again. That delicate-seeming frame housed a passionate and fiery spirit.

*She'd fought on Bajor, as part of the resistance, and re-
fused to be content with simply driving the Cardassians
from her homeworld. That wasn't enough. She joined
the Maquis, to track the Cardassians down wherever
they might be terrorizing other worlds, other people.*

"Vallia," Kaz said, his voice deep and hoarse with
emotion.

As if she were physically present, he could smell her
scent, a combination of sweat and the metallic tang of
the weapons she always carried and her own unique
fragrance; felt the brush of soft, full lips on his—

Kaz made a fist and slammed it down. Vallia was
dead, that much he knew from Gradak; was dead,
was the lover of someone else, not him, not Jarem
Kaz. . . .

Gradak had backed off when there were injured requiring treatment. He'd respected the needs of others
that much, at least. But now that there was nothing to
really occupy Kaz's thoughts, Gradak had come right
back again, settled down in Kaz's tall, strong body as if
he belonged there.

Kaz looked again at Patel's tricorder with a renewed
appreciation for the information it contained. Patel had
managed to take some scans of the creatures. Maybe
analyzing the data would be enough to send Gradak
back into a sulky retreat.

Kim and the others hadn't been able to tell him
much. Chakotay might have gotten a better look at the
creatures, but this was clearly not the time to ask him.

There wasn't much Kaz could surmise from the injuries alone.

It would occupy his thoughts. And it was better than seeing and feeling the lithe, lost Vallia in his arms.

"Computer," he said, his voice trembling but sounding in his ears like his own again, "transfer data from the tricorder to main computer."

Chapter 6

THE CARDASSIAN TURNED as she entered the lab. Sekaya looked around curiously. She'd never seen so much technology crowded together in one place in her entire life. She had no idea what most of it was for, and she was almost dazzled by its colorful shininess.

"I'll be right with you, just a moment." The voice was pleasant, soothing, and the Cardassian speaking threw her a quick, benevolent smile. Some of Sekaya's defensiveness abated. This was the first time she had met the head scientist of the project, Crell Moset. She had previously only interacted with lab technicians, underlings who made little attempt to hide their arrogance and scorn. This man radiated a different attitude entirely.

Her people had always been blessed—or cursed, depending on how one looked at it—with an insatiable curiosity about the world around them. Maybe this Moset shared that sentiment. Maybe there really wasn't anything sinister going on, just a scientist and his inquisitiveness.

Musing on the nature of this man and his possible sense of curiosity helped take her mind off of Blue Water Dreamer. He had promised to show up at her father's hut last night, ready to sing the chant of Asking, headdress in hand, prepared to formally court her. But he hadn't appeared. She wondered if she'd done something to annoy him, displeased him in some manner. As soon as the thought came, she dismissed it. They'd loved each other since childhood, though they hadn't realized it and neither of their tribes would have wanted them to marry. Probably he'd wandered off somewhere and simply lost track of the time. He'd done that before; time seemed to mean little to him when he was caught up in his flute playing or quietly observing birds and animals. That would be more like him than mysteriously and silently being angry with her.

"Have a seat." The Cardassian looked her full in the eye and smiled. She found herself smiling back. "I'm Dr. Crell Moset." He extended a hand, and after a brief hesitation Sekaya shook it.

"We've been told who you are," she said cautiously, still feeling him out.

"And I'm sure you're wondering what it is that we want," he said. She didn't answer, just gave him a look.

"Would it make you feel better or worse to know that I'm not sure what we want?"

Sekaya had to laugh, charmed by his forthrightness. Maybe her instincts had been wrong.

"I respect your honesty, Doctor."

"And you've avoided my question entirely. A diplomat in the making, I see."

"What were you singing? I heard it coming down the hall."

He looked slightly abashed. "An aria from a Cardassian opera. It's based on a story rather like your human tale of Beauty and the Beast."

"I'm not familiar with that," Sekaya said. "But we do have a story about a girl who falls in love with a bear."

"There are similarities across all cultures, it seems. In this tale a young woman is kidnapped to be the wife of a powerful man. She expects to be ravaged, but instead he woos her gently, and she falls in love with him."

"A happy ending, then." Sekaya wondered if they were talking about more than stories.

"I love happy endings, but unfortunately they seem to be few and far between in opera. Tragedy makes for better theater."

He nodded to two of his assistants, who stepped forward and, to Sekaya's shock, began to fasten her to the chair in which she was sitting. She gasped and tried to bolt out of the chair, but they were too quick. Frightened and furious at the same time, she gave Moset an angry, accusatory look.

"So sorry my dear, I'll make sure they're not too tight. It's just that some patients inadvertently move during the proceedings, and this prevents anything like that from happening."

Quickly he stepped forward and pressed a hypo to her throat. Suddenly she couldn't feel anything.

"There we are," said Moset kindly. He felt at her restraints and loosened them a bit. "I'm keeping them on just in case the medication wears off before I'm through."

Sekaya was utterly paralyzed. She couldn't even move her eyes or close her eyelids. She felt her tongue relax against the back of her throat and with a burst of terror wondered if she would choke on it. Moset was looking at her with concern, somehow wanting her approval for what he was doing.

Blue Water Dreamer was supposed to meet with the Cardassians the same day he was to come to Kolopak's hut. Great Spirit, *thought Sekaya,* has this sick man imprisoned him?

Killed him?

Tears welled in her eyes at the thought and spilled down her cheeks. At once Moset dabbed at them with a soft cloth, looking unduly distressed.

"There, there, dear, please don't cry, I don't mean to frighten you. Don't worry, I'll make sure you keep breathing and that your heart continues to beat. Poor child. I'd sedate you if I could, but we really must be able to monitor your brainwaves while you're conscious or else we will have gone to all this trouble for nothing."

61

She watched him, her eyes fixed and staring, as he moved in and out of her range of vision. Humming something. She heard the snip of scissors or shears, she couldn't tell which, and then the buzz of a razor.

"I like the older tools," Moset was saying, as if she cared, as if she wasn't terrified and helpless and being violated. "I like the contact. I think modern medicine and research has wandered too far away from that sort of intimacy between doctor and patient."

In and out of her field of vision he drifted, reaching in to touch her skull, his fingers coming away red, humming, humming the song about the frightened maiden, and then came the descent of agony, not blocked by the paralysis—

Sekaya gasped and tried to bolt upright, slamming painfully against the restraints.

"Sekaya!"

Chakotay—

It took a few seconds for her to remember. She was not aboard Moset's ship in orbit about Dorvan V. She was with Chakotay, her brother, deep underground on a distant world. Sekaya lay back, trying to gather her thoughts and not let the primal terror overwhelm her. Moset was not a fool. She'd need all her wits about her if she and her brother were to get out of this alive. Even as she had the thought, another came hard on its heels: *But you're not going to get out of this alive.*

She looked around. They were alone, for the moment. "Where is he?" she asked.

"I don't know," said Chakotay, keeping his voice soft. "He left just a few moments ago."

She turned to look at him. Part of his head was shaved and there were glowing inserts implanted in his skull. Sekaya couldn't feel hers, but she was willing to bet she had them, too. She suppressed a shudder.

"Sekaya, was this what he did to you on Dorvan V?" Chakotay asked.

"Among other things." She took a deep, steadying breath. "Have you learned anything?"

"Not much," her brother replied. "Sekky, this is important. Did he perform an analysis on everyone on our world?"

She nodded. "Everyone. He seemed most interested in those from our tribe, though. But even new mothers were required to bring in their infants. The only person he didn't get was you, because you weren't there."

"He knows about the Sky Spirits," said Chakotay. "Both of them do. Ellis—Katal—the Changeling used the *chamozi* as bait to get me down here." He laid his head back down on the bed.

She couldn't tear her eyes away from the blinking green and blue lights in his skull.

"So much makes sense now. Ellis seemed a bit upset when I ordered him to lead the away team, which puzzled me at the time. That decision was by-the-book regulations. He ought to have been delighted. When I made it clear that I wasn't planning to visit the surface, he had to think of another way to get me here."

He turned to look at her again. "Sekaya, I'm so sorry I dragged you along. You shouldn't be part of this."

"It's all right," she said, and meant the words despite her terror. "I can help."

Chakotay sighed. "I'm not sure anyone can." He paused, his face thoughtful. "Our doctor created a holographic simulation of Moset."

"Yes, I remember you said that."

"It was based only on the information we had at the time. There was a lot about Moset we didn't know, that we found out later."

"How close a version was it, do you think?"

"Very close indeed. The simulation had an ego. He liked to think of what he did as heroic, as advancing the sciences and helping people. He was a classic example of 'the end justifies the means' thinking."

Sekaya recalled Moset's face hovering over hers, concerned that she like him and approve of what he was doing even as he sliced into her brain.

"Yes," she said, her voice cold. "That sounds about right."

"Something's wrong with the Changeling," said Chakotay, continuing to share his thought process with her. "I heard Crell say something about him soon being his old self again. I wonder if he's infected with the disease?"

Sekaya shook her head. "Chakotay, there's so much

going on here that I'm not at all familiar with. I mean, we heard about Changelings. That they were also called the Founders, and pretty much the ones who led the Dominion. I know the Vortas and the Jem'Hadar thought of them as gods."

Chakotay nodded. "But even gods can die. Starfleet created a bioweapon—a disease that would kill all the Changelings. There was one Changeling who grew up, for lack of a better word, in the Alpha Quadrant. His loyalties stayed with the Federation. He was cured, and after the war he went to the Great Link and spread the cure among all the Changelings.

"But if this Changeling didn't get back to the link," Chakotay continued, "he may still have the disease."

"And Moset's a doctor," Sekaya finished, following her brother's train of thought. "He brought Moset in to help him."

"That's a good theory, but maybe not the only one. It could be something else."

"I know what Moset did to us," Sekaya said. "But it sounds like he's done a lot of other things, too."

Chakotay chuckled humorlessly. "He didn't get the nickname the Butcher of Bajor for nothing. Are you sure you want to know?"

"Yes. I do."

"He used to be chairman of exobiology at the University of Culat and won the Cardassian Legate's Crest of Valor. He liked to use live subjects for his experiments, and during the occupation of Bajor, hundreds died because of those experiments."

Sekaya made a small noise in the back of her throat. When her brother paused, she said quietly, "Go on."

"He exposed subjects to nadion radiation, to observe how they died. He blinded people to watch how they adapted to their disability. He's known for curing the fostassa virus, all right, but only because he infected hundreds of Bajorans with it."

Sekaya turned her head so he wouldn't see the tears in her eyes. *Blue Water Dreamer . . . oh, Great Spirit, was that how you died?*

"The *Enterprise* captured him during the war. He was performing experiments on Betazoids—trying to see if he could create a telepathic race of Jem'Hadar."

Sekaya inhaled swiftly. "That's a terrifying thought."

"The worst part was, he succeeded. Thank goodness the Jem'Hadar couldn't handle all the sensory input. Everyone thought he was killed when Picard had him transferred to another ship and that ship had a warp core breach. I think it's pretty obvious now that the breach was a ruse by the Changeling to liberate Moset."

"What's in it for him?" Sekaya asked abruptly. "Why is he doing this for the Changeling? You said it's been years since Katal freed him."

"That I don't know. Maybe a sense of honor; he's got one, though it's twisted. Maybe he feels he owes Katal something for freeing him."

Sekaya shook her head. "I think it's more than that.

There needs to be some powerful reason Moset hasn't trumpeted his return from the dead."

"Being a Cardassian mass murderer doesn't have quite the cachet it did when the war was still going on," Chakotay reminded her.

"No, but . . . he has an ego. When he . . . experimented on me, he wanted me to be all right with whatever he was doing. He wanted to stick these things in my head, to slice open my skull, and for me to *like* him for it." The words were like ash in her mouth. Her stomach clenched and for a moment she thought she was going to be sick.

"That rings true with what I saw of the holographic simulation," Chakotay agreed. "Katal knows he's committed murder. That he's doing things society calls evil. He doesn't give a damn. But Moset always wanted to explain himself. So what about spending three years helping a Changeling heal? Gratitude only goes so far."

"I wonder if Katal has something on Moset, to force his cooperation."

"Again," Chakotay countered, "the man's a mass murderer. It's hard to think of something worse than that to hold over someone's head."

"Sorry. I guess I'm not much help after all."

"Sekky, look at me." She did so and saw her brother gazing at her with love in his eyes. "You're my sister and I love you. I'm sorry you're in this situation, but not sorry for your company."

She forced a smile past the fear in her heart. A noise

67

in the corridor brought that fear back full force. Then the sound that chilled her, that had haunted her nightmares for years, filled her ears and turned her blood to ice:

Pretty little maiden, why do you weep
When delight and joy surrounds you?
Fear not, fear not, for the Lord of the Keep
Has wonders to astound you,
Has wonders to astound you.

Chapter 7

ONCE, when Tom Paris was very, very young, he had been permitted to attend an important social function. An ambassador from a planet whose name he tried to block from waking memory even now had specifically extended the invitation to Tom. It seemed that the presence of sons, particularly those who had not yet reached puberty, were considered quite a blessing among this species. Clearly, the son of one of Starfleet's most famous admirals would bestow much good energy upon the gathering.

Tom remembered his mother fussing over him as he dressed, trying to get a recalcitrant cowlick to stay in place, running after him so that he wouldn't spill something on his formal suit, going over manners and eti-

quette until he rolled his eyes. He remembered transporting into a room that seemed bigger than his whole
house. Columns of blue lusarite held up incredibly high
ceilings that seemed to stretch for meters. The carpeting was so thick that he sank about a centimeter in it.
Mirrors, gold trim, statuary, burbling fountains of the
pink celebratory liquor, an alien version of champagne,
all served to dazzle the young Paris's senses and make
him feel tiny and lost.

He hated feeling tiny and lost. So he did what he
normally did when he felt that way.

He misbehaved.

Tom quickly detached himself from his parents and
hooked up with a bored-looking Andorian kid about his
own age. Before Tom really quite knew what was happening, he, the Andorian kid, and a human girl whose
name Tom never learned but whose fragile beauty hid
a wild interior, were splashing in the fountain of the
pink liquor, having consumed sufficient quantities of
the stuff so that this seemed like the logical thing to
do.

His father went through the roof, but when Tom and
his parents transported home, Tom was so sick from the
alien alcohol ("Sorry, Dad, it tasted like raspberry ice
cream") that Owen Paris decided that the crime was its
own punishment.

Tom had since learned to enjoy alien alcohol. Sometimes quite a lot. But he'd always stayed away from
anything pink.

The memory of that ignominious incident flashed in his mind as he, Janeway and Tuvok, all clad in their dress uniforms, materialized inside a room that was, if not a clone of that long-ago and faraway embassy, at least a kissing cousin of it.

"My," said Janeway as she looked around admiringly. "Starfleet is pulling out all the stops."

She barely got the words out before a server with a tray of champagne appeared at her elbow. She and Tom took one, Tuvok politely declined. Paris took a sip of the beverage and raised an eyebrow approvingly. Starfleet was indeed pulling out all the stops.

"So, Mr. Paris," Janeway said quietly, "tell me about our cast of characters."

There was a wild butterfly of panic in his stomach. Janeway clearly expected him to point out all the people he'd read up on during the flight. Fortunately, Tom was a people person and he had a good head for names and faces.

"That's Ambassador Mnok, from Ysa," he said, his gaze falling on a humanoid female who would have seemed quite attractive to him except for the tusks poking out of her mouth. "They've been among the most outspoken of the secessionists. In fact, Mnok has been credited—or accused, depending on your opinion—of spearheading the movement."

"Very good. Who's that over there?"

"That's Clan Leader Kai," Paris replied promptly. Maybe this wouldn't be so hard after all. "He's got all four of his hands full. He and his advisers want to stay in the Federation, but his people want to secede."

He looked around, and suddenly grinned.

"And that," he said, "is Admiral Montgomery. He's very gruff and bristly but a softie when it counts."

"I heard that," Montgomery growled, turning around to glare at him, and Paris went pink. "You don't look quite so dashing with that foot in your mouth, Paris."

"Sorry, sir," Paris stammered, snapping to attention and feeling nervous perspiration dewing his forehead. "I was attempting to inject a little levity into the situation. My apologies if I've offended you."

"God knows this gathering could use a little levity," Montgomery said as he strode toward them, snaring a glass of champagne from the seemingly ever-present waiter. "You look as red as a Skakarian tuber, Paris. Consider yourself properly chastised."

"Aye, sir," Paris replied, relieved. Underneath it all, Montgomery really could be a softie.

"Any updates, Ken?" Janeway asked.

Montgomery grimaced and knocked back the champagne. "Unfortunately, yes. I've just received word that the governing body of Parnasi has refused to come."

Paris searched his memory. The Parnasi, the Parnasi . . . oh, yes, the joined species. It took three of them to form a single entity. This interesting fact made "governing body" a more revealing, and literal, term than usual.

"That's unfortunate," Paris said. "The Parnasi have great influence in their sector."

"And there are at least two other neighboring planets considering secession," Tuvok said. "Unfortunate indeed."

Montgomery sighed and helped himself to a small, unidentifiable appetizer from yet another omnipresent waiter. Popping it into his mouth, he said around the morsel, "This is a tough call. On the one hand, you want each species, each world, to do what's really right for them. On the other, it's hard for me to understand how withdrawing from the Federation can be right for anybody."

Janeway smiled gently. "We're slightly biased, Ken."

Montgomery grunted. "Maybe. But we're no starry-eyed fools, either. All you need to do is look at the history of the Federation to see how much better things are for its member planets."

"Such a statement is subject to interpretation" came a cool, smooth female voice from behind them. Startled, Tom looked to see a woman with orange-red skin and hair in the most elegant garb he'd ever seen. The gossamer-like silver material hugged her figure in the places where it ought to, but seemed to float to the floor from her back and hips. Her mouth was quite wide, covering most of the lower half of her face, and as she delicately clasped a glass of champagne, he saw that she had only four fingers on each hand.

Janeway turned, her face composed. "Amar Kol,"

she said in a pleased tone of voice. "I'm delighted to finally meet you in person."

The wide mouth widened further in a smile. "Admiral Janeway," Kol replied. "I assure you, the pleasure is all mine." She extended a hand and Janeway grasped it.

"Amar, may I present Admiral Kenneth Montgomery. Admiral, this is Amar Merin Kol, the leader of Kerovi."

"Admiral," Kol said graciously. "I understand you are a famous war hero."

Montgomery looked slightly embarrassed. "I did what I had to do. What my duty demanded of me."

"As do we all," said Kol in her pleasant voice.

"This is Commander Tuvok, my former security officer, and Lieutenant Commander Tom Paris, my former pilot."

Kol greeted them all in turn. "I see you agree with a quote from my world, Admiral Janeway: 'Old friends are the best friends.' "

"Kerovi is an old friend of the Federation indeed," said Janeway smoothly. "I do hope that we won't see that friendship severed."

"Perhaps it will be strengthened even as it changes," Kol said.

Tom was suddenly and peculiarly reminded of an ancient dance form called a *minuet.* It was formal, precise, elegant, and usually performed by people who were just as formal, precise, and elegant. It didn't take too much imagination to imagine Janeway and Kol engaging in such a dance.

He tried not to sigh as he was reminded all over again how difficult diplomacy was. *Give me the conn any day,* he thought, and gathered his wits as Kol turned to him.

"Lieutenant Commander, what do you think?"

I think I need another glass of champagne was what he really thought, but he said aloud, "I think that the Federation would be distressed to lose Kerovi. Clearly, her people are attractive, insightful, and intelligent, and such individuals can only be an asset to the whole."

Montgomery looked startled at the eloquent response. Janeway looked pleased and not a little surprised. Even Tuvok raised an eyebrow. Paris felt better. Maybe this diplomacy thing wasn't so hard after all.

Kol seemed amused. "Admiral," she said to Janeway, "would I be right in suspecting that our Mr. Paris is quite popular with the ladies?"

Before Janeway could answer, Tom replied, "I am a happily married man, Amar, with a lovely daughter. They are presently the only ladies in my life, and I adore them both."

Her eyes twinkled. "But you haven't forgotten how to flirt."

Slightly panicked, Tom looked from Kol to Janeway. Neither was giving him any hints as to how to proceed. He gave up and asked frankly, "Is that a bad thing?"

Kol laughed and everyone visibly relaxed. "Not at all, Mr. Paris! I only wish that we were gathered this evening for no other purpose than to enjoy dancing, feasting, and harmless flirtation." Sorrow showed in her eyes. "Since my husband's death, when I became Amar to complete his term in office, I haven't had much time for dancing and flirting."

"My condolences," Paris said sincerely.

Surprising him, she slipped her arm through his. Her smile was bright, though there was still sadness in her eyes. "The real negotiations begin tomorrow," she said. "Tonight is simply a social occasion, and I shall embrace it as such. Tomorrow, we may all find our voices raised in argument and even perhaps anger. But tonight, I think I'll consider it a success if I have a handsome human leading me through a dance or two. May I borrow him, Admiral?"

"As long as you return him, Amar," said Janeway. "I'm going to need him in the future."

Hope surged through Tom at the words. He gave her a grateful look as he led the leader of Kerovi to the dance floor, and saw Janeway nod approvingly.

So far, so good, Kaz thought as he sat alone in sickbay perusing the data Patel had collected. Gradak seemed to intrude only when there was a lull, when there was nothing pressing to capture Jarem's attention. That had been his worst fear—that he would be rendered useless as a physician by this other person sharing his consciousness. But tending to Patel had been no problem, and even this, studying Patel's data, was enough to hold the Maquis at bay.

For now.

It was much as he had expected. The creatures that had attacked the away team were this planet's version of a primate, evocative of both the Earth species known as an orangutan and also with characteristics associated with the more dangerous *mugato,* although it had no trace of that creature's poison.

Kaz frowned as he delved deeper. Surely this couldn't be right—this thing had more in common with Earth-based primates than ought to be the case with a species that had evolved on an entirely different world. Maybe Patel had somehow contaminated the data—although with her reputation, it seemed highly unlikely. Devi Patel wouldn't be that careless, not even when a huge, clawed creature was charging her.

He adjusted the parameters and ran the information through again. This time, when the computer returned the results, Kaz sat down heavily in his chair and wiped his forehead, staring at the data displayed on the screen.

Humanoid DNA.

Kaz swallowed, running a hand through his thick dark hair as he tried to make sense of what he saw. How could these primates have humanoid DNA? Granted, it was the thinnest of lines that stood between humanoids and primates—for instance, there was a 98.5 percent genetic similarity between humans and chimpanzees on Earth—but it was a line that was not crossed. How, then, did these creatures on Loran II show up as being humanoid?

Evolution from some sort of primate was common,

if not entirely universal among humanoids, but as the process was usually long and slow, it was hard to pinpoint when a species made that transition. Kaz liked the term humans had given this in-between state—"The Missing Link." They'd never found concrete evidence of that point in their evolution when the monkey became the man. Few other species had, either; this evolutionary moment was so subtle, so fleeting, that concrete evidence was rarely found.

He wondered if that was what he was seeing here. The idea excited him. He thought about waking Patel to tell her what he'd discovered, but decided to wait until he was certain.

"Computer," he said, his voice taut, "run a comparison with this DNA against all known samples in the database. Cite closest matches."

Even as fast as the computer was, this was a huge request, and it took several seconds before the crisp, feminine voice cited the answer.

"Submitted DNA sample has been identified as human."

"What?" Kaz yelped, as if the computer was a person and not a machine.

And then the computer delivered the most shocking statement yet: "Closest matches in database: Marius Fortier and Captain Chakotay."

Chapter 8

IT WAS STARTLING, to think how much the quadrant had changed in a mere three years.

When Crell Moset had been transported out of the *Adventure*'s brig onto the small cloaked ship that belonged to his future friend the Changeling, the Cardassians were still a proud and powerful race. Now, Cardassia was broken, beaten, struggling with idiotic notions of democracy. They were a defeated people.

The thought appalled and infuriated Moset. Once he had thought of a pleasant scientific alliance with some of the more advanced species of the Federation. Now, even if such a thing were possible, he would spit upon the idea. Humans, Vulcans, Trill, Bolians, Bajorans— *Betazoids*—he had nothing but contempt and hatred for them all. The only value they had was what they could do for him, for his experiments.

Which was why these new beings were his hope.

He cooed to them as they huddled in their cell, staring at him with wide black eyes. One of them ran a clawed paw across a streaming nose.

Moset turned off the forcefield and beckoned to one of them. It was the youngest, one of only a few young ones they had found and the only one that had survived. Moset had named him Kaymar, after his father. Kaymar was his favorite.

Kaymar looked at him and then lumbered forward, placing his forepaw—no, thought the scientist, his hand—in Moset's.

"That's my good boy," Moset said approvingly. "Now, you know what to do."

Indeed it did. Kaymar hopped onto the slightly raised table and sat patiently, bleating from time to time and scratching at the occasional parasite.

Moset touched the computer, adjusting the proportions of the components for the next treatment. A tweak here, a nudge there—he began to hum, nodding his approval at what he saw. The touch of a padd prepared the hypospray.

"Now, my boy," he said to Kaymar, "give me your paw."

Obediently the creature stuck out a foreleg. Moset felt for the soft, fleshy part of its upper arm and pressed the hypo. Kaymar looked at him expectantly. Moset chuckled, went to the replicator, and programmed a Cardassian delicacy—a ripe, juicy *ulyu*. He handed it to Kaymar, who hooted softly and began to devour the scarlet fruit.

While the little fellow was thus occupied, Moset scanned him with the tricorder. A little better: the DNA from Chakotay seemed to be having a slight effect. But not nearly as much as he hoped.

Kaymar finished the *ulyu* and sniffed about for more. Gently Moset guided him back to the cell and erected the forcefield. He had had it programmed so that it was visible to the naked eye; the creatures needed to be able to see the barrier or else they would wander into it. And the absolute last thing Crell Moset wanted was to cause these precious children any pain.

Clearly, a simple infusion of Chakotay's DNA would not suffice. More drastic manipulation was called for.

He turned around, his eyes still on the tricorder, and almost bumped into Chakotay.

Moset gasped and dived for something, anything, he could use as a weapon, but the human was faster. Chakotay reached and gripped both of Moset's wrists, crying, "Calm down, Crell, it's just me!"

Though the voice was Chakotay's, the sense of arrogance that wove through the words was familiar to Moset, and he slumped in relief.

"Don't ever do that again!" he snapped, rubbing his bruised wrists. "You nearly scared me to death." Suddenly the full implications of the Changeling's presence struck him. "Is something wrong? Aren't you returning to Earth?"

"Nothing's wrong. I just left a shuttle on the surface." He grimaced. "If I'd been thinking properly I'd have piloted it back. I couldn't risk anyone else transporting down here, so I came myself. It's put me behind schedule. On the plus side," he added, "you can give me another treatment."

"I'm not sure that's such a good idea." Moset had recovered—mostly—from the shock and was in control again. He stepped to the computer. "It has only been a few hours since your last one. I'd feel better if we could wait."

"Chakotay" shook his head. "I'm not going to let this opportunity slip by."

Moset thought fast. The real reason for his reluctance was the fact that he'd been working on the creatures, not on the Changeling's predicament. But he didn't want his benefactor to know that.

"I don't know if the treatment will be much different. I haven't had a lot of time to work on this, you know." He knew he sounded defensive and that worried him. But he was getting awfully tired of the Changeling's demands.

"Let me have it anyway. And give me some more for the trip, too," the Changeling added.

"More?" The treatments Moset had stockpiled were supposed to be used on the creatures.

"More," demanded the Changeling. He bent his neck

to the side to give Moset easier access. Resentful but seeing no alternative, Moset prepared the hypo and pressed it into the skin.

The Changeling closed his eyes as the chemicals coursed through his body. Moset stepped back warily. "Chakotay's" features blurred and ran together. They reformed themselves into those of Moset. The Changeling grinned at Moset's annoyed and discomfited expression. Then again he assumed the form of Chakotay. No, not quite; this form was more slender, with long black hair, larger eyes, curved red lips.

Moset's eyes widened. Was he doing it?

The Changeling growled and suddenly snapped back into Chakotay. He slammed his fist into the wall.

"I almost had it," he muttered.

"Sekaya?"

The Changeling nodded. "I couldn't reduce the mass sufficiently for a female humanoid. I don't dare even try to do an insectoid or anything else."

"But you came closer than I've ever seen you," Moset said, trying to encourage the Changeling. The scientist wanted him out of here so he could continue with his experiments on his children. When the Changeling and *Voyager* were safely out of this area of space, Moset would breathe more easily.

"True," the Changeling said thoughtfully. It extended its hand and the fingers grew smaller, more slender, with longer nails. He smirked a little. "Got her hands, at any rate."

83

"You probably shouldn't delay," Moset nudged, none too subtly. Chakotay's dark, intense eyes regarded Moset thoughtfully. Moset stared back, trying not to reveal his unease.

"You're right. Chakotay's crew is obedient and they're fond of him, but some of them are starting to question my decisions. Give me the injections and I'll be on my way."

Moset could think of no way to refuse him. Swallowing his disappointment, he stepped to a cabinet and opened it. Inside were several containers.

"How many do you need?"

"All of them. And the reversal ones, too."

Moset's heart sank and for a brief moment he was furious. This was a very delicate formula to replicate; the containers he now regarded had taken him weeks to create. Still, for the moment, he needed to let the Changeling feel in control. Grinding his teeth at what he was being forced to do, Moset gathered all the containers and handed them to the Changeling, who had brought a satchel for this very purpose. Moset watched as several years' worth of research, of trial and error, of long nights spent deep in thought, disappeared into the depths of a Starfleet bag. Almost as an afterthought, "Chakotay" grabbed a handful of hypos and tossed them into the bag as well.

"You have access to hyposprays!" Moset protested.

"It would look suspicious if equipment began disappearing from sickbay, wouldn't it?" the Changeling countered.

Moset sighed. "Remember, since you've just had an injection, you have to wait at least an hour before you can take the reversal formula. Stay away from anything that could scan you at that time." He didn't know why he was giving the Changeling all this helpful advice. It might be convenient if "Chakotay" was caught—it could leave Moset free to work in peace.

It was just part of his inherently decent nature, Moset supposed.

"Right, thanks for reminding me." "Chakotay" shouldered the bag. "How are our guests doing?"

For a moment, Moset was tempted to gush about the exciting discovery he'd made regarding Chakotay's DNA. He loved to share his discoveries, bask in the glow of impressed regard and comments of "Moset, that's amazing!" But not this time. Better that the Changeling not know. He might change his plans—again—and decide he wanted to stay here.

"They're fine," Moset said after the briefest of hesitations.

"Just fine? I went to all this trouble—"

Hastily Moset said, "I've only just begun examining them! You must have patience, my friend. I'm sure they will prove to be worth every risk you took."

"Chakotay's" dark eyes flashed. "I have been locked in Solid form for seven years, Moset. You have no idea what—" His voice broke. "I have been patient long enough. I want *results*."

"You're getting them!" Moset's own voice was high

with strain. "You were almost able to take on Sekaya's form just now!"

"*Almost* is a very big word, Moset. Don't forget that."

Moset swallowed nervously. He'd seen the Changeling murder with a casual ease before, and he had no desire to be next in line.

"You know I am doing everything I can," he said. "I'm certain that with just a little more time I will make great progress."

Suddenly, strangely, the Changeling smiled. "By leaps and bounds," he said.

Relaxing slightly, Moset smiled as well. "Yes," he affirmed. "By leaps and bounds."

As he watched the large, powerful form of Chakotay stride back down the hall, Moset sagged in relief. He turned to regard the creatures sitting in their cell.

"Soon," he promised them, "it will just be us."

The Changeling stepped out of the holographic boulder, lost in thought. He didn't like what he was starting to see in Moset. It was a good thing he had taken all the available amounts of the formulas. Moset would make more. There'd be enough for the Cardassian to continue his work on the creatures, which, too, was for the Changeling's benefit. But his need to be cured came before the creatures' need to be perfected.

Now that the fruit of ultimate victory was dangling within reach, the Changeling felt almost panicked. He thought he had grown used to living in a Solid body during the many years he had spent locked into the form of Andrew Ellis. But then he'd freed Moset and, after a year or so, he'd been able to change his features, feel, however briefly, like a true Changeling again. The elation that had surged through him at that moment was akin to nothing he'd ever experienced, and he realized he'd only been fooling himself if he thought he could learn to be "content" living as a Solid.

Another year, another development. By this point he could look like any male human of a certain height. And then, just last year, he'd been able to shift sufficiently to broaden his range to other males of humanoid species. That ability had broadened his options, but was not enough.

He wanted to feel again what it was like to have no form, no limbs, no skin, no eyes; to just *be*. For too long he had valued the ability to shape-shift over simply being what he was. These last, bitter years had taught him how sweet was the simple nothingness he had so scorned.

He clutched the bag more tightly to him in a protective gesture. He could see the rock with the "Sky Spirit" symbol etched in chalk upon it. He wondered if he ought to have Moset give him a nice light rain, enough to wash away the symbol, then decided it wasn't that important. Just over the rise was the shuttle. He picked up the pace. At that moment his combadge chirped.

He touched it. "Chakotay here," he said.

"Captain, it's Kaz." The Trill's voice was strained.

"Go ahead."

87

"It's imperative that you call a senior staff meeting the moment you return," Kaz continued.

"Chakotay" bristled. "Why? What's so important?"

A pause. "I'm reluctant to say quite yet. I'd like to present my findings to everyone—make sure I'm on the right track."

A chill went through him. What had Kaz found? Had he gone ahead with the autopsy after all?

"I've shown my findings to Astall, and she can see it, too." A shaky laugh. "I wanted to make sure Gradak wasn't playing around with me."

Gradak . . . the Changeling fought to recover the name. Ah, yes, one of Kaz's previous hosts, if he remembered correctly. He'd known Gradak when he was Arak Katal, before his punishment. Gradak had been among a handful who had escaped destruction at Tevlik's moon. But why would Gradak be "playing around" with Kaz?

Was Kaz losing his mind? That would be a good thing. Any excuse to discredit or relieve the doctor of duty would be useful.

"Jarem," he said, recalling that Chakotay and the Trill doctor were personal friends, "you must understand that I can't call a meeting unless I know what it's about."

Kaz sighed and didn't continue immediately. Chakotay reached the shuttle. The door slowly opened and he stepped inside, settling himself at the helm.

"Patel took some really good scans of the creatures that attacked her," Kaz finally continued. The Changeling grimaced. "I've been analyzing them, and . . . Chakotay, I don't know how it's possible, but somehow, those things are humans."

Damn it, he'd figured it out. These *Voyager*s were too smart.

"There's got to be some mistake." He'd do his best to see that the information was discredited. "We'll discuss this more when I get back. I'm in the shuttlecraft preparing to launch right now. El—Chakotay out."

He'd almost said Ellis. He'd almost said First Damn Officer Andrew Ellis. The slip horrified him. Quickly, automatically, he went through the launch sequence and lifted off, not giving the planet that had been his secret base so much as a glance.

Chapter 9

"YOU'RE NOT," ASTALL SAID. Kaz was staring moodily into the computer screen, going over and over the documentation that Patel had found on the creatures.

"I'm not what?" he asked absently, his blue eyes roaming over the evidence.

"Going crazy," said Astall.

He chuckled and turned to look at her. "Coming from you, that's reassuring," he said. He turned back to the screen. "But the facts certainly seem insane. How could these things be human? And match Fortier's and Chakotay's DNA so closely? It boggles the mind."

Astall shrugged her narrow shoulders. "The concept of life on other worlds boggled the great minds of every single civilization, once. I'm just curious as to *how*. And speaking of 'how,' how did the captain react?"

Kaz thought about it. Chakotay was as much an explorer and an adventurer as he was a leader, and yet he didn't seem to have much of a reaction beyond . . . annoyance.

"He wants to talk to me before we say anything to anyone."

"Too late," said Astall brightly. "I've already told Patel. I thought you heard her whoop of delight all the way from her quarters."

Oops, thought Kaz, but he wasn't really worried. He couldn't imagine Chakotay not wanting to dive into this mystery. And yet . . .

"I know you haven't had a chance to talk to him about his sister's death," Kaz said. "But what's your general impression?"

"It was odd that he insisted on being the one to recover the shuttlecraft," Astall said. "My assumption was that he wanted some time alone, to collect himself before stepping back into his role as captain." She hesitated slightly, but Kaz was getting to know the Huanni pretty well by this point.

"But?" he pressed.

"I don't know him particularly well. But it just didn't seem like the sort of thing he would do. And it *definitely* strikes me as odd that he didn't want to retrieve poor Sekaya's remains." Quick tears filled her eyes. "I liked her a great deal. I would have liked to have paid my own respects. And it's what her people would have wanted."

A flash of a memory filled Kaz's mind; a memory that was not Jarem's. A betrayal by someone he trusted.

"You all right, Gradak?" The voice belonged to Arak Katal, who was looking at him with concern in his eyes.

Gradak Kaz ran his hands though his graying hair. Funny, *he thought;* it hadn't been gray so very long ago. It had never been gray while Vallia was alive. *His heart contracted and he wondered if he would ever recover from the shock his system had endured when he learned what his beloved had undergone at the hands of the Butcher, Crell Moset. He hadn't believed the rumors; hadn't wanted to believe them. Surely, not even the Cardassians could be so without compassion. Surely, the rumors of vivisection, of deliberate mutilation and callous observation, of planned infections, surely these were just frightening tales dreamed up by a frightened people.*

"Jarem?"

This man had offered sympathy, had offered a means of revenge. Had convinced so many to trust him, and yet he had deliberately set the Cardassians and the Jem'Hadar upon innocent children. No one could be trusted. Everyone was planning something behind his back. There was a conspiracy. These creatures were tortured beings, like Vallia had been tortured, by the monstrous Cardassians—

He whirled at the touch of a hand on his shoulder, and it took fully three seconds before he recognized Astall.

"Jarem, I'm really worried about you. I think we should bring Vorik into this."

He ignored her statement, staring with fresh, suddenly seeing eyes. He stabbed a finger at the screen.

"Gradak thinks it's a conspiracy," he said hoarsely. "And I'm not so sure he isn't right."

The Changeling braced himself when he entered sickbay. To his irritation and sudden worry, he saw not just Kaz, but the Huanni and Patel all clustered around the computer. As one, they looked up when he entered.

"What's this all about, Kaz?" "Chakotay" demanded.

"Atrocities," said Kaz promptly. Astall nudged him and he amended, "or at the very least a tragedy that demands investigation."

The Changeling was suddenly glad he'd taken the time to order Tare to head for Earth at warp eight. It would buy him a little time, at least. He had a sick feeling he knew what was coming.

"Explain."

"Our levelheaded science officer Patel kept her wits sufficiently about her to get a good, solid scan of one of the creatures even as it attacked her."

Little Patel stood up slightly straighter, and although her eyes were modestly cast down, she was clearly appreciative of the compliment.

The Changeling knew what response was expected

of him, and even as he wished he could throttle the troublesome human, he said, "Good work, Patel."

"Thank you, sir."

"Things were fairly quiet, so I analyzed the data she'd collected," Kaz continued. "Captain—I told you that I found human DNA in these creatures. Not humanoid—*human*." He paused to let his captain absorb this information. "And there's more. It's *specific* human DNA. And I've identified it."

"Who?" demanded "Chakotay."

Kaz swallowed and exchanged glances with the two women who flanked him. "Marius Fortier's. And . . . yours."

It was a huge leap. How the hell had Kaz managed to make it? This was not supposed to happen. He should have been well away from here with no one the wiser. And yet, thanks to the curious Patel and the startlingly astute Kaz, the Changeling realized he had two choices: He could continue to proceed according to plan, thus arousing suspicions even more, or he could act like Chakotay would.

He wished he'd let the creatures kill Patel and the others after all.

Fortunately, he'd been expecting this, judging from what Kaz had said so far, and he was ready with an explanation. But he couldn't make it look as though it came too quickly. So the Changeling opened his mouth slightly in an expression of shock, and leaned a bit heavily on Kaz's desk, and wiped his forehead. Astall went up to him and placed a hand on his shoulder, squeezing gently. He wanted to slap her.

"I don't understand. How is this possible?" he replied, feigning shock. He felt Astall watching him closely. "There's got to be an error somewhere."

"Believe me, Captain, that was our first thought," said Patel. "We double- and triple-checked everything. It's all there."

"Chakotay" rubbed his chin, thinking frantically. How much had they learned?

"Kaz, what made you run a specific DNA check?" he asked finally.

Kaz laughed a little, but it was cold laughter. "Call it a hunch," he said. "If you had the memories of a Maquis who'd lost a Bajoran wife to Cardassian experimentation, it might have occurred to you, too."

Damn the man. Damn his dead wife, and damn himself for not remembering this. He'd *known* Vallia Kaz, known exactly how she'd died. It was what had brought Crell Moset and his work to the Changeling's attention in the first place. He was slipping, slipping badly, and if he didn't watch himself, it would be his undoing.

"Of course," he said, putting a hint of sympathy into his voice. "I hadn't though about that."

"My theory is that the colonists were somehow transformed into the creatures that attacked the away team," Kaz continued. "It's the only explanation for why there's Fortier DNA in that creature. Whether it was some bizarre accident—I don't know, a transporter malfunction or something—or deliberate genetic manipulation, I can't tell."

"That theory provides at least a tentative explanation for why there's Fortier DNA present," said Patel. "But what's really puzzling me is how Captain Chakotay's DNA got into the mix."

"Me, too," said the Changeling earnestly.

"This does lend credence to the genetic-manipulation theory versus an accident," said Patel.

"Chakotay" sighed and straightened. "Kaz, you were right. We should bring the rest of the senior staff in on this."

"And Fortier's people as well," said Astall promptly. "They have a right to know what we think happened to their families. If the evidence can be trusted, then Patel was attacked by Marius's brother."

"Chakotay" fought the urge to grind his teeth. Informing the colonists would be exactly what Chakotay would do. He was open, forthright. He didn't like to keep secrets unless it was necessary to security, and the Changeling suspected that this was poised on the brink of metamorphosing into something very big if he didn't navigate carefully. Cries of "but why?" would go up if he didn't tell Fortier what was going on.

"Of course," he said, trying to sound sincere. "Kaz, Patel—I want you two to work up a presentation. I'll call a meeting of the senior staff at 0600 tomorrow."

"Tomorrow?" they said, both in chorus, like some sort of musical theater performers.

He put a puzzled expression on his face. "I assume it would take you that long to prepare."

"We can be ready in, what, Patel, an hour?" said Kaz. Patel nodded her head vigorously. "I've done most of the research anyway on my own," Kaz continued, "before bringing it to you."

"Chakotay" smiled easily. "Of course you would have. Two hours, then. Just to double-check your research." He hesitated, then motioned to Kaz. The doctor rose and the two walked a little bit away from the others.

"How are you doing?" the Changeling inquired solicitously. A fair question, and, he hoped, one that would make Kaz give him necessary information.

"Well enough," Kaz said. "My isoboromine levels were elevated, but I've been able to keep them down with medication. I've told Astall I'm prepared to call Vorik in for assistance if Gradak becomes too big of a problem." He paused, then added, "I'm still quite fit for duty, if that's what you're wondering."

The Changeling thought frantically. What were isoboromine levels? Something to do with the Trill symbiont, judging from the context. What would Vorik be able to do about it? Gradak was becoming a problem? Was he trying to assert dominance over Jarem Kaz?

He looked up and met Astall's concerned gaze. He waved her over as well, wondering if Patel would feel excluded. He needn't have worried. She plopped herself down in Kaz's chair and immediately set to work, much more engrossed in solving a scientific mystery than in getting involved in real people's problems.

Which suited his needs perfectly.

"Astall, what do you think about Kaz?" he said, again posing an open-ended question that would give him the information he needed without revealing the level of his ignorance.

She flapped her long ears gently. "As well as can be expected," she said. "When he told me what he'd found, I thought he was . . . what is the human phrase . . . moving around the curve?"

"Chakotay" laughed. He'd been around humans long enough to know this one. "Going around the bend," he corrected.

"But then I saw it myself and, well." She threw up her hands in an eloquent gesture. "He's all right for now. Gradak seems to be kept sufficiently at bay when Kaz is occupied. When there's nothing for him to do. . . ."

"He comes out again," Kaz said quietly.

The Changeling regarded Kaz. The Trill met his gaze evenly.

The Changeling thought about it. Gradak resurfacing could be a bad thing or a good thing. Gradak and Chakotay had known Arak Katal, had liked him, had trusted him. It was Gradak's sense of paranoia that had caused Kaz to think about genetic manipulation rather than a freak accident. That sense of paranoia could be dangerous.

On the other hand, if Kaz were fighting his own personal demons, he might not notice or care if his captain said or did something out of the ordinary.

"I trust both of you," he said, as Chakotay would. "You're Starfleet officers. You'll put the safety of your fellow crewmen above all else. I trust that neither of you will let this get out of hand."

"No, sir. Thank you, sir," said Kaz.

"Report to the briefing room in two hours," said Chakotay. "And be prepared for the sounds of jaws hitting the floor during your presentation." He strode toward the door.

"Captain?" called Kaz.

The Changeling froze. "Yes?" he said, turning around.

"Now that you're back from Loran II, I'd really like to treat those injuries."

"Chakotay" laughed, one hand going to his face to touch the "wounds." "I'd forgotten about them. Don't worry about it, Kaz. You need to concentrate on preparing that presentation for the senior staff."

"Yes," said Patel absently, staring at the computer screen. "He does."

Kaz hesitated, clearly torn between two aspects of his duty as doctor.

"It's all right," the Changeling said. "There'll be plenty of time to examine me once your presentation is over. I'll be a good patient, I promise."

The smile bled from his face as he turned and strode out of the room. He was grateful for the inadvertent reminder Kaz had given him. He needed to get to his quarters and take the reversal drug as soon as the proper amount of time had elapsed. Then he could safely submit to any scan Kaz might want to put him through.

"Hurry up, Moset," he muttered under his breath. He didn't know how much longer he could wait, now that success was so very near.

Chapter 10

CHAKOTAY WAS NOT SURPRISED to see Kathryn. After all, they were stranded here on this planet, alone together, possibly for a few weeks, possibly for the rest of their lives. Joy, shyness, delight, worry, longing for his friends, secret pleasure at being alone with her—all rushed to flood him as he regarded her.

She sat atop a rock overlooking a lake. She must have just emerged from its cooling depths, as water still glistened on her bare shoulders and long hair. She looked, he thought, like a mermaid, or a siren from legend.

But how was it that she was dressed in a traditional swimming sarong of his people?

Kathryn smiled as she saw him approach, and then suddenly he realized that he, too, had a sarong *wrapped around him. It was then that he knew he was dreaming, and sorrow, sweet and haunting in its gentle melancholy, wrapped him.*

The poignant sound of a flute reached his ears. He turned toward the sound, not at all surprised to see Blue Water Boy playing on the grassy shoreline of this tranquil lake. Chakotay's childhood friend was fifteen, the age he had been the last time Chakotay had seen him. The age at which he would forever be emblazoned on Chakotay's memory. Unlike Sekaya, Chakotay had been denied the privilege of seeing Blue Water Dreamer, the adult man. He wondered what that man had been like. Sekaya had told him a little, but her story was deeply personal, and she had not gone into detail.

He was therefore surprised when the boy morphed into a man. His hair was not as long and had more than a few silver strands entwined in the glossy black. Blue Water Dreamer was of average height and build, shorter and less muscular than Chakotay. There were wrinkles around his dark eyes, but those eyes were every bit as untroubled and clear as Chakotay remembered; as untroubled and clear as the lake before them.

A dream? Chakotay wondered.

Or a vision?

"They're the same thing," said a voice. Chakotay turned to see himself. A deep shudder went through him. Was it he? Or was it the Changeling, a being he

had known as Arak Katal the Barjoran and Andrew Ellis, the priggish first officer?

The other Chakotay knew what he was thinking. "I'm you, don't worry," he said reassuringly, and Chakotay believed himself. He looked again at the figure standing before him, clad in the standard Starfleet uniform, the number of pips on his collar marking him as a captain. He looked down at himself, seeing bronze skin and a colorful wrap around his loins.

Which am I?

"They're both you" came Kathryn's voice. She, too, had a twin now, a short-haired, no-nonsense woman clad in the formal dress uniform of a Starfleet admiral. Chakotay glanced from one to the other, knowing he cherished both the woman and the admiral.

"You keep trying to compartmentalize us." He knew this voice, too, and turned from Kathryn's warm smile to see Sekaya sitting next to Blue Water Dreamer. He was still playing his flute, the music a score to the drama that was unfolding in Chakotay's dream/vision. Chakotay's heart hurt as he beheld his sister and his childhood friend. They looked good, sitting side by side. If only Fate had permitted them to be together.

"Not fate," growled his other Self, dark eyes flashing, arms folded across his uniformed chest. "Moset. Moset killed him." And suddenly that other Self split in two, and Chakotay now looked at a Maquis captain. The Starfleet Self was now calm and cool, in control. The Maquis blazed with fury, with a burning desire for vengeance.

103

And still Blue Water Dreamer played, calm and peaceful, as the drama of the Chakotays unfolded. Three of them there were now; his cultural Self, his Starfleet Self, and the Maquis. Traditionalist, adventurer, rebel. He was all of these. Janeway, too, was more than one aspect of her personality. They were all Changelings, in their way, transforming from one to the other as the need surfaced.

Even Blue Water Dreamer had made the transition from boy to man in Chakotay's mind. And that was a transition he had never witnessed.

Chakotay's mind drifted, oddly at this moment, to his friend Kaz. Was this how it was to be a joined Trill? To have all these aspects at play in your mind at one time? It was amazing to him that Trill didn't all go mad.

As the thought struck him, pain shot through his head and he groaned aloud. He brought his hand to his temple, and his questing fingers found not short, almost spiky hair and skin but hard nubbins of technology.

We are the Borg. Prepare to be assimilated. Your biological and technological distinctiveness will be added to our own. Resistance is futile.

Even as the chilling voice of thousands speaking in perfect harmony shuddered through his bones, Chakotay knew it to be wrong. The things in his head were not the Borg's doing, not this time. This time someone else had put them in. Someone who didn't have the excuse of having his mind taken over by a hive mentality. Someone who was most definitely an individual.

Kathryn disappeared. Blue Water Dreamer disappeared. Slowly, fading reluctantly, Sekaya followed suit. Chakotay saw himself staring at the chamozi *on a log, the image he'd spotted while on Earth with his father. The* chamozi, *scrawled on a rock on a distant moon. The* chamozi, *written in chalk on the surface of Loran II. The best bait imaginable, it combined Chakotay's curiosity, deeded to him by the Inheritance of the Sky Spirits, and guilt over his father's death.*

The pain in his head changed. It softened, slightly, but became warmer. Suddenly standing before him was the alien whose name he had never known, but whose ancestors had genetically bonded with his ancestors, and who pressed his hand to Chakotay's heart and—

Chakotay's eyes flew open and breath rushed into his lungs with a gasp. All at once, he knew. He would have figured it out before, but at the outset he had been so groggy, and then later distracted by worry for his sister and the pressing need to escape.

The Changeling, in the form of Arak Katal, had somehow contrived to send a Gul after Chakotay. Not to capture and punish the crew of a Maquis ship, though that's what Evek had believed, but to capture and analyze one single, specific human being. For whatever reason, Crell Moset wanted to take samples from Chakotay, to finish his analysis of the colonists of Dorvan V.

Did you know that you were the only inhabitant of

Dorvan V who ever left the planet? And I'm a completist.

Chakotay had wondered at that comment, about the megalomania that would drive a man to such lengths just to experiment on a lone representative of a not-in-considerable population. He had thought it trivial, an example of a mind so obsessed by ego it could think of nothing else. But now . . .

"Chakotay?" Sekaya's voice, rich with concern. "Are you all right? I thought when he put you under that . . ." Her voice trailed off.

Normally he would speak quickly, to reassure and comfort her. But now Chakotay was too busy sorting out his thoughts, trying to grasp them and mold them into something coherent before they slipped through his fingers.

He turned his head to regard his sister. "I know what Moset wants," he said, his voice harsh and raspy, as if it had been unused for some time. "What the Changeling wants. They want—"

"The Sky Spirits," the Changeling said at the briefing, after the troublesome Kaz and Patel had finished their presentation and every single member of his senior staff had turned to stare, slightly open-mouthed, at their captain.

Kim, Campbell, and Vorik nodded after staring only a short time. They had been the only ones on *Voyager* when Chakotay had had his little ancestral adventure. The Changeling looked around at the others, forced

SPIRIT WALK, BOOK TWO

himself to look a little amused and abashed, and said, "It's a long story."

"I think we should hear it even if it takes a hundred and one nights," said Astall.

"A thousand and one," said Lyssa, softening the correction with a friendly grin.

"Oh," said Astall. "Well, perhaps we don't have quite that much time. But I'd like to hear any explanation for this, Captain."

"As would I," said Marius Fortier, staring at Chakotay with what the Changeling thought was rather a rude and blatant curiosity.

He sat back and sighed. Fortunately, this was a tale he knew perhaps even better than Chakotay himself. It was a tale he'd immersed himself in for years.

Ever since they'd trapped him in that hated body of Andrew Ellis, and he'd dreamed of becoming free . . .

"It seems that over forty-five thousand years ago, Earth was visited by benevolent aliens. They saw a race of primitive people in the far reaches of the world. These people didn't have a language, and knew only how to use the crudest tools and fire. But apparently, there was a passion for the land and the natural world that impressed these aliens, and they decided to give this primitive race—my long-distant ancestors—a gift. A genetic bond with the aliens. This bond gave my people a sense of adventure, of curiosity." He spread his hands. "It's no wonder I wanted to join Starfleet and see the quadrant. I was genetically predisposed to seeking out a life of adventure."

"Captain," said Fortier, a little edgily, "this is fascinating and I am certain quite meaningful to you. But I don't understand what it has to do with your DNA being found in that of an ape-like creature on a world far from Earth."

His dark gaze wandered back to one of the images displayed on the viewscreen, that of the charging creature who had attacked Patel, who bared an open mouth crammed full of teeth and extended clawed forepaws.

Who was Marius Fortier's brother.

"I know you're angry and confused, Mr. Fortier," said the Changeling, as he knew Chakotay would have. "But it's important that you understand the background, or else what I'm going to say isn't going to make sense."

Fortier choked back his anger, and "Chakotay" continued.

"This much is fact. But as facts often do, over time, it became legend. I grew up on tales of the Sky Spirits, and I gave those stories about as much credence as we give Greek myths today. But then, when I was fifteen, my father and I went to Central America on Earth, the place where my genetically enhanced ancestors eventually settled. We went there looking for the descendents of these ancient ones, known as the Rubber Tree People. And to my shock, we found them."

He touched his forehead, his temple and the space

between his eyes. "I first saw this tattoo that I now wear on their faces. Their faces, which had a strange cleft here, between their eyes. I didn't think anything of it at the time." He smiled sadly. "I was too eager to be gone, to get back home. To go to Starfleet Academy. But I was to recall that strange cleft several years later, in the Delta Quadrant.

"You can imagine my shock when, while *Voyager* was visiting a moon in search of polyferrinide, I stumbled across an ancient symbol of my people called a *chamozi*." He rose and went to the screen, tapping in a command, and the image appeared.

"We followed up on it, and that was how I learned that the legends of my people were real after all, in a sense." He manipulated the controls and another image of the *chamozi* appeared. "Harry, you never asked specifically why Sekaya and I went to the planet's surface."

Kim frowned. "You said that Ellis had found something of archeological interest."

"Chakotay" nodded. "Yes," he said. He pointed at the image. It was the one he'd had Moset write. "He found this."

Kim stared. "You're kidding," he said.

"No, I'm not. I wish I were. If I hadn't seen that symbol and felt compelled to investigate . . . well." He decided not to push the oh-my-poor-sister's-dead angle too much and contented himself with blinking quickly and swallowing hard. He saw the faces around the table soften with compassion.

He cleared his throat and continued. "Anyway, we saw evidence that the Sky Spirits had been here as well. Kaz is fairly certain that the creatures that attacked the away team were once the colonists who chose to stay behind. I think that they, like my own ancestors, genetically bonded with the Sky Spirits."

He'd hoped there would be nods and this would placate them. But he didn't get that lucky.

Kaz was the first to voice his concerns. "That would explain the combination of Fortier DNA and the close match with yours, Captain. But there are a lot of questions that this theory doesn't answer."

"I thought you said that the alien told you his people hadn't been back to the Alpha Quadrant for thousands of years," said Campbell.

"And the aliens have successfully and harmoniously bonded with humans before, as you just said," said Astall. "Why would such a bonding now have so disastrous an effect on the colonists?"

"Yes," said Fortier, a hint of amusement in his voice. "There is not that great a difference between a Frenchman and a Central American Indian—although we make better wine."

The real Chakotay would have responded to Fortier's attempted witticism with a friendly, heartfelt smile. The Changeling had no time for that. They were closing in on the truth, and he had to stop them before they unwittingly uncovered it.

"Who knows?" he replied to Astall's comment.

"Maybe something went wrong this time. Maybe there was something in human DNA forty-five thousand years ago that's been diluted, or something new that's developed. I know this is a terrible tragedy and a great shock, but I think it's obvious that Loran II is now a dangerous place. Recolonization there is impossible."

Fortier's brows drew together and he opened his mouth to protest. The Changeling held up a hand. "I know what you're going to say, Marius. But what's going on down there is too important for me to get involved in right now. We need to return to Earth and consult with Starfleet Command before I can put any more lives at risk."

He felt Astall watching him with great intensity, and saw Kaz looking confused. No, this wasn't what Chakotay would have done. But it was what the Changeling had to do.

"Permission to speak freely?" That damned Kim, at it again. The Changeling wanted to say no, but instead he nodded, bracing himself for what the security chief was going to say.

"Sir, there are members of the Federation down there who need our help. Those colonists went to Loran II because we told them it was safe. Granted, there was no way we could have anticipated that things would unfold as they did, but now that it's happened, we can't just walk away and leave them there."

"With all due respect, Captain," said Kaz in his most formal voice, "Lieutenant Kim is correct. These

111

beings were once human. There's a chance that if we can examine them, we can isolate the alien DNA and make them human again. At the very least, we need to try."

The Changeling realized that he should have known better. If he insisted on returning to Earth now, judging by the way both Astall and Kaz were looking at him, they'd pronounce him unfit for duty and relieve him. With "Ellis" gone, the next in line would be Kim, and that would spell disaster.

Sighing, the Changeling rubbed his eyes. "I'm sorry. Mr. Kim, you're right, of course. I just don't want to risk anyone else after we've lost Ellis and . . . and Sekaya. But my personal feelings shouldn't get in the way of my duty to your people, Mr. Fortier. They need our help. So let's give it to them."

He turned to his helm officer. "Lieutenant Tare, set a course for Loran II. Warp five. Let's get back to our stations, everyone."

They rose, concern on their faces, and more than a few gave their captain glances as they left. To the Changeling's vast annoyance, both Kaz and Astall stayed behind. Although he knew the two had just met on this mission, they had apparently bonded quickly and now presented a united front.

"Captain, I think you should come to sickbay," Kaz said quietly. "I want to run some tests on you and treat those injuries."

"Certainly," the Changeling agreed readily, surprising Kaz a little bit. A sufficient amount of time had passed that he knew he would read as entirely human. Thank goodness for Moset.

"And while the doctor treats you," Astall said, "I'd just like to chat a little with you."

"Chakotay" folded his arms across his broad chest and sighed, looking amused. "You two are pretty obvious, you know that?"

They both tried and failed to look innocent.

"Seems like the Gradak incident has brought you closer together," he continued. Keep the doctor off balance; remind him that he, too, was perilously close to being relieved of duty for his mental status.

Kaz wasn't ruffled so easily, however. "It has, but as I told you, Gradak stays in the background when I stay busy with work. And treating my captain's injuries certainly qualifies on that account."

"I know what I sounded like," the Changeling said. "And I admit it—I'm grieving. I'm upset and a bit rattled by what happened down there, and I don't want it to happen to anyone else."

"That's a completely normal and understandable reaction," said Astall.

"Then why do I get the feeling that there's a *but* in there?" the Changeling replied.

Astall laughed, a bright, silvery, happy sound. The Changeling decided on the spot that he hated Huanni.

"Let's go," Astall said, still chuckling. "We've got some time before we get back to Loran II. Everyone will check everyone out, and I'm sure we'll all decide we're all fit for duty."

"Sounds like a plan," said Kaz.

"Chakotay" extended a hand, indicating that they should precede him. As he followed them to the turbo-lift, he desperately wished he could figure out a way to justify killing them both.

Chapter 11

"IT HAS TO BE," Chakotay said, feeling his way along the path of logic. "Think about it, Sekky. You and I and everyone else on our world—we're all only human. There's nothing different about us."

"Yes," said Sekaya slowly. "That's what I told Father. That's why it struck me as so odd that they'd want to have samples of each of our DNA. We were just human."

"Except we weren't," Chakotay said. "We aren't. And what's made us different from other humans is we still have a trace of Sky Spirit DNA in our makeup. Moset noticed it when he examined the members of our tribe." His mind raced, and he struggled to keep up with the thoughts. "And I've got more than a trace. I've gotten . . ."

The words came to him in an instant, making him almost ill. He was furious that he hadn't figured it out earlier. "Moset spoke of a fresh infusion," he said slowly. "When they walked down the corridor and thought we couldn't hear them."

"I remember," said Sekaya.

"And that's exactly what I've got. Less than seven years ago I got a fresh infusion of Sky Spirit DNA, directly from the source. I had the bonding, the same bonding our ancestors had. The gift, he called it. Just like it happened over forty-five thousand years ago."

Exhausted and in pain as she was, as they both were, Sekaya was able to follow along. "Your Sky Spirit DNA is much more pure than any of ours," she said. "And because of it, you are genetically similar to the first human who had the bonding."

"That's what Moset wanted, all those years ago. He discovered a trace of it when he started testing our people and wanted to make sure that he got everyone, just in case my DNA was somehow better for his purposes. The irony is, if he'd gotten me then, I'd have been no different from any other member of the tribe. The question is, why does he want this so badly?"

"You are a curious fellow, Captain," came Moset's voice, startling Chakotay into silence. "But that comes with your DNA, I suppose. Tell me, Chakotay, did you notice if anything was different after your encounter with the Sky Spirit?"

He stood over them now, a padd in his hands, taking

notes as if this were nothing more than a traditional, sanctioned experiment.

Chakotay laughed. "Why the hell would I tell you anything, Moset?"

The Cardassian smiled mischievously. "Because you *are* a curious fellow. You want to know what's going on. We have more in common than you think, Captain. What I learn here because of you and that amazing DNA you carry could help cure diseases we haven't even heard of yet. It could move technological development forward at an accelerated pace."

Chakotay regarded him. He'd tried to, as the Changeling had put it, "play" Moset earlier. It wasn't likely the Cardassian would be stupid enough to fall for it if he tried again, but there was nothing to lose. He was certain that he and Sekaya would die here unless he could somehow convince Moset to free them.

He decided to try the obvious first. "I'll make a deal with you, Moset. I'm the one you missed the first time around, and I'm the one with the fresh infusion of Sky Spirit DNA. Let my sister go. She's of no use to you. I'll tell you everything you want, as long as I know she's safe."

Moset regarded him with a mixture of contempt and pity. "Surely you must know I can't do that. She'll lead your friends right to us. And besides, she's quite useful as a control subject. I can compare and contrast results. I'm sorry, but you must both stay here."

Chakotay smiled. "I had to try," he said.

"Of course you did. That's part of your nature, Captain."

Chakotay found it disconcerting to be addressed by the respectful title while he was bound and being experimented on, but that was part of Moset's nature. Anything the Cardassian could do to pretend that they were all on the same side, working toward the same noble goal, he would.

"You're right about one thing," Chakotay continued. "I *am* curious. I know a little about the gift that the Sky Spirits bestowed on me and my people, but I'm willing to bet you know more. It looks like the Cardassians have been studying it for some time."

Moset brightened at the compliment, then took umbrage. "The Cardassians? No, the whole thing was entirely my idea. I tell you, if people like me had led our Union, then we'd still be a force to be reckoned with in our quadrant. After my successes on Bajor and my little side trip to Betazed, I recommended that we perform a thorough analysis of every population that came under our control. It was time-consuming and expensive, but I felt it would be worth it."

He was getting excited now, talking about himself and his shrewdness. "Successes on Bajor" indeed.

"By examining every individual, by collecting exhaustive data, we could discover who had recessive traits that might prove useful one day. We might be able to cure diseases, prevent birth defects, create ways to inoculate people against biological weapons. Who knows, we might be able to find individuals able to resist assimilation by the Borg. Now, mind you, most of those we examined had nothing of interest to offer us, other than being useful test subjects."

Chakotay had been watching Moset intently, as if highly interested in anything he had to say, but out of the corner of his eye he saw Sekaya flinch slightly. *Stay calm, Sekky,* he thought. *Don't let your anger out, not yet. This could be our chance.*

At the same time that he watched with feigned interest and cold calculation, Chakotay also experienced regret. This was the Moset who had so charmed the Doctor at first. Waxing eloquent about saving unborn generations from illness and destruction, his eyes shining with passion, this was a man who had once been capable of doing great good. Instead, he had let his head get in the way of his heart. He had either failed or refused to see that the cold-blooded murder of innocent people—defeated enemy or not—couldn't possibly be excused by the discovery of a cure for the fostassa virus. Moset wasn't as far gone as the Changeling, though; he still desperately craved approval and acceptance. Katal, for that was how Chakotay thought of the being, had no such weaknesses.

Chakotay was more than willing to exploit Moset's.

"But there were others, like your tribe, who had something unexpected and utterly fascinating to offer us. They told me I was obsessive, single-minded, but I persisted. I knew that it would be useful to have every single one of you on file. You were worth chasing, Chakotay."

"Good thing I went into the Delta Quadrant before you found me," Chakotay said. "Otherwise, I never would have had my encounter with the aliens."

"Absolutely!" exclaimed Moset.

"I know that the bonding gave us a sense of adventure, of curiosity, and encouraged our love and respect for the land and its creatures," Chakotay continued. "But it sounds like you found something else. If my sister and I are going to die because of this, can't we at least know what it is we're dying for?"

Moset looked from one to the other, considering. He was clearly bursting to share what he'd learned, but at the same time was wary that somehow telling them might be dangerous. At last he shrugged.

"I do think you have that right," he said. "It's comforting to know that you're dying for a good cause."

Sekaya made a small sound and turned her head so Moset wouldn't see the hatred in her eyes. Chakotay looked at the blinking lights set deep inside her skull and shuddered inwardly.

"Captain, you reported that you encountered storms when you attempted to land on the Sky Spirit's planet," said Moset.

"Yes, that's right. They were afraid that we'd come to cause them harm and wanted us to leave. So whenever we tried to transport or land a shuttle, a storm would appear at those precise coordinates." Despite himself, Chakotay knew he really was curious.

Moset grinned. "And being the intelligent people

that you are, you no doubt noticed that something similar happened here. That there was a storm centered over the colony site."

Chakotay nodded.

"Our . . . technology . . . isn't quite as exact as that of the Sky Spirits, but we're working on it. Would you like to see how we controlled the weather?"

"Yes," Chakotay replied. Even Sekaya, hate-fueled and in pain as she was, was listening in on the conversation with growing interest.

Moset grinned even wider and hastened out the door. A moment later he returned with a small ape-like creature loping at his heels and holding his hand. The creature reminded Chakotay of a cross between a chimpanzee and a young *mugato*. It opened its mouth to chitter, and Chakotay saw long, sharp teeth. The small hand that curled trustingly around Moset's fingers was tipped with long claws. A strange and unusual creature, no doubt, but why had Moset brought it when they had just been discussing weather control technology?

"Kaymar," said Moset in a voice full of affection. "Kaymar, eyes here." He brought his fingers to his own eyes, and the creature looked at him intently. "Good boy." He stepped forward and brought up an image on one viewscreen of a storm raging, and a second image that showed the colony site. The sun was bright and the sky blue.

"Kaymar," Moset said, pointing toward the first screen, "make a storm."

The creature hooted softly and screwed up its face. A second or two later, Chakotay saw the image of the colony site grow dark as clouds rushed to fill the sky. He couldn't hear the thunder, but he saw the flashes of lightning and the torrential downpour.

Kaymar grunted and held out his hand for a treat.

"This," said Moset proudly, "is Kaymar. *He* is our weather control technology."

"But—how—" Sekaya asked, then bit her lip.

"These creatures are my latest experiment. They're my reward for helping Katal." Moset turned to the replicator and instructed, *"Ulyu."* A few moments later a large, red, soft-fleshed fruit appeared. He handed it to the creature, who began to devour it with delight.

"They were once just human, but now they're better than that. This one controls the weather technology. Another, when his brain is hooked up to a scanner, can telepathically communicate with us."

Moset looked at Chakotay, his eyes bright with passion and triumph. "The Sky Spirits gave you just the slightest hint of what they can do, Chakotay. Even you, with your fresh infusion, can't hold a candle to what they really are. In your logs, which Katal was kind enough to obtain for me while he was masquerading as Ellis, you mentioned that the aliens lived very crudely, very close to the land. Well, this is why. They could mentally create anything they needed. Their shelter was just the most basic symbol. They could control the tem-

perature inside the shelters, whether or not the rain penetrated—even telepathically summon animals to be
their meals, or locate fruits and vegetables that were
safe to eat. And frankly, my research is leading me to
believe that they could actually *create* their food and
other items out of thin air."

"Great Spirit," breathed Sekaya. "They *were* gods,
after all."

Moset gave a condescending chuckle. "I believe you
have a saying, and we have a similar one: Any sufficiently advanced technology is indistinguishable from
magic. Think of how a transporter or a replicator might
appear to primitive people, of how—"

"But this isn't technology," Sekaya interrupted.
"These are mental abilities."

"Quantum physics in action," said Moset, settling
back and assuming a professorial air. "The Sky Spirits—I do hate calling them that, but you never did get a
proper name for their species, Captain—have certain
physical genetic markers that interact with their brain
chemicals to do with thoughts what it takes us limited
beings tools to accomplish. I've been hard at work over
the last three years attempting to create a race that is
able to do what the Sky Spirits can. Fortunately, my
work on the Betazoids enabled me to become familiar
with the abilities of a powerfully telepathic mind. Even
with that background, this has been the greatest challenge of my life, and, when I am finally able to an-
nounce that I am not dead after all, it will be my

greatest scientific triumph. The breakthroughs I'll be able to achieve will be staggering."

Chakotay looked at the small primate-like being who was busily nibbling the fruit. "The Sky Spirits weren't apes," he said. "The genetic bonding didn't turn me or my ancestors into creatures like this."

"Yes," said Moset, and frowned. "That's one thing I haven't figured out yet. I used other sources than Sky Spirit DNA; the interaction could be what's causing this side effect. I'll need to do more work before I can say definitively."

"You said this—this creature was human," Sekaya said. "Who was he?"

Moset looked affectionately at the creature. "He was born Paul Fortier, son of Guillaume Fortier. But I call him Kaymar, after my father."

Fortier—this must once have been Marius's nephew. "The colonists," Chakotay said. "You've been experimenting on the colonists. That's why we lost contact."

"Of course."

"And somehow we weren't able to detect them with our sensors," Chakotay continued. His mind went back to when he had landed on the Sky Spirit's planet. There had been no trace of humanoid life-forms. Not until the aliens had decided they were ready to make contact. He and the rest of the *Voyager* crew had assumed it was technology at work—of course they had. He remembered Kim talking about unusually large EM readings, and they'd simply, logically assumed it was some sort of cloaking device. But brain waves produced measurable activity, too, didn't they?

"You can measure it," Chakotay said. "Their brain activity. To someone who doesn't know exactly what they're looking for, it'll register as standard equipment readings."

Moset was looking at him admiringly now. "Yes," he said. "You catch on quickly. Maybe it's that special boost you got."

"You made them into animals, not gods," said Sekaya bitterly. "Look at him. He used to be a little boy and now look at him!"

"Kaymar and the others are works in progress," Moset admitted. "All I had was the diluted DNA to work with. I'm certain I'll make tremendous strides soon, once I can isolate the genetic markers that are more developed than the common ones."

"How the hell did you get our DNA anyway?" Sekaya continued.

Chakotay wished she would stay quiet. His goal was to befriend Moset, as much as he could, anyway. He feared she would antagonize him and he'd clam up. But she raised a good question.

"You're supposed to be dead."

"My dear, there was nothing easier," said Moset, completely unruffled by her hostility. "When Cardassia Prime fell, there was utter chaos. Our friend the Changeling was able to hire a more unsavory type to break into a certain laboratory, where I had stored the

DNA. It was hardly anything of import to anyone else, and Starfleet didn't know the significance of what was stolen."

"But he's a Changeling," said Chakotay, feigning incomprehension of the situation. "Surely he could have impersonated anyone he wished. There would have been no need to hire a third party to get the DNA samples."

"He hasn't been himself for some time," said Moset. "About seven years, in fact. He rescued me from imprisonment and provided me with everything I needed to continue my research into the Sky Spirit DNA. And I've been able to use what I've learned to great effect."

"What do you mean, not himself?" asked Chakotay, keeping his voice conversational, mildly curious. He didn't want to let on how desperately he wanted to know this piece of the puzzle.

"He wasn't able to shape-shift," Moset said blithely. "He was stuck as Andrew Ellis for years. Absolutely hated it, apparently. I was able to help him recover some of his abilities. He can now shape-shift into humanoid male form, but that's it. He says he's at least happy for a change of face."

Moset threw back his head and laughed uproariously at his pun. Chakotay felt sick at the revelation. For almost his entire Starfleet career, "Priggy" Ellis had been an impersonation. Quickly he did the math—the Changeling had assumed Ellis's form when he was twenty-two or twenty-three. A fake. All the kudos Ellis had received, the reputation he'd built—it was all a fraud.

Moset wiped at the tears. "My, it's good to laugh. It hasn't been all fun and games the last few years, let me tell you."

"How did the Changeling lose his powers?" Chakotay probed.

"He doesn't talk about it much. Something about how they were taken from him. But let's not dwell on the negative. Things are taking such a positive turn. I'll soon have the Changeling back to normal, and I'll have lived up to my end of the bargain. Then I can devote all my time to my little friends."

Chakotay felt as if he'd awoken to madness. This couldn't be happening. It was right out of one of Tom Paris's Captain Proton scenarios, the one about the mad scientist. Moset was even laughing maniacally at a mildly humorous pun. He was creating monsters à la Victor Frankenstein, attempting to fabricate a master race à la Adolf Hitler. He was helping a murderer recover his ability to murder more effectively.

And he was using Chakotay's body to do it.

Even as the thoughts passed through Chakotay's mind, Moset approached with a hypospray.

"Let's get back to work, shall we?"

Chapter 12

KAZ STUDIED THE COMPUTER SCREEN, which displayed
the scan he'd just taken of Chakotay. *At least he's all
right physically,* the doctor thought. The wounds were
superficial and easily healed, and a scan with the medical tricorder had revealed nothing serious. But to have
lost his sister—that had to have been awful. Well, judging Chakotay's emotional state was Astall's field. Kaz
at least could pronounce that Chakotay was physically
fine.

While he was conducting the tests, he quickly did a
read on himself and grimaced at the results. The damn
isoboromine levels were dropping again. He rubbed his
eyes, and when he opened them, a shadow had fallen
over him.

"I think it may be time to call in Vorik," said Astall, very gently.

Wearily Kaz nodded. He rose and returned to where Chakotay sat on the biobed.

"Captain, you're fine physically," he said, "although I, apparently, am not. With your permission, I'd like to contact Lieutenant Vorik and ask him to perform a mind meld."

Chakotay glanced from Kaz to Astall. "What do you think?" he asked the Huanni.

"I think it's a good idea," Astall replied. "Vorik will be able to interact directly with Gradak. Perhaps he can convince him to settle down for a bit."

"Very well. And, Counselor, how am I doing?"

She smiled sweetly, compassionate sorrow in her eyes. "You're doing as well as anyone could expect."

"Good." Chakotay managed a grin. "I don't think my ego could take it if young Kim had the run of the ship."

As Chakotay slipped off the bed, Kaz asked, "When will you contact Starfleet Command and Admiral Janeway?"

Chakotay hesitated. "It's late, and we're all tired. We won't get back to Loran II until the morning anyway at this rate."

Not for the first time, Kaz wondered why Chakotay was going at such a comparatively slow speed. Maybe to give them time to digest what had happened.

"I'll contact her in the morning. In the meantime,

this has been a grueling day for everyone. I suggest we all get some sleep."

Chakotay headed for the door, but Kaz called after him. "One last thing, Captain."

Chakotay froze. "Yes?"

"I'd like to contact Seven of Nine and the Doctor. Get their think tank going on this."

"Tomorrow, Doctor."

"But, sir, it's midday in San Francisco right now," Kaz protested. "Surely—"

Chakotay turned and Kaz almost shrank from the anger in his eyes. Maybe Astall hadn't diagnosed him correctly after all. Almost immediately, though, Chakotay softened his expression.

"It's late. We'll discuss this in the morning, when you're rested and have a chance to make a good presentation." As Kaz drew breath to protest, Chakotay added, "That's an order, Doctor."

Kaz stiffened. "Aye, sir," he said.

The door closed behind Chakotay. For a moment Astall and Kaz simply stared at the door.

"Golly," said Astall, in a heartfelt tone of voice.

Kaz had to smile; the Huanni gravitated to such amusing slang when speaking Federation standard.

"Golly indeed," he said.

"When we return to Earth, I'm going to insist that he take some time and discuss this with someone. Preferably me," Astall said. "It's really tearing him up inside."

Kaz shook his head. "I just didn't think he would

take it like this," he said. "He's being illogical and not acting like himself at all."

Astall nodded. "I agree. But we all react differently to grief, Doctor. Sometimes in quite unexpected ways." She turned to face him. "Now, are you going to contact Vorik tonight?"

"No," said Kaz, and added quickly, to forestall her comment, "Chakotay was right about one thing. It is late. I know Vorik likes to meditate before retiring, and he's probably already well into it. I'll head to bed myself and talk to him in the morning. The isoboromine levels are still within normal parameters. I'm in no danger."

Astall sighed. "Very well. But if you haven't done so by 0800 hours, I'll go down to engineering and fetch him myself."

"Understood, Counselor."

She reached and squeezed his shoulder. "Good night, Doctor. Pleasant dreams."

The dream was pleasant, at first. Kaz found himself walking along a beach at sunrise. The waters, lilac at this time of the morning, lapped rhythmically at his feet. The beach was rocky and it wasn't warm yet, but it was still relaxing to be here. He breathed deeply of the sea air, and absently reached to toss a stone out into the waves. A breeze ruffled his thick, dark hair and gently made the trees sway.

"I thought I'd find you here" came a voice, harsh and blunt. It wasn't unexpected, though.

Jarem Kaz sighed. "Gradak," he said. "Not only are you interfering with my waking moments, but apparently now you're stealing my sleep as well. I'm trying to be patient with you, but I'm starting to resent this."

He turned to look at the man who had shared the Kaz symbiont. Gradak returned the gaze with his habitual expression of controlled anger and thinly veiled hostility.

"Let's not get into who resents whom here," he said, "considering you're alive and I'm not."

The resentment melted. "Gradak, I am truly sorry. I did everything I could to save you, but finally I had to save the symbiont."

Gradak laughed harshly. "You think that bothers me? No, you idiot, I understand that. But you haven't heard me out. No one has heard me. And you're shoving me aside and not listening to me when I'm seeing things that you're not!"

That got Jarem's attention. "What sort of things?"

"Give me free rein and I'll show you."

"You know I can't do that," Jarem answered.

"Can't? Or won't?" challenged Gradak.

"Either way, it doesn't matter," Jarem shot back. "It's not going to happen. When I have the time, I'll listen to you. I promised you that and I didn't lie. But there's too much going on now for me to just drop everything and put you in charge of this body."

Gradak grunted in exasperation. "Even when I spell it out for you, you're not seeing it. How was it that you thought to test for the DNA? It was my memory of what

132

the Cardassians did to my Vallia that caused that to even occur to you."

"True, but—"

"No buts. Things just aren't what they seem. I trusted Arak Katal, and he betrayed me. He wasn't what he seemed, either."

It was the raving of a madman, who saw lurking Cardassians behind every boulder, and thought everyone was a traitor. And yet, in this dreamscape, where logic couldn't quite be grasped and things could shift at any moment, it seemed an appropriate statement to Jarem Kaz.

"Things aren't what they seem," he murmured.

Gradak leaned in closer, his eyes almost fever-bright. "You know it in your bones," he said. "Something's off, isn't it? You find monsters who used to be human, and someone you trust is behaving oddly. You can't just ignore this, Jarem. You have to take matters into your own hands. Our hands."

"Into our own hands," Jarem echoed.

"If you're wrong, there's no harm done. If you're right, then you have a chance to stop something."

"Stop what?"

But now it was Gradak's turn to walk along the beach and toss stones into the purple waters. As Jarem turned around, ready to head into his waking stage, Gradak said, "You're a doctor. Do what a doctor does."

* * *

Jarem awoke feeling oddly at peace for the first time since this strange mission had begun.

You're a doctor. Do what a doctor does.

It was so simple, so obvious. He had been neglecting his duties—at least, one duty in particular. Even though he had been ordered to so neglect this duty, it had been bothering him. He glanced at the chronometer and realized that it was only 0237, but he felt as refreshed as if he'd gotten a full night's sleep.

Do what a doctor does.

Kaz entered sickbay at 0254. The third-shift doctor on duty seemed surprised to see him. "I thought you were asleep," Karen Ashton said, concerned.

"I was," he said bluntly. "I'm not now. You're relieved, Karen. I'll let you know if I need your assistance."

"If you're sure. . . ."

He smiled. "I'm fine," he said, and for the first time in what seemed like forever, he believed the words. "Really. Go on."

"All right, then. Thank you, Doctor. Good night."

He watched her go, then went to the replicator and ordered coffee. As he sipped the steaming beverage, he thought of the time he'd met with Kathryn Janeway, the two of them conspiring to help save the world as they knew it, meeting in a little Santa Barbara coffee shop. That seemed like ages ago now, though it had only been a few months.

He knew what he needed to do. He rose, went to a

cadaver drawer, and pressed. Slowly the drawer slid out, and Kaz gazed sadly down at the face of Andrew Ellis. The body would continue to be kept in stasis until such time as a proper burial at sea could take place. The lighting was dim in sickbay at this hour, and by its soft illumination, Ellis's face looked younger than Kaz had remembered. He didn't look asleep; the dead never looked asleep. Kaz, in all his incarnations, had seen his share of the dead, and he knew that that conceit was a pretty fiction meant to comfort the survivors. Ellis looked dead, stasis or no.

Chakotay had told him not to perform an autopsy because there were too many other things going on. Well, right now there was absolutely nothing going on, and Kaz wasn't about to try to go back to sleep. The autopsy would need to be performed eventually. He might as well do it now. It was his duty, and he was going to perform it.

Besides, it was likely that he'd be able to find further DNA samples from the creature who killed Ellis, and that would assist in any attempts to return the colonists to their normal state.

"Full lights," he called, and winced a little as the computer complied. Another touch of a control panel gently maneuvered the stasis-enclosed body to the biobed. Kaz prepared himself, sanitizing his hands and selecting his tools. Normally, he'd perform an in-depth scan and create a holographic replica on which to conduct the entire autopsy. But this time he was looking for more than cause of death. He was looking for something that might have been left behind, and he'd begin by examining the actual body.

"Computer, prepare to record audio and visual input."

"Recording begun."

He gave the time and the stardate, then his name, the estimated time of death, and finally, "Autopsy for Commander Andrew K. Ellis. Computer, perform standard analysis and alert doctor to any discrepancies in previously entered information."

"Stasis time incorrect," said the computer.

Kaz blinked. "What? Repeat."

"Stasis time incorrect," the computer repeated obligingly. "Estimated time the subject has been in stasis is not nine point four hours, but six years, seven months, two days, four hours, nineteen minutes, and twenty-seven seconds."

Kaz stared at the body, disbelieving. He shook his head. Ellis had died only yesterday. The computer had to be in error. It happened, from time to time, and *Voyager* was fresh out of space dock after having been gutted to within an inch of her mechanical life. Hadn't Campbell recently said something about "ghosts" in her system? Kaz was supposed to talk with Vorik in the morning anyway. He'd mention the computer and have the chief engineer run a thorough diagnostic.

Six years in stasis, indeed.

And yet . . .

Ellis *did* look younger to him. Kaz could have sworn

he remembered seeing some wrinkles around the first officer's eyes and mouth that had seemingly vanished. Perhaps those were just a by-product of the way Ellis held his expressions. But the hair seemed a little thicker, didn't it, and wasn't there less gray in the pale gold strands . . .?

The computer had to be wrong. He'd seen Ellis just yesterday. And yet . . .

Things aren't what they seem.

His mouth suddenly went dry. He grabbed a medical tricorder and ordered the computer to drop the stasis field. He scanned Ellis's body, and his heart sped up at what he discovered.

Everything on the tricorder pointed to indications of long-term stasis. Certainly longer term than a few hours. Slight tissue dehydration, lack of cellular reproduction—

"The computer was right," he whispered aloud, and he started to tremble at the implications.

There were a variety of hypotheses, of course. One was that they had somehow passed unknowingly through a space-time continuum, and that Ellis's body, in stasis, was the only thing that revealed the passing of time. Another was that somehow both the tricorder and the computer were malfunctioning . . . in the exact same way. . . .

He wasn't what he seemed, either.

Could the being before him somehow be an impersonation? A clone?

"I need all the facts," he said, realizing that he was

talking to himself but not caring right now. He needed to complete the autopsy. Perhaps it would reveal something that solved this bizarre puzzle.

Kaz would start with the clothing, which had carefully been removed from the body earlier and was in a separate compartment. It was blood-soaked and torn from the attack that had claimed Ellis's life. With more focus than he thought he'd ever brought to bear in his life, Kaz removed the clothing, spread it on the sanitized surface, and ran the medical tricorder over it.

Chakotay had said he watched, helpless to interfere in time, as Ellis was attacked and mauled to death by the creatures whom they now knew to be the colonists. Logic dictated that the clothing and the injuries would be teeming with DNA from the attack.

Kaz found nothing.

He looked closer, using his eyes and gentle fingers instead of tools. The cuts in the clothing were startlingly clean and uniform, looking little like what a rent from an animal's claw would produce. If he didn't know better, he'd say these cuts came from a precise instrument, such as a knife or a scalpel.

Kaz replaced the clothing in the sealed container and placed it in the cadaver drawer. Now he bent over the unclothed body, examining the actual wounds themselves. Again, there was no hint of DNA-rich dirt from under a supposedly unsanitary claw, no scattering of animal hair that could point toward Ellis's attacker. It was, in fact, unnaturally clean, as if Ellis had been killed with a sanitized weapon by an assailant who had no DNA of his own to deposit.

Kaz stood back, wishing with all his might that he could somehow contact Ellis and ask him just what the hell had happened. He knew that on Earth, several centuries ago, it was widely believed even by medical professionals that the eyes of the slain retained the image of their attacker. Would that it were so simple.

"Autopsy addendum," he said, "0342. Initial visual, tactile, and tricorder examinations reveal no indication of DNA from alleged attacker." He cringed as he said "alleged," but it was the truth. Even if it meant, in a very real way, that he was calling Chakotay a liar.

A thought came to him. Holograms had no DNA, yet they were quite capable of causing physical injury. Perhaps the creature who had attacked Ellis was a *hologram* of a creature, not an actual, physical being.

A possibility, certainly, but a strange one. For a hologram to exist, someone had to program it. Who would want to create and operate such a precise and peculiar program? Kaz shook his head and continued.

In more barbaric times the body would actually be sliced up and the organs physically removed, weighed and measured. Even now there were times when such a procedure was warranted, but from here on in, Kaz felt he could utilize a holographic version of the corpse to complete the regulation autopsy.

"Computer, prepare to construct accurate holographic replication of the body on the biobed. All weights and textures must be exact."

The biobed closed over the body, and a lavender beam washed through the form.

"Prepared and awaiting data," replied the computer in its cool female voice.

"Project the subject's skeletal structure," Kaz ordered. "Keep it in the same position as it would normally be if held in place by tissue."

Immediately the skeleton appeared on the empty bed. Kaz bent over the holographic projection. "Visual inspection reveals a three point four centimeter slash across the clavicle and sternum," he said. "There is also a second slash entering above the fourth rib and cutting through the costochondral cartilage. Computer," he said, slowly, carefully, "extrapolate from available data provided on autopsy what caused lethal injuries."

"Lethal injuries most likely caused by lacerations from a surgical scalpel, type A-49."

Kaz's mouth went dry, but he continued. "Likelihood of injuries being caused by three-centimeter claws from an alien species?"

"Statistical odds are 4,298,443.987 to one."

Kaz cleared his throat. "Statistics in favor of lethal injuries being caused by surgical scalpel type A-49?"

"Statistical odds are 1.0043 to one."

In a slight daze Kaz said, "Add internal organs."

The computer did so, and he beheld the matching injuries to vital organs. Again, he asked the computer to extrapolate what had caused them; again, it insisted that Ellis was slain by someone—or something—wielding an A-49-type scalpel.

"Apply epidermal layers," he rasped. A third time the computer asserted that the injuries were caused by a scalpel.

There was a lot more he was supposed to do in order to fulfill the requirements of a Federation standard autopsy, but Kaz had had enough. The damn procedure had raised more questions than it had answered—questions that seemed illogical and bizarre. He terminated the holographic program of the body and instructed the computer to reinstate the stasis field around Ellis and return the corpse to the cadaver drawer.

Making his way to the replicator and requesting another cup of coffee, Kaz went over what he knew—or, at least, what he thought he knew.

One: The body showed signs of being in stasis for at least six years, but Ellis had been aboard *Voyager* yesterday.

Two: Chakotay claimed that he saw Ellis attacked right before his eyes, attacked by one of the creatures that Devi Patel had had the wherewithal to take scans of. The creatures existed, Kaz had no doubt about that. But there was no speck of dirt, no shred of DNA, anywhere on Ellis's body.

Three: The computer insisted—and, he thought, rubbing his eyes tiredly, he would have agreed had he not been told differently—that the clean slices in the body that had gone deep enough to nick the bone had been caused by a scalpel, not animal claws.

It all added up to a mystery, one he was determined to solve. But again, he needed more information; more than just examining the body could provide.

Chakotay would still be asleep, and Kaz was glad of that. He didn't want to have to bring any of this to his captain's attention until he had more evidence and a theory that stretched wide enough to accommodate all the evidence. Commander Data had told him that he and Geordi La Forge had enjoyed playing the roles of Sherlock Holmes and Dr. Watson on the holodeck. Kaz felt like that fictional detective right now, although he doubted that Holmes ever felt as befuddled as he.

"The phasers," he said aloud. He'd check the phasers that Chakotay said he and Ellis had fired in self-defense. Quickly he went to the computer, gave it the proper access codes, and it told him which phasers had been assigned to Chakotay and Ellis yesterday.

Unfortunately, he didn't have the security clearance to examine the phasers physically. But he knew someone who did, someone who, like him, was expressing some worry about Chakotay.

It was time to bring in an accomplice.

Chapter 13

Harry Kim was awake the instant he heard the door to his quarters hiss open.

He lay, unmoving, keeping his breathing regular, and not for the first time wished he could permanently kick his habit of sleeping with an eye mask on.

He heard the sound of the door closing. The footsteps, soft and careful, came closer to his bed. Still Kim feigned sleep, his eyes wide open beneath the mask, his body ready to jump.

A hand touched his shoulder. In one smooth motion Kim erupted from the bed, grabbed his attacker around the neck with one hand, ripped off the mask with the other, and cried, "Lights!"

A nanosecond later he realized that his intruder was

none other than the ship's doctor, who gazed up at him with startled blue eyes. At once Kim loosed his grip.

"Sorry," he said.

Kaz sat up, rubbing his throat gingerly. "Good thing I have spots here or else I'd be wearing your finger-prints," he muttered. "Mr. Paris indicated that you weren't a light sleeper."

Harry's mind went back to the time, so long ago, when Paris had done almost the exact same thing—walked in on him in the middle of the night to drag him off to a make-believe French bistro. He was hit with a sudden longing for those times, difficult as they had been, and a keen sense of missing his old friend.

"I was an ensign then," Kim said. "Now I'm a lieu-tenant and chief of security. Speaking of which," he added archly, "how did you get in here, and oh, by the way, do you know what time it is?"

Kaz shrugged. "Gave my clearance code and told the computer to override the lock as it was a medical emer-gency," he replied. "And I know what time it is. Harry, I need your help."

Kim was alert at once. Tom might have busted in on him for a lark, but Kaz wouldn't. He wouldn't be here if there weren't a problem. A big problem.

"What's going on?" he asked.

"I'll explain while you get dressed," Kaz said. "We don't have a lot of time." He hesitated. "Now that it's come to it, it's hard to know what to say."

"Let me see if I can help you," said Kim, reaching

for his uniform. "You're worried about Chakotay. You think he's acting strangely."

"Yes, I do. And I suspect you share that opinion."

Kim ran a comb through his hair. "I do. I've known Chakotay for seven years, Doctor. I would never have expected him to behave the way he is. This reluctance to return to Loran II, his refusal to contact Starfleet Command or even Admiral Janeway—hell, you know what good friends they are. Chakotay should have told her about the situation immediately." He shook his head. "I don't know what's going on with him."

"Neither do I, for certain," Kaz said. "But I'm here because I need you to check on a couple of phasers for me."

"What?"

Kaz sighed. "This all sounds preposterous, but . . . I couldn't sleep tonight, so I began the SOP autopsy on Commander Ellis."

Kim frowned. "I thought the captain ordered you not to do it."

"Well, he actually said for me not to spend time on it, since it was such an open-and-shut case. But he didn't exactly forbid me to do it. So I started, and Harry, what I found . . . I can hardly believe it. The body shows every indication of having been in stasis for six years."

"What?"

"I know, I know, I thought there had to be a computer error, too. But my tricorder confirmed it. Also, there were no traces of the creature that killed him. And I mean none—not a hair, no skin cells, nothing."

145

Kim, who a moment ago had been the model of Starfleet efficiency, now stared at Kaz with his mouth slightly open. Slowly he sank down on the bed.

"Isn't that impossible?" he asked weakly.

"It ought to be," Kaz replied. "Then, as I examined the rips made in Ellis's clothing and the corresponding injuries on his body, I realized they were too clean to have been made by animal claws. The computer said they were made by a scalpel. Even gave me the type. And I have to agree."

Kim ran a hand through his just-combed hair, rumpling it. "So what you're saying," he said, groping his way to a conclusion, "is that the body has actually been in stasis for several years and was fatally injured by someone wielding a scalpel who managed to leave no DNA behind?"

"That pretty much sums it up."

Kim gave him a faint smile. "Either you're insane or I am," he said.

"I wish it were that simple," said Kaz. "I'm trying to get more evidence, to figure out just what the hell is going on. This seems ludicrous to me, fantastical, impossible, but the facts are there. That's why I need you to get me into the weapons locker. Chakotay said that both he and Ellis fired their weapons at the creatures who attacked them. I want to make sure . . ."

His voice trailed off and he looked slightly sick. Harry could empathize.

"You want to make sure that this man, our captain and our friend, isn't lying to us," he finished.

Kaz nodded. "I can't believe it's come down to this, but there it is. Yes, I want to make sure he was telling the truth. I want very much to believe that he's acting so erratically for one of the most basic of human reasons—simple, honest grief at losing a loved one, nothing more."

"You realize that I could put you under arrest for proposing this to me," Kim said, testing the waters.

"Of course I do," Kaz replied, "and frankly, that would be a relief. There's nothing I could do in the brig to keep investigating. And, of course, if you do what I ask of you, you'll be involved, too."

Kim sat for a moment, gathering his thoughts, although he knew in his heart his mind was made up.

"Let's go," he said.

The lights were dim and the corridors were quiet as the two conspirators approached the weapons locker. Kim entered the clearance code, and the door slid open.

"Lights," Kim called. The air was cool and slightly more stagnant than elsewhere on the ship, and Kaz looked at the rows of weapons neatly lined up on the wall. He'd told Kim which two phasers to look for, and Kim located them quickly.

Kim examined the first one. "This one's been fired within the last twenty-four hours," he confirmed. Kaz was disproportionately pleased; it meant Chakotay hadn't lied about that. Feeling more hopeful and confident, Kaz watched as Kim examined the phaser that Ellis had carried with him on his final mission.

147

Kim's face revealed the answer.

"That one hasn't been fired?" Kaz asked.

Kim shook his head. "Negative. This is about as un-used as a phaser can be, fresh from the armories. You're certain it was this number phaser?"

"Ask the computer yourself; I could have been mis-taken." But he wasn't, and Kim knew it, and even as Kim went through the motions of reconfirming the phaser's number and who had last been assigned it, they both knew what he'd learn.

Kaz felt cold. Chakotay had told him a bald-faced falsehood. But why? *Why* would he lie? None of this made any sense! It was like being in a bad dream.

Things are not what they seem.

He shivered.

"What would you like to do now?" he asked *Voyager*'s chief of security.

Kim's full lips tightened, and Kaz saw a flash of anger mixed with a sense of betrayal in his dark eyes.

"I'd *like* to go wake up the captain and get him to explain all this, but my gut is telling me that that would be the absolute worst thing I could do."

Kaz nodded; he shared the sentiment. Something was very wrong here, and until they figured it out, they couldn't trust their own captain.

"We can't trust him," Kaz said, finally speaking the words, his voice sounding hollow in his own ears. Looking miserable, Kim shook his head. It was probably worse for him than for Kaz, as he'd been so close to Chakotay for so long.

"Well, then," Kaz continued, "I do know someone we *can* trust."

Kim knew exactly who he meant.

"That's a huge breach of protocol," Kim said, needed to say it even as Kaz knew he was more than willing to go along with it.

"I don't give a damn about protocol right now," Kaz said recklessly, hearing Gradak's words in his voice. "I think there are more important things at stake. Are you game, Harry?"

Kim nodded.

"Then let's do it."

The Changeling dreaded sleep, but in his completely human form, he required it. He lay on Chakotay's bed, staring out the window at the stars streaking past, wishing he were heading to Earth instead of back to Loran II, to Earth, where he could disappear without a trace. His eyes closed and the dream, as it always did, broke upon his sleeping mind like a wave crashing on the shoreline.

It had all gone so well, better than he had dared hope. The massacre on Tevlik's moon base was not part of the original deal struck between Dukat and the Dominion, of course, but the Changeling who now wore the face of Ensign Andrew Ellis felt certain that was a minor technicality. Gul Dukat had made it clear what he wanted by allying with the Dominion. He hated the

Maquis with an obsession, and he wanted them eradicated. Over the last three days the Jem'Hadar and the Cardassians had done almost precisely that.

Over the last year the Changeling had managed to kidnap and place in stasis not only Ellis—a rising young star not long out of the Academy; the wife and infant Ellis had were trivial obstacles as far as the Changeling was concerned—but others as well. No one too noticeable, no one too important, just people in certain handy positions he could become for longer periods of time. He kept them in stasis, realizing that when the time came for him to stop impersonating any one of them, he could arrange a tragic "accident" and produce a fresh body.

Ellis was a transitory body. It was good to have a Federation alias, and as things were about to heat up here in the Alpha Quadrant, it would be easy enough for "poor Ellis" to have a hero's death in some battle somewhere.

The Changeling was the proudest, though, of Arak Katal, who was completely fictitious. He had created the face and body from his own imagination, making a "character" as real as any of the actual people he could impersonate. It had been good enough to fool all those trusting Maquis. He'd picked out the moon base, he'd led them all there, he'd convinced them it was safe enough to bring their children.

And now he'd shown the Cardassians right where they were. A few had survived, but only a handful. The Changeling was proud of his handiwork.

He'd watched the destruction from the safety of a

cloaked ship. Even if anyone had been able to detect him, it was unlikely anyone would care, considering what was happening on the moon and in the space around it. Now that it was all over but the body count, he was happily heading back to Earth, where "Ellis" would rendezvous with his starship.

He was startled when he heard the hail, but relaxed slightly when he realized who it must be. And sure enough, there was the pale, dark-haired image of a Vorta on the viewscreen.

It was one of the Elani clones. She was young, younger than most, and quite attractive. Her eyes were large now with reverence and wonder, and her voice betrayed her nervousness as she spoke.

"Great One, it is an honor to behold you."

He was feeling good, so he inclined his head graciously. "What is it you seek from me?"

Elani licked full lips. "I come from the Founders on an important mission, to guarantee safety."

His eyes narrowed. "Safety? From what?"

"Please, Great One, may I board your ship? I will explain all."

So he let her aboard, and she was as obsequious in person as she was on-screen, perhaps even more so. She was dressed in long, flowing robes and carried a bulky piece of equipment.

"What's this?" he asked.

"A weapon," she said. Strangely, her voice cracked with grief. "To ensure the safety of the Founders."

There was a brief moment when he could have stopped it. A second, a fraction of a second, when he realized what it was and could have shot out a tentacle to dash it out of her hand as she stood on the transporter pad, could have snapped her elegant neck. Could have saved himself.

But in that moment of hesitation, of disbelief that a Vorta, a Vorta, was planning on doing this to him, she lifted the weapon (clumsily, it was heavy and awkward, and she had tears in her lovely eyes) and fired.

The sheer agony was unexpected.

He dropped to the floor and writhed, too much in pain to even scream. He felt as if he were being turned inside out. It burned through him, twisted him . . .

. . . Solidified him . . .

And then she was bending over him, sobbing aloud, touching his Solid face and apologizing.

"They told me to do this to you," she cried, "they told me! They said, one of the Founders has fallen from grace, and he must be punished or he will bring destruction upon all, he will obliterate the Great Link. . . . Oh, please tell me you forgive me . . . I must obey them!"

He couldn't believe what he was hearing. The other Founders had sent her to do this thing? To distort him, cell by cell, molecule by molecule, to turn him into a Solid? He'd recognized the technology, but the last he knew of it, it could only generate a forcefield that would hold him in Solid form as long as the field was active. But this Elani had brought hell upon him. They had somehow managed to change the Changeling, to distort him from a fluid entity into a Solid one.

"Never!" he cried. "I will never forgive you! I will hunt you down and . . ." The words dissolved into gibberish as the pain increased.

She froze, her hand on his forehead, and her eyes widened in pain. "You will not forgive me? Even though I have no choice but to obey the Founders?"

Even in the depths of his torment, the Changeling remembered a human insult. He summoned saliva and spat in her pretty Vorta face.

Slowly Elani sank back on her heels. She looked stunned, stricken. "I cannot live with this," she said. "I have destroyed one of my gods. You are right, Great One. There can be no forgiveness for me." And as he watched, she placed a long, lovely index finger behind her ear and pressed her thumb under her chin—activating her termination implant.

When she collapsed upon him, lifeless, his satisfaction slightly eased the pain.

Chapter 14

"I CAN'T BELIEVE I'M DOING THIS," muttered Kim as he and Kaz entered sickbay and he sat down at the computer. "It goes against everything I believe."

"I couldn't agree with you more," said Kaz, "but that fellow in the cadaver drawer and poor Sekaya deserve the truth. What that will end up being, I haven't the slightest idea."

"I should warn you, Campbell's pretty damn good at her job," Kim said as his fingers flew over the controls. "She's going to spot this when she comes on duty."

"You had her job for seven years, Harry," Kaz reminded him. "You know the communication system of this vessel better than anybody. All you need to do is be better than she is. Besides, didn't you say she was having some problems earlier?"

"Yeah, we call those ghosts," said Kim, brightening a little at the reminder. "I'll do what I can to make this look like one." He shook his dark head. "Damn it, Kaz, I hope we're doing the right thing."

"So do I, Harry," said Kaz, "so do I."

They were silent for a few moments, then Kim stiffened. "What time is it on Vaan?"

Kaz did the math. "Fifteen hundred hours," he said.

"Well, at least we're not getting her out of bed."

"No, just calling her away from a key negotiation situation that could affect the future of the Federation."

"You're not making me feel any better, Doctor." Kim paused, then said, "There. The request was put through, top priority."

After a few nail-biting moments, the attractive features of Admiral Kathryn Janeway appeared on the screen. "Dr. Kaz. Lieutenant Kim. This had better be important."

"Good afternoon, Admiral," said Kaz. "Believe me, I wouldn't have put Harry up to this if it weren't." Quickly, knowing that every second that the conversation lasted could lead to someone detecting this unauthorized transmission, Kaz told her what was going on. He left nothing out; not the deaths of Sekaya and Ellis, or Chakotay's inexplicable behavior, or what Kaz had learned during the autopsy. Her eyes widened slightly as he spoke, but she didn't interrupt.

"What's your theory?" she asked calmly when he had finished.

"I haven't got one, other than we're all going mad," Kaz said.

"Admiral, I'm with the Doctor," said Kim. "You know how well I know Chakotay. Something's very wrong. He's just not himself."

"I agree with both of you. Certainly, Seven and the Doctor need to be brought in on this, if nothing else. Figuring out a way to get the colonists back to normal needs to be a top priority."

She sighed, looking into the distance for a moment, her sharp mind already working on the problem. "All right, let me think about this and I'll get back to you. Is this a secure channel?"

The two *Voyager*s exchanged glances. "Not exactly," Kim admitted. "We're, um, kind of going behind everyone's back."

A smile tugged at Janeway's lips. "I see." More seriously, she added, "If that's the case, then you'd better send me everything you have documented. We might not get a chance to speak again. I'll do my best to be in touch. Janeway out."

Both men breathed a sigh of relief. Kaz knew that he certainly felt better, knowing that Kathryn Janeway, of Borg-thrashing fame, was on the case.

Kim's fingers flew over the controls. He was sending everything they had to Janeway: the report on the autopsy, the DNA from the creatures who had once

156

been Federation citizens, everything. Kaz knew it was because he, like the Trill, thought this might be the only chance to do so.

"Okay, that's everything," Kim said.

"Any sign that anyone's on to us?"

"Nope. Not yet, at least."

"Then let's contact Seven and the Doctor," said Kaz. "Give them everything, too."

"The longer I stay here doing this, Kaz—"

"The greater the chance of discovery, I'm well aware of that, Lieutenant. But this could be our only chance. I'd feel a lot better if I knew those brilliant minds in addition to our humble ones were working on this problem."

"You have a point," Kim conceded. Again doing everything he could to misdirect anyone who might be snooping, he sent a message through.

The lovely Seven herself answered the hail. Her usually perfect hair was slightly mussed, and Kaz thought she looked exasperated. She seemed surprised and pleased to see them, though.

"Doctor. Lieutenant. What can I do for you?"

Something whizzed past her in the background, and she closed her eyes briefly, then opened them again, clearly forcing herself to stay calm and professional. Kaz bit back a laugh, wondering what exactly went on in these "think tank" sessions.

Kim, however, was all business. He was already touching control panels as he spoke to his former colleague. "I'm sending you some information," he said.

"We've got a situation here that we want your group brought in on."

"We're doing this clandestinely, Seven," Kaz added. "Do not under any circumstances contact this ship. Especially say nothing to Captain Chakotay."

The urgency of his voice chased away any distractions she might have been experiencing. Despite the fact that she and Chakotay had once been more than fellow crewmates, she didn't bat an eyelash at Kaz's statement. "Understood" was all she said, slipping into the icy demeanor that Kaz had seen only once or twice before.

"We're sending everything we've got," Kaz continued, "and Janeway's in on this as well."

From the side the Doctor poked his head in and beamed when he saw his friends. "Please state the nature of the medical emergency," he said jokingly.

"It'll be clear enough when you have a chance to—" began Kaz.

Kim swore and immediately terminated the conversation. "That's it. Someone's on to us."

Now Kaz, too, swore in his native tongue. "Were they able to track it?"

"I don't think so. I made it look as much like a ghost as possible the entire way through. But like I said, Lyssa's one sharp cookie. It may be a matter of time till we're thrown in the brig for what we've just done."

Kaz said nothing, but he thought that being thrown in the brig might be the least of their worries, if what he suspected was the case. He just hoped they survived.

Satisfied, Gradak? he thought.

Not yet came the reply from the dead Maquis whose consciousness vied with his own. *Not quite yet.*

Tom Paris noticed a slightly distracted expression on Admiral Janeway's face when she returned to the conference. He himself was screamingly bored and doing his damnedest to feign interest. A species that, for some reason beyond his fathoming, spoke a language that could not be translated by the apparently misnamed Universal Translator was holding forth, and the process of human translation was excruciatingly dull.

As Janeway slid into her seat beside him, he asked softly, "Anything I can assist you with, Admiral?" Tuvok, with his extremely sensitive hearing, gave him a glare. Tom ignored the Vulcan.

"You sound almost hopeful, Mr. Paris," Janeway whispered, keeping her eyes on the furry yellow alien and pretending to be interested in his laboriously translated diatribe.

"Well, actually . . ." he admitted.

"As a matter of fact, there might be. Keep on your toes, Mr. Paris. I may need to send you on a secret mission."

Tom felt happier at that pronouncement than he had all day.

The Changeling awoke feeling as if he hadn't slept.

Ever.

He hated this period of time, when he was as locked

159

into Solid form as if he had never met Moset. Fortunately, it was time for another dose of Moset's concoction, and he reached eagerly for the hypospray. He closed his eyes as he felt the stuff hit his system, felt it changing the very molecules of his body. Breaking them out of the prison of Solid form and releasing them to fluid freedom.

How had he endured it for so long? Sometimes he marveled at the strength of his own will. He was made of sterner stuff than the Vorta who had enforced the punishment; he had resisted the seductive call of suicide. And now he was finally starting to reap the rewards of his determination.

He had barely stepped onto the bridge and greeted his crew when Campbell said, "Incoming message, Captain."

"Source?"

"Admiral Janeway, sir."

He covered his surprise. "I'll take it in my ready room." He felt puzzled eyes on him as he rose. Half the people on this bridge had served under Janeway and liked and respected her; they would have been pleased to see her.

"Chakotay" reached the ready room, and the doors closed behind him. "Put her through, Lieutenant," he told Campbell. He smiled with what he hoped would be perceived as pleasure as the image of Admiral Janeway appeared on the small computer screen.

"Admiral Janeway. I hope things are going well at the conference. Looking for an excuse to step away from it for a bit?"

She smiled. "Something like that. It's going as well

as can be expected. I hadn't heard anything from you, so I thought I'd just check in and see how you were doing. Were you able to locate the colonists?"

He put a sorrowful expression on his face. "Unfortunately. They're all dead, Admiral."

Her face softened in sympathy. "I'm so sorry to hear that," she said. "Do you know what happened?"

"Not yet, but we're conducting an investigation. I'll be keeping *Voyager* here until we've got enough evidence to figure it out."

She smiled sadly. "This reminds me of the time we came across those bodies on Amasri. Do you remember that?"

The name of the place was unfamiliar to the Changeling. He was sure he hadn't seen it in any of the official logs. Was this something that Chakotay and Janeway had kept between themselves? He had suspected that they had shared more than they'd reported in the official logs.

"How could I forget?" he said, stalling.

"All those poor people." She sighed. "We never did find out what happened to them."

"Chakotay" shook his head in utterly faked remembered sorrow. "No, and I know we both felt pretty bad about that." It was a safe guess.

"How's your sister? Are you enjoying her company?"

He smiled. "Of course. She's got her hands full with the colonists, though, after this bad news. I wish I could see more of her, but we all have our duty."

CHRISTIE GOLDEN

"Indeed we do, Captain, and mine is calling right now. Let me know if you make any progress in your investigation. Janeway out."

The Starfleet insignia appeared on the blue screen and the Changeling flopped back in his chair, breathing a gusty sigh. That was close. Too close. He couldn't risk it happening again.

When he returned to the bridge, he said quietly to Campbell, "Lyssa, I've got an important job for you."

She straightened. "Of course, sir. How can I help you?"

"For reasons I can't go into right now, I need you to make sure that no one other than myself has any communication with anyone outside this vessel. And I want every single incoming message, no matter how trivial, brought to my attention. Is that clear, Lieutenant?"

"Perfectly, sir. I'll take care of it."

He smiled easily. "I knew I could count on you."

The Changeling took his seat with the ease of one used to it. Despite the direness of his predicament, he mused that it was good to be the captain.

Janeway stared at the screen, only now aware of how powerfully she had wanted Kaz and Kim to be wrong.

She and Chakotay had never discovered any dead bodies on Amasri. Hell, there *was* no planet named Amasri. She'd made the whole thing up on the spot, hoping against hope that Chakotay would stare at her and say, "Kathryn, what are you talking about?"

162

Instead, he . . . whoever, whatever it was, because she knew for damned sure it wasn't Chakotay . . . had looked her full in the eye and lied. Lied, too, about the death of his sister. His *sister.*

No, whatever that thing was sitting and looking earnestly into her eyes a moment ago, it wasn't Chakotay. There was no question about that. The questions before her were, what was it, what did it want, and how was she going to stop it?

She was relieved that by the time she returned to the conference, there was a twenty-minute break scheduled. She'd already missed five of those minutes, so she quickly headed for the cluster of people who had come to the conference with her. Just as she was about to reach them, she felt a hand, feather-light and respectful, on her arm. Janeway turned to see the smiling face of Amar Merin Kol.

"I was hoping we might use this break time to talk, just the two of us," Kol said. "I certainly enjoyed our conversation at the gathering the other night. I was particularly interested in following up on a comment you made."

Janeway gazed at the other woman, her heart sinking. This was precisely the sort of opportunity she had hoped would crop up at this conference. Until now, it had largely been one group holding forth, and then another, each entrenched in their own opinions and using the time while the other was speaking to prepare fresh arguments instead of really listening to what was being said.

Kol wanted to talk to her about a point she had

made. Perhaps it was an indication that she had changed her mind, at least about some things? Under any other circumstances, Janeway would seize this chance, steer Kol away someplace where they wouldn't be overheard, and listen with all her being to what the Amar of Kerovi had to say.

But there was an impostor sitting in place of her friend, on a ship she still regarded, she had to admit, as hers. Her crew, and people who had entrusted their safety to that crew, were in danger. The need to help them overrode any political coup she might count at this conference.

As sincerely as she could, Janeway looked into Kol's eyes and said, "Believe me when I say I am deeply sorry that I can't do that right now. I've had a dire situation crop up, and I must attend to it immediately."

The Amar's face still held that pleasant expression, but Janeway, who knew how to read people, saw disappointment in her eyes.

"I understand," she said. "I hope you resolve it successfully."

"Amar, you know that it would have to be something very important for me to miss a chance to talk one-on-one with you."

"Of course, of course. I understand that emergencies can arrive at inconvenient times. That's why they're called emergencies. Do not worry about it, Admiral. There will be other breaks in the proceedings. Perhaps we can chat then."

"Let's plan on it," Janeway said. But even as she

164

spoke the words, she knew that the golden moment had fled. She continued heading for Tom, Tuvok, and Montgomery, and as she glanced back over her shoulder, she saw Merin Kol deep in conversation with Ambassador Mnok, one of the strongest proponents of secession. Janeway wondered if she would look back on this moment as a turning point in the negotiations, and not for the good.

But there was nothing to be done. She had made her decision and knew in her heart it was the right one. Conversation between the three men stopped abruptly as all of them saw the expression on her face.

"What happened?" Montgomery demanded.

She motioned to them to follow her and led them away from the others. In a low voice she told them what was going on. Tom and Montgomery stared in growing anger and horror as the tale unfolded. Tuvok, of course, merely raised an eyebrow.

"I'm willing to bet that this is the last communication we'll have with anyone on *Voyager*," Janeway finished grimly. "The impostor would be a fool to let any communications out or in after this point. And we don't have the luxury of thinking he's a fool."

"Agreed," said Tuvok. "It will be necessary to intercept *Voyager*, perhaps even to challenge it."

"I'll take a ship and challenge him," Montgomery growled.

"That might be an extreme, final option," Janeway said, "but this is still a delicate situation. We don't know who this is, or why he's impersonating Chakotay. We don't know where the real Chakotay might be. I think a friendly hello might be better received. Ken, Tuvok—you two and I were specifically requested to be at this conference to help represent Starfleet. We can't leave without causing a stir."

Her blue eyes fell upon Tom Paris, who straightened under that appraising gaze.

"But you, Tom, were simply here as my guest. There would be a few questions, but it wouldn't raise any suspicions if you left."

"Aye, Admiral."

"Take the *Delta Flyer*. She's fast, maneuverable, and capable of defending herself, but no one on *Voyager* would deem the return of that vessel a threat. You'll be my eyes and ears, Tom. I think we can rig a way for you to communicate with us without being detected. As long as you don't use any of *Voyager*'s systems, you should be all right. You know you can trust Kaz and Harry, but everyone else should be regarded with suspicion. Who knows—you may end up helping lead a mutiny against this false Captain Chakotay. We'll get you backup, but it might take some time. For a while, it's going to be just you. You up for it, Tom?"

"I've had six months' leave, Admiral. I'm more than ready to get back in the saddle."

She grinned. "That's exactly what I thought."

Chapter 15

"WHAT HAPPENED?" asked the Doctor, staring along with Seven of Nine at the suddenly blank computer screen.

"They alerted me that they were sending an unauthorized transmission," Seven said. "A reasonable assumption would be that they were detected and had to sever communications abruptly."

"But why would Dr. Kaz and Lieutenant Kim be sending an unauthorized transmission?"

"Speculation on the issue would be futile and a waste of our time," said Seven, using the cold rationale to cover her own growing sense of apprehension. She turned to face her friend. "I was instructed not to contact the ship, and they especially cautioned me against having any communication with Captain Chakotay."

"Chakotay? But why would—"

"Doctor," she said icily, "do not persist in asking me questions to which you must know I do not have the answers. I am as confused as you are. I can only assume there is a dire situation aboard the vessel."

He looked at her with his dark eyes, full of apprehension and determination. She felt herself soften. She was quite fond of the hologram.

"How can we help them?" he asked.

Seven permitted herself to smile slightly. "That is a question to which I *do* have the answer. They transmitted a great deal of information, which they requested our group analyze."

The Doctor looked over his shoulder at his coworkers. "These may be brilliant minds," he muttered, "but there are times when they behave like children."

"They focus when it is required of them," said Seven, keeping her voice equally soft. She straightened in her chair. "And now, I think, we will *demand* it of them."

The Paris family had, for the entire time they had been present on Boreth, been the only ones who had visited the library. Tom and B'Elanna had preferred it that way, and B'Elanna realized that she'd come to think of the place as "hers." It was just the ancient books, the scrolls, and her . . . well, her and the cranky librarians, but she'd gotten used to their mostly silent disapproval. All the others who had come to Boreth seemed to have a single focus—the lava caves, and the visions that they hoped to achieve there, and that was just fine with Torres.

In the last day or so, however, two other pilgrims had joined her in the quietude of the library. The place was large enough so there was no crowding or jostling for seats, but she still found that she was slightly intimidated by their presence. She didn't know what the two large, burly males were researching, and frankly, as she stole a surreptitious glance at them now, she thought they seemed as out of place as a *targ* in a china shop.

They didn't wear armor, but it was clear they were more warriors than scholars. One, the larger who stood more than two meters tall and weighed well over a hundred kilos, was missing two fingers on his right hand. From beneath her lashes, B'Elanna watched as he reached for a scroll.

Those hands would be much more comfortable curled around a bat'leth, Torres thought as the large newcomer grasped the scroll assertively. She thought she heard poor Lakuur hiss in fear, as if he expected the warrior to crush the priceless scroll in his single, powerful hand as he might crush an enemy's windpipe.

The other Klingon was no less intriguing, though slightly less massive than his companion. He seemed the more "book learned" of the two, whispering to his companion now and then and pointing to a line in the scrolls or one of the massive tomes. Both Klingons took copious notes. They seemed to studiously avoid B'Elanna, and that suited her admirably. She had no desire to engage in chitchat with her fellow pilgrims. She was here on a mission.

This quest to learn about the *Kuvah'Magh* had started as a way to humor Tom, to find something that might interest him enough so that she didn't feel too overwhelmingly guilty about forcing him to come to Boreth. Torres had fully intended to abandon the effort once his interest waned. Instead, she spent nearly every waking minute in the library now, barely taking time to eat, drink, sleep, or nurse her child. More than once Kularg had given her a reproachful look when she'd come to collect Miral after leaving the girl with him for hours at a stretch. She felt the stab of guilt, but rationalized it by telling herself that she was investigating her daughter's future.

A future that could, if the scrolls were to be believed, prove to be very interesting indeed.

She hadn't heard anything from Tom, but then again, she hadn't expected to. Communications on Boreth were usually for emergencies only, or at least highly important messages. Conversations along the lines of "Hi, sweetie, the conference is interesting, talked to a Ktlonian today" just weren't going to happen.

But that was all right. B'Elanna buried the pangs of missing Tom in her research, and the more she learned, the more excited . . . and, she was forced to admit, apprehensive . . . she became.

"And then she fired some sort of weapon on him," Moset was saying excitedly. Sekaya watched him with a strange, detached amusement. When she had first awoken to this living nightmare, she had burned with hatred and fury. As the hours crawled by, that burning had subsided to embers. It wouldn't take much to stir the embers into a raging flame, and she knew it; she cherished her hatred of Crell Moset. But she had now figured out what Chakotay was doing, and had no desire to hinder her brother in what was likely their best shot at freedom.

Chakotay was courting the scientist. There was really no other way to say it. He was flattering, admiring, without being so over the top that the Cardassian would catch on. There was just enough dislike, just enough judgment in his tone, that Moset still felt secure.

Secure enough to—oh, what was the slang word Chakotay had used a few hours ago when Moset had left the room—spill his guts.

Sekaya thought, with a surge of the old rage, that she wished she could literally spill Moset's guts. It was alarming how gratifying an image that was.

She returned her attention to what the scientist was saying, and it was shocking enough that it kept her attention.

"There's a way of holding a Founder in solid form," Moset rattled on. "Relatively simple, actually. All you needed to do was set up a device that emits a quantum stasis field. That inhibits the biochemical process by which Changelings can shape-shift. But Ellis—that's how I think of him, as that's the appearance he's had

171

for most of the time that I've known him—was shot by something much more sinister. It changed him on the molecular level and locked him permanently into human form." He preened a bit as he amended, "Well, it *would* have been permanent had not I come along."

"But why?" Chakotay sounded sincerely curious. "What had he done that the Founders would be so upset with him?"

"Blazed ahead without orders, apparently," said Moset. "Gul Dukat's deal with the Dominion included the destruction of the Maquis. The Dominion gave him the coordinates, and most of them were wiped out."

"But Tevlik's moon was supposed to be spared."

Moset's eyes brightened as he regarded his apt pupil. "Exactly! This was the place where, if they could manage it, most of the Maquis sent their children, to keep them safe. There were more children on the moon than adults, many times more. In fact, most of the Maquis who operated out of the base were elsewhere at the time of the attacks."

"The Founders were concerned about the lives of Solid children?" Sekaya tried to sound as curious and interested as Chakotay, but she knew she sounded more skeptical than intrigued.

His comment proved her attitude the correct one. "Oh, no, it wasn't any kind of a moral issue. It was a practical one. The Dominion knew that Starfleet would, albeit unhappily, accept the massacre of adult Maquis, who were, after all, technically outlaws. But they feared that an attack against children might rouse the Federation into retaliation. That didn't happen, of course, at least not at that time, but that was their worry. So Tevlik's moon was never considered as a target."

"But the Changeling—Arak Katal at the time—took it upon himself to tell the Cardassians about it anyway," Chakotay finished.

"Precisely. He acted on his own initiative, as an individual, not as part of the Great Link. And that," Moset finished, as if he had just told an exciting story to a group of wide-eyed youngsters, "was why he was condemned to be locked into Solid form."

"But the weapon wasn't perfect," said Sekaya. "That's why you were able to somehow reverse the process."

"It's indeed lucky that the Changeling found me. I doubt if anyone else could have done it."

Or would have, Sekaya thought bitterly. *Genetic tampering like this has been illegal for decades among all civilized, sane people.*

"That's why he's given me my wonderful little friends," Moset finished. "They're my reward for all my hard work on his behalf."

Chakotay started to open his mouth, then closed it again, frowning. Moset didn't miss the gesture. He jumped on it like a bird on an insect.

"What?" he asked, concerned.

Chakotay said, "Nothing."

"What?" Moset insisted.

Chakotay hesitated, and then said, "You think Ellis

gave you the colonists to experiment on to thank you for helping him, right?"

"Of course, that's what he said, and I have no reason to doubt him. I've done him an enormous favor." His bright eyes narrowed. "Don't you think I deserve that much for what I've done?"

"Oh, it's not about whether or not you *deserve* it," said Chakotay, as calmly as if he were talking to an old friend. "There's no question that you do. I'm just wondering if you're going to get it."

"Why wouldn't I?"

"I think the appropriate question would be, why *would* you? What's in it for the Changeling?"

The idea clearly angered Moset. "Not everyone does things simply to gain by them," he said.

"You and I don't, that's true enough," said Chakotay amiably.

Despite her new determination to play along with Chakotay's game, Sekaya tensed in her bonds. The thought of classifying Moset and Chakotay as being of equal status from a moral standpoint infuriated her, but she kept quiet.

"But the Founders have never really been about doing things just to be nice, have they? They like to be the ones pulling the strings. Frankly, my gut's telling me that he's just using you and that the minute you've given him a viable option with this new race you're creating, he's going to take them away from you and use them for his own purposes."

For the first time since she had met him, Sekaya thought Moset looked unsure of himself. Chakotay let his comments sink in, then continued.

"It sounds like he's been a bit of a renegade from the beginning. A Founder defying the other Founders? That's someone I'd be very, very careful of. He didn't liberate you to be a nice guy, he did it because he wanted something from you. I think he still does. I think he wants your creations. And once he's gotten what he needs from you . . ."

He let his voice trail off, but he didn't need to say anything more. Crell looked nervous and the silence stretched between them. Finally the Cardassian rose.

"You're trying to get me to betray him," he said. "You're sowing the seeds of mistrust. Ellis has done nothing but help me. I'm not going to turn my back on him now." He strode out of the room, a bit too quickly.

"Think about it, Moset," Chakotay called after him. "The Founders regard Solids as inferior beings. Once you're no longer an asset to him, you're a liability."

Moset hastened back to his creations, fuming. It was so obvious what Chakotay was trying to do! Did he really think that Moset didn't notice? Of course he was trying to get between Crell and his benefactor. Turn them against one another. He would do anything, say anything, to free himself and his sister. The only reason Moset even listened to him was because he was lonely, with no one else to talk to, to share his accomplishments with.

But still . . .

Even an enemy could speak the truth.

When *had* the Founders displayed more than condescension to a Solid?

The Changeling had betrayed people who trusted him in defiance of his own kind. Why had he done that, if not to lay the foundation for his power base in the Alpha Quadrant?

Why *wouldn't* he want a superior race, telepathic and telekinetic, capable of almost godlike powers, who would willingly obey anyone who led them?

Fear, icy and choking, now crept into the scientist's heart. He had reached the holding cell of his creations, and now regarded them with fierce protectiveness.

"I made you," he said to them softly. "I made you and I'm going to keep you."

Chapter 16

"HEY THERE!" Astall said brightly, peering over Kaz's shoulder.

He gasped and started in his chair. "Damn it, Astall, I didn't hear you come in." He quickly closed the screen, hoping she hadn't seen what was on it. He wiped a hand across his forehead.

She eyed him speculatively. "You seem a bit jumpy," she said. "How is Gradak?"

"We've reached a truce, I think," he said. He was going to have to keep so much from his friend now that he was glad of being able to tell the truth about this, at least. The two hosts had indeed seemed to reach a sort of truce. Kaz was going behind his captain's back, practically committing mutiny, and the Maquis was satisfied with this development.

"Talked to Vorik yet?"

Damn. "No, not yet. I'm working on something here."

The Huanni folded her arms and cocked her head. Her long ears were pricked forward, indicating the strength of her current focus.

"We had a deal," she said. "You promised you'd do a mind meld with him."

Kaz gazed at her, his thoughts racing. He had no practice in mental control. There was no doubt in his mind that once Vorik had initiated the intimate contact, the Vulcan would immediately know everything that Kaz knew. And he might feel differently about the information.

Vorik might take it to Chakotay. And that would be disastrous.

"Look," he said at last. "There are things going on, things I can't tell you about. Important things. Right now, everything is under control. But I can't take the time to—"

It was the wrong thing to say. "Can't take the time? Jarem, you've got another person sharing your mind and you're telling me you can't take the, what, fifteen minutes to mind-meld with Vorik?"

She can be annoying, can't she? The thought was Gradak's, but right now Jarem shared the sentiment. He knew and liked the Huanni, knew that she was just looking out for his well-being and that of the crew they had both sworn to serve. But right now, well . . . *annoying* was an excellent word.

"Astall," he said as calmly and as carefully as he could, "I know you are aware that on a military vessel, which is essentially what this is, sometimes there are things that happen on a need-to-know basis. And right now there are things that you don't need to know."

"I know that you're in a difficult place right now," she said gently, totally disarming him. "I want to help you, Jarem. Don't shut me out like this."

Jarem Kaz deliberately pushed Gradak to the back of his mind and closed the door. He reached for Astall's pale purple hands, running his thumbs along the short, soft fuzz that coated them.

"You've been a wonderful counselor, and a good friend to me," he said, looking into her eyes. "But you can't help me right now. I need you to trust me."

Her huge purple eyes searched his, and tears welled in them. She blinked them back, striving to maintain her professional demeanor despite her almost overwhelming emotions.

"I'm worried about you," she said.

"I know, but right now it's all right. I need you to behave as if nothing is going on. If you feel you have to check in on me from time to time, that's fine, but you can't take me off duty. Not now."

Quietly she said, "How do I know you're not suffering from delusions, Jarem?"

He smiled slightly. "Like I said. You're going to have to trust me."

She sighed deeply, squeezed his hands, and released them. "I'm popping in every hour," she warned him, "and if I see something going on that I think you can't handle, anything that might make you a danger to yourself or this crew, you're going off duty so fast your head will roll."

His smile turned into a grin. "I think you mean *spin*."

"No, I mean *roll*, with all that that implies," she said. "Darn it, Kaz. You'd better be right."

She stalked out of sickbay, her ears flat against her head shouting her annoyed distress.

Kaz let out a sigh of relief. That had been close—too close. If only someone would get back to him. He had done all he could do at this point.

It wasn't just a matter of knowing the right codes, Libby Webber thought to herself as she continued to re-search into the identity of the mole. She was curled up on her bed surrounded by padds, munching on cheese and crackers and absently brushing off crumbs. Captain Skhaa, who had been several worlds away at the time, seemingly had accessed sensitive documents from *Voyager*. His fingerprints and retinal scan had all been utilized in order for him to gain access. Those were hard things to forge. It could be done, but—

Libby froze.

Her thoughts tumbled over one another. She sprang from the bed and raced to her computer, eager to see if her hypothesis was correct. Her eyes flew over the information as she called it up. She was assembling the pieces now, and they were starting to form a complete picture.

A terrifying, dangerous picture.

If she went on the assumption that the mole was her chief suspect, suddenly everything fell into place.

For the first time in her career with covert ops, she put her emotions ahead of her duty. She had to contact Harry, make sure that he was all right.

"Sir, I have an incoming message," Campbell said.

Kim's stomach clenched and his hands began to tremble slightly. Through sheer willpower, he forced them to steady, forced himself to continue to stare at his console, revealing nothing. He felt sweat gather at his hairline.

"Who's it from?" Chakotay's voice was sharp. He sounded as tense as Kim was feeling. Surreptitiously he glanced over at Campbell. She was grinning and winked at him.

"It's for Lieutenant Kim, sir. Libby Webber."

Kim blushed furiously. He usually loved hearing from Libby, but of all the times she could have tried to contact him, this had to be the worst. He felt every pair of eyes on the bridge staring at him.

"You'll take it here, Mr. Kim," said Chakotay. "Please keep it brief."

Libby's face appeared on the screen, and she seemed

startled and embarrassed to realize she'd be talking to the whole bridge crew.

"Um, hi, Harry," she said. "I just wanted—"

"Libby, I can't talk to you right now," he said, aware that Chakotay was watching him intently.

"Oh," she said, trying not to look surprised and hurt and failing. "Sure. I'm sure you're very busy with your new duties."

Against his better judgment, he said, "Libby, I'm sorry. There's just a lot going on right now. I'll talk to you later, okay?"

She blinked hard and smiled courageously. "I understand. Okay. Talk to you later."

The screen again filled with stars streaking past as they continued on to Loran II. Kim kept his eyes on his console, but he wasn't surprised to hear Chakotay say, "Until this mission is concluded, let's have no more personal messages in or out, shall we?"

"Of course, sir. Understood," Kim said. Lyssa looked uncomfortable, and the newcomers to the bridge, Patel and Tare, studiously attended to their stations.

Suddenly Lyssa made a small sound of annoyance. "Another message, sir."

"Please tell me it's not a personal one."

A frown marred her pretty face. "I wish I could, sir, but . . . sir, it appears to be from Irene Hansen."

Kim's head whipped up, but Chakotay appeared not to have noticed.

"Irene Hansen," Chakotay repeated. "On-screen."

Was it Kim's imagination, or was Chakotay drawing a blank at the name? Chakotay—the real Chakotay— would know exactly who this was. Everyone knew Seven's jovial aunt. But why would she be—

Irene Hansen's lined face appeared on the screen. Normally, she always had a hint of her smile and her eyes twinkled. Now, however, she had put on no makeup. Her hair was unkempt, and her eyes darted about.

"Chakotay?" she said in a shaky voice. "Chakotay, is that you?"

"Yes, ma'am. What can I do for you?"

"Annika . . . I want to talk to Annika. . . ." Her gaze wandered off to the right, and she fell silent.

For the briefest instant Kim was terribly worried. Then he realized what was going on—what had to be going on. Irene Hansen had a sharp mind and was in full possession of her faculties.

"Ms. Hansen," said Chakotay, his voice starting to sound harsh, "I don't know what you're talking about. Seven isn't on *Voyager* anymore."

Irene set her mouth, looking like a stubborn child. "That's just silly. You shouldn't try to trick an old woman like that, Frederick. I want to talk to Annika, and you should put me through to her right now."

"Mute," Chakotay said to Campbell, who quickly obeyed, looking surprised and embarrassed for poor Irene Hansen.

Kim swallowed and followed his gut hunch. "Sir," he said, "Seven's aunt has been this way for some time."

183

Now I've done it, he thought. *If somehow this really is Chakotay, he'll know I'm lying. Irene Hansen was at his send-off party, for pity's sake. . . . Good thing no one else on the bridge was there. . . .*

"I'm sorry about that, but she's got no business interfering with a starship on an important mission," Chakotay snapped irritably.

A huge wave of combined relief and horror washed over Kim.

It really *wasn't* Chakotay.

"May I alert Seven? She'll want to talk to her aunt," he said, shocked at how casual his voice sounded.

"Chakotay" considered this. "Let me do it," he said, and Kim's hopes fell. He had thought that Seven might be trying to contact them privately by sending her aunt as a "front." But if Chakotay contacted her, there'd be no chance for her to tell Kim what they might have discovered.

"I've got Seven, sir," said Campbell.

Seven of Nine's lovely, cool face appeared on the viewscreen. "Captain Chakotay," she said. "What a pleasant surprise. What can I do for you?"

Kim didn't dare risk looking up at her; he didn't want to give the game away. He concentrated instead on his console—and his eyes widened.

The woman was brilliant. She'd anticipated every possible problem. She was currently sending him an encrypted message, piggybacking it along the official channel. Quickly he began to download it.

"Seven, your aunt is trying to contact you," Chakotay said bluntly. No *hellos*, *how are yous*.

Her eyes widened slightly. "I apologize, Captain. My aunt has been having . . . some difficulty lately. I hope she did not cause any problems."

"No, but I thought you might want to know."

"Thank you. I will contact her immediately."

Kim almost had it. *Keep talking, Seven*, he thought fiercely.

"Is there anything else, Captain?"

"No. Chakotay out."

Kim hoped he was the only one who caught the flicker of distress that passed over Seven's face, like the faintest ripple in the surface of a pond when a stone was tossed into its depths. He hadn't gotten all of the message, but he'd gotten most of it. Now to crack the code and share whatever information was there with Kaz.

"That was weird," said Campbell. "I didn't know Seven's aunt was having problems. I'm so sorry to hear it."

"You're on duty on the bridge, Campbell," said Chakotay. "Attend to your station."

Campbell's fair face turned bright red. "Aye, sir. My apologies, sir."

The strain of the façade must be getting to the impostor, Kim thought. He wasn't even trying to ape Chakotay's mannerisms and demeanor anymore.

Kim burned to get at that message, but he didn't know how he would manage to excuse himself from the bridge and escape the eagle eyes that belonged to someone who wasn't Chakotay.

Libby thought Kim's voice was so controlled it was almost cold. She was startled, but immediately logic kicked in and she thought: *He knows something's going on. I should have realized that would happen. Harry's not stupid. At least he'll have his wits about him.*

She wanted so badly to discuss it, to ask him what he knew, what was going on, but she couldn't. She had to play the role of pretty, bright, talented girlfriend, and besides, it was obvious she wasn't going to get a chance to speak to him privately. So she let her face register the hurt she knew she ought to be feeling. *It's too bad we can't be allies. I hate deceiving him like this.*

Once his face had disappeared from the screen, she shifted gears immediately, going into the detached, emotionless state that had become such familiar territory over the last few years. She knew she was going over Fletcher's head but didn't care. Libby would be able to explain it to him; they had a good working relationship and he relied on her judgment.

Libby sent the message.

Chapter 17

IRENE HANSEN BEAMED as she regarded her niece. "Well?" she asked brightly. "How did I do?"

"You were convincing," said Seven.

"From Seven, that's high praise," said the Doctor. "I thought you did a magnificent job, Ms. Hansen."

"I confess, when you first proposed the scheme, I was a bit nervous," the older woman said. "I don't like the idea of trying to fool Chakotay. But when I did it, I have to admit, it was a lot of fun. Made me feel positively young again." Somewhat wistfully she added, "You will tell me what all of this is about? When you can?"

"Of course I will, Aunt Irene," Seven assured her. "Once everything has been declassified."

"I'd better let you be about . . . whatever it is you're about," said Irene. "Do keep me posted."

"I will. Thank you again." Seven hesitated. "You did a fine job."

Irene smiled, waved, and signed off.

"Do you know if Lieutenant Kim was able to get the message?" the Doctor inquired.

"What I am certain of is that he was unable to receive the complete message," Seven said, her fingers flying over the pads. "Even though he is no longer head of operations on *Voyager*, I have no doubt that he has remembered his skill at that post. It is entirely up to him now."

"At least we can get this to Admiral Janeway," the Doctor said.

Janeway wished she could have been aboard the *Delta Flyer* instead of being forced to sit in a conference hall and listen to the same argument being played out again and again.

The hope had been, on the Federation's part, to convince the planets that had expressed a desire to secede to remain. Unfortunately, the plan was not achieving that goal. If anything, it was causing those who had been on the fence to opt with the Secessionists. Janeway knew that the representatives of at least two member planets had gone from unsure to certain—about leaving. She desperately hoped that there would be no more added to that number, especially not Merin Kol.

She spotted the Kerovian amar in one of the front

rows and vowed to somehow find a few minutes to talk with the woman. She seemed to want to have a reason to stay, but if Janeway didn't give her one, and a good one at that, Janeway knew that Kerovi would also turn its back on an alliance of over forty years.

The presentation ended. Janeway blinked. She'd been so lost in thought—about Chakotay, about Paris, about Kim and Kaz and the colonists—that she hadn't paid much attention to what was going on right in front of her.

Break time, she thought. As she rose, stiff from sitting, she caught Merin Kol's eye. The other woman smiled in acknowledgment, but was quickly obscured by the exiting crowd.

Janeway tried to make her way toward the amar, but she felt a light touch on her shoulder and turned to see Tuvok. He looked even graver than usual.

"You have another message, Admiral. Priority channel gamma one."

Her eyes widened. Not only was this an urgent message, but it came from an untraceable source. She tasted disappointment at once again being unable to talk privately with Kol, but her duty was clear. Tuvok followed her, his silent presence a comfort, as she reached the private room where she could take the message.

"No, stay, Tuvok," she said to her old friend as the Vulcan turned to leave. "I have a feeling I may need you, now that I've dispatched Paris."

Tuvok inclined his head. "As you wish, Admiral."

She licked lips suddenly gone dry and entered her

personal data code. Old-fashioned lettering, white against a black background, scrolled across the screen.

Admiral: There is a traitor on Voyager, *a mole who has been accessing confidential information about the crew and ship for several months and who has been active for years. He is Commander Andrew Ellis. He is believed to be dangerous. Take all precautions when apprehending.*

The message was signed: *Peregrine.*

"Our elusive friend from a few months ago," Janeway said. She recalled that the mysterious "Peregrine" had appeared before at a crucial time, his or her untraceable messages always accurate, always helpful. Previously Peregrine had given them information that had helped save their lives—and, perhaps, the lives of everyone on Earth.

"This could be a trap of some sort," the ever-cautious Tuvok warned his former captain. "There is no way to document that this is the same Peregrine. And whoever it is, is not as up-to-date on the situation as we are. Commander Ellis is dead."

Janeway listened to Tuvok; she always listened to Tuvok. But she was also thinking furiously, staring at the white lettering as if trying to brand it into her brain.

"Yes, Ellis is definitely dead, according to both Kaz and Kim. Not, apparently, according to Chakotay." She turned to regard him with an intense gaze. "Dead by cuts inflicted by someone or something wielding a scalpel and leaving no trace of himself behind; dead just recently but somehow showing signs of long-term stasis."

She pointed at the screen. "Peregrine says he's been active for years. That's quite a feat for someone who's been in stasis for so long. I'm wondering if we're looking at something much more sinister than a mole, Tuvok."

"While we do not yet have all the facts, and the facts that we do have are perplexing and seemingly contradictory," Tuvok said, "logic still supports your conclusion."

He is believed to be dangerous. Take all precautions when apprehending.

So lost in thought was Janeway, her mind examining the options and coming up with only one that would fit all the evidence, she jumped when the computer chimed. At once Peregrine's warning vanished from the screen. She had committed the few words to memory, knowing that once the message was gone, it would be gone for good. Peregrine was not about to let himself— herself?—be traced.

"Another message on my private channel," said Janeway. "I'm in for a busy afternoon."

Seven of Nine and the Doctor appeared, looking serious.

"For people I no longer work with, I'm seeing quite a lot of you two," Janeway said. More seriously, she added, "What do you have for me?"

"Dr. Kaz was correct," Seven said bluntly. "The DNA is from Guillaume Fortier. It's been restructured and crossed with a variety of other sources of DNA to create a new species."

Janeway forced herself not to shudder. This monstrosity was exactly why genetic engineering had been made illegal in the Federation. It was too easy to go too far, to do something horrific in the name of advancing science.

"Is it possible to reverse the damage?"

The Doctor and Seven exchanged glances. "Fortunately, Opharix is a specialist in the field of genetics. It's hard at work on that right now," the Doctor said. "Naturally, we have been able to offer valuable input as well. But as you know, Admiral, it's easier to destroy than create."

"Whoever did this to Guillaume Fortier thought he *was* creating," Janeway said.

Seven's eyes flashed in outrage. "Whoever did this needs to be found and brought to justice. What happened to the colonists is not creativity, nor science. It is a crime."

"I couldn't agree with you more, Seven," Janeway said. "I've learned a little something myself. If," she added, with a nod in Tuvok's direction, "my source can be trusted."

"Who might that be?" the Doctor inquired.

"Someone who calls himself Peregrine," Janeway said.

The Doctor and Seven exchanged glances. "Peregrine was accurate in his suspicions the last time he communicated with us," Seven said. "What does he have to say this time?"

Janeway recited the message, and again the two old friends exchanged glances. The Doctor sighed heavily.

"Admiral," he said slowly, "our group has come to the conclusion that the murderer of Commander Ellis has to be—"

"A shape-shifter, possibly a Changeling," Janeway finished for him. The Doctor's eyes reached for his hairline, and even Seven looked surprised.

"May I ask what made you reach that conclusion?" she asked.

"It's the only answer that fits the evidence. Ellis wasn't a mole. He couldn't have been. The poor man has been in stasis for six years while someone else has been impersonating him. Chakotay is acting completely unlike himself and I tripped him up on a 'remember when' story when I last spoke to him. There's no trace of DNA on the body that isn't Ellis's own, and the mole Peregrine warned us about has been reading up on *Voyager*'s crew. How this all ties in with the genetic manipulation of the colonists, I've no idea. But I'll find out."

Seven and the Doctor were solemn. "What would you like us to do, Admiral?" Seven asked quietly.

"Keep doing what you're doing. There's got to be a way for us to return those colonists to their human state. Tuvok, Paris, and I will do what we can on our end."

"Admiral," said Tuvok, "Starfleet Command must be advised of the situation."

Janeway thought hard. "Not yet," she said, "and I'll take that responsibility on myself."

Controlled as his features were, Janeway knew her friend well enough to recognize surprise and disapproval on that familiar, dark face. "Admiral, I strongly suggest that you reconsider."

She shook her head. "Think about it. The shape-shifter murdered Ellis in cold blood, after apparently going to great lengths to keep him alive in stasis for six years. Why would he do such a thing? Why kill him now, and not before? My guess is: in order to produce a freshly killed corpse when it was convenient for him to do so. How many others does he have, hidden away for just such an occasion? Chakotay for one, I'm certain of it. I'm daring to hope that he's still alive, but if the Changeling gets wind that we know what's going on, everyone on that ship is going to be in jeopardy. Tom's on his way there right now. I'll let him know what he's dealing with. He can monitor the situation until help arrives."

"If you are not going to contact Starfleet Command, what form will that 'help' take?" Tuvok wanted to know.

"I'm not sure yet, Tuvok," Janeway replied honestly. "I'm not sure."

Kaz was starting to see the beach when he closed his eyes for even a moment.

They walked together now, he and Gradak. Stride for stride, feet sinking into the soft sand washed smooth by the ceaseless purple tides. They were growing more alike with each step, the doctor and the Maquis. Jarem glanced at Gradak as they walked, and almost before his eyes the lines of care and fear seemed to melt from around his eyes and mouth.

Jarem was starting to listen.

He sighed and opened his eyes. Hours had passed since they had spoken to Janeway, Seven, and the Doctor, and they'd heard nothing. It wouldn't be much longer until they reached Loran II, and who knew what would happen then. Maybe it was time for another attempt.

"Kaz to Chakotay." He marveled that his voice didn't sound the least bit shaky.

You're getting good at this, Gradak thought approvingly.

"Chakotay here. What is it, Doctor?"

"Is Lieutenant Kim at his station?"

"Yes, he's here."

"I've processed the data I took on the away team, and I think he may have the beginnings of a mild case of Umari flu," he said. "Of course I should have caught it at once, but we've all been a little distracted recently. I'd like to examine him again and stop the flu in its tracks."

A pause. Kaz's heart raced.

"Very well, I'll send him down. Chakotay out."

Kaz leaned back in his chair and blew out a breath. A few moments later Kim burst into sickbay.

"That was brilliant, Kaz!" the younger man exclaimed. "What the hell is Umari flu?"

"Completely made up," Kaz said. "I thought we might try to contact—"

Kim held up a hand. "I'm way ahead of you. We had an interesting message about an hour ago. From Irene

195

Hansen. She was incoherent and trying to reach Seven of Nine."

"But Irene Hansen is fine! She's one of the sharpest people I've ever met. She's in full control of her faculties."

Kim grinned. "Exactly. But whoever's sitting in the command chair right now didn't know that, and contacted Seven of Nine so she could tend to her poor auntie. While Seven was talking, she sent me an encoded message. I don't think I quite got it all—Chakotay was pretty keen on wrapping up the message quickly—but I got something."

"You know," said Kaz, "it's never a dull moment with you *Voyagers*."

"Don't be too judgmental," Kim retorted, sliding into Kaz's seat. "You're one of us now." His fingers flew over the control pads. "The trick," he said, "is for me to be able to access this message without sending up a red flag at Campbell's station."

"Any way you could distract her?"

Kim shook his head. "We've attracted enough attention by getting me down here with Umari flu. Better not risk it." He sighed and frowned in concentration. "I can't believe I'm saying this, but right now I wish Lyssa Campbell was less competent."

The Changeling was a creature of instinct.

Instinct—not a thorough, scholar's knowledge of anatomy or cell construction—was what made a

Changeling a shape-shifter. In order to be a stone, one had to know a stone; in order to be a person, one had to know a person. It wasn't a question of getting the freckles or moles or laugh lines right; it was understanding what made a person unique that gave a Changeling its real power.

And right now his instincts were telling him that something was about to go very wrong if he didn't figure out what was going on and stop it immediately.

Odd, two personal messages so hard on the heels of each other. Especially odd was Irene Hansen's appearance. Even with the medical strides made by the Solids over the years, the Changeling knew that some mental illnesses remained untreatable.

But not very many.

His fingers drummed on the arm of his chair as his thoughts raced. Not very many at all. What were the odds that Irene Hansen had one of those diseases?

And what was it Campbell had said? "Weird," she'd called it, and weird, indeed, it was. Hansen's condition had taken Campbell by surprise, but Kim seemed fully aware of the situation, as had Seven of Nine.

They were still some time away from arriving at Loran II. He'd wanted to drag that time out, to try to come up with a plan, but nothing had materialized. Suddenly the thought struck him that he might be better off on the planet surface, safe from detection, with Moset and his creatures to protect him.

The thought of the entities Moset was creating

thrilled him. Who needed to be part of a Great Link when one had beings like that under his command? Moset was a brilliant mind, but gullible, like all Solids were gullible. The Cardassian thought that the creatures he was hard at work perfecting would belong to him.

The Changeling almost snorted in derision. As if he'd hand over such a treasure trove to a scientist.

No, they were his, although Moset didn't know it yet. They, and the scientist who had made them, would protect him.

"Lieutenant Tare," he said, "increase speed to warp seven."

"Aye, sir," she replied, her fingers moving knowledgeably over the console.

As unobtrusively as possible, "Chakotay" touched his computer screen. The beaming face of the elderly woman he'd just spoken to appeared. She looked quite healthy, both physically and mentally.

He read her bio. There was no indication there of anything wrong with her.

Irene Hansen was just fine. And, come to think of it, how had she been able to so casually contact a starship engaged in a mission?

Kim had been the first one to react as if Hansen's mental state was not unexpected. And Kim had been called down to sickbay, to be treated for Umari flu. . . .

He searched the computer banks for information on the illness.

Nothing.

They were playing him. They knew something, and the two were playing him like—

"Captain?" Lyssa Campbell's voice, puzzled, unsure.

"Yes, Lieutenant, what is it?" His mind was racing at light speed. He didn't dare act until they had reached the planet. He was glad he'd instructed Tare to change speed.

"You asked me to monitor all incoming and outgoing messages."

He wished he could form a tentacle of his arm and wrap it around her slender neck. Forcing himself to remain calm, he replied, "Yes, I did. What have you got?"

"It may be nothing, sir. I had a ghost earlier, this may just be more of the same." She shook her blond head. "They really did a number on this ship."

The Changeling decided that if he had the opportunity to do so without putting himself at risk, he would indeed kill Lyssa Campbell.

"Lieutenant, make your report."

"Well, it looks like I'm detecting unauthorized activity. It's as if—but that can't be right." Her brow furrowed.

"Chakotay" couldn't take it any longer. He rose and strode to her station, pushing her out of the way firmly.

And that's when he saw it.

Seven of Nine had sent a hidden message, encrypted and deeply embedded in the ordinary, everyday conversation she'd had with Chakotay about her "mentally ill" aunt.

A message that was now being decoded and read in sickbay. Where Harry Kim and Jarem Kaz were.

He was so furious that for a moment, he almost lost his form. It was with a monumental effort of will that he retained it, kept calm, forced himself to sound mildly curious.

"I see why you're confused, Lieutenant. This is quite odd. Tare, how much longer till we reach Loran II?"

"About two minutes, sir."

"Enter standard orbit when we arrive. I'm going to duck into sickbay and talk to Kaz. Maybe one of his computers is acting up."

He strode to the turbolift. Once the doors were securely closed, he gave vent to his fury. His form shifted, then rearranged itself into Chakotay.

The clever bastards were on to him. Through his rage, he smiled, his lips twisting.

At least now he ought to be able to finally kill someone.

Chapter 18

Tom ran his hands over her sleek curves, deeply content. "I've missed you, sweetheart."

He truly had missed the *Delta Flyer.*

It was fortunate that Vaan was in fairly close proximity to Loran II, or else Tom knew that even with the sweet ship that was his beloved *Flyer,* he wouldn't be able to make it in time.

Sighing, he turned his thoughts away from admiring the *Delta Flyer* to the more sobering thoughts of Chakotay's strange behavior.

Lying to Janeway. Failing to notify Starfleet when his first officer had been killed. Leaving the planet at high speed. Janeway had been right—whoever it was who'd been sitting in the captain's chair, it wasn't

Chakotay. Or at least, it wasn't the Chakotay they knew.

There were all kinds of scenarios: possession by an alien, an impostor who could *be* an alien, a malicious clone, or simply a human with his features surgically altered.

Tom had never met Sekaya, but he grieved for her death. Chakotay had always spoken with such fondness, such wistfulness of his sister. It was inconceivable that he'd just abandon her remains on the planet.

Whether Chakotay was held hostage in the literal sense, or whether it was merely his mind that had been hijacked, Paris burned with determination to rescue and free his friend.

"Janeway to Paris."

Tom glanced at the small viewscreen to see Janeway's face. She looked more serious than he thought he'd ever seen her.

"Aye, Admiral, go ahead."

"We've got some new information about the being who's impersonating Captain Chakotay." A pause, then, "Tom, it's a shape-shifter. Maybe even a Changeling."

Tom's blue eyes widened. "A shape-shifter? But how—when—"

Janeway held up a hand, forestalling his barrage of questions. "There's a lot we don't know, and even this is nothing more than our best guess. But it's a guess that fits all the known facts. I've been talking with Seven and the Doctor, and the think tank's theory is that Andrew Ellis has actually been impersonated by a being able to assume his form for years. It kept Ellis's body in stasis, so it could produce a just-killed corpse when being Ellis was no longer convenient. There was no trace of DNA on the body other than Ellis's own—one reason why we believe it's a Changeling rather than another species. This, plus the fact that it's obviously not Chakotay. We think he switched places on the planet."

Tom's mouth opened and closed. He was dying to ask questions: *Who else do you think he was? How could he slip past security as the same person for so long? What does he want with Chakotay?* Instead, he chose the wiser option of silence.

"The shape-shifter poses an extremely high risk to everyone on board that ship. I'll be talking with Starfleet Command here shortly. We'll be getting you backup, but not yet. We have to do it as surreptitiously as possible. No matter what, do nothing to alert the shape-shifter that we are on to him. But you are to apprehend him if it's at all possible. Is that understood?"

"Aye, ma'am. Understood."

Her serious expression softened. "You're going to be on your own for a while yet, Tom. Be careful. But your duty is to prevent any more lives lost."

He nodded. "I know. I'll keep things as quiet as I can."

"Above all else, you can't let him leave the ship. If he's not contained, he'll disappear, and there's a chance we'll never find Chakotay." Her eyes revealed her pain. "Except perhaps the way we found Ellis."

Pain stabbed Tom, too. Righteous anger surged to replace it. "I'm not going to let that happen, Admiral."

"I know I can count on you, Tom. Janeway out."

Paris looked out at the stars racing past. The damn shape-shifter better watch out.

"How's it coming?" Kaz inquired.

Kim gave him an angry look. "About as well as it was two seconds ago when you asked me that. I'm going as fast as I can." He shook his head. "Seven did a good job. Maybe too good a job.

"Show me what you've got," Kaz said. Kim muttered something underneath his breath, then touched a pad. Kaz's eyes flew over the words:

After a thorough analysis of the data presented, the think tank has come to a consensus. The conclusion we have reached is that

"Why didn't she just tell us what the conclusion was?" Kaz asked, exasperation permeating his voice.

"That's Seven for you. She's so concerned about making sure her comments are comprehensive that she sometimes forgets about being concise."

"Well, that little trait of hers is costing us precious time that we don't have," Kaz said.

"I know, Kaz, I'm going as fast as I can," Kim said.

Kaz ran a hand over his face, finding it to be covered in sweat. He walked away a few steps, trying to collect himself. *Why are you standing here?* Gradak's voice demanded in his brain. *You're the chief medical officer.*

He's the head of security. You're suspicious of Chakotay; why isn't he in the brig right this moment?

"We don't have enough evidence," Kaz said under his breath.

Kim shot him a glance. "We may have what we need right here. This is the last of it."

Kaz hastened back to look over Harry's shoulder as the younger man deciphered the message.

. . . Captain Chakotay has been killed or abducted and is currently being impersonated by a

Kim's shoulders sagged. "And that's all there is."

Kaz pounded a fist on the table, making Kim jump. White-hot fury rushed through him. "Damn it!" he swore. *"Damn it!* Captain Chakotay is being impersonated by a *what*?"

"A Changeling" came a smooth voice.

Both men turned, shocked, to see Chakotay—the Changeling—standing in the entrance. He had a gentle smile on his face, but Kaz saw the hatred in the dark eyes.

Kaz and Kim sprang into action. As Kaz reached for a laser scalpel, a poor weapon but the best he could find here in sickbay, out of the corner of his eye he saw Kim doing something on the computer. Gradak's outrage washed through him. *What is he doing?* Gradak demanded. *He's chief of security, why isn't he fighting the intruder?*

Whatever Kim was doing, he paid the price for his delay. More swiftly than Kaz could have imagined, the Changeling sprang. He backhanded Kim so hard that

· 205

the security chief went flying. He crashed into the wall and slid in a crumpled heap to the floor, unconscious— or dead.

Kaz took advantage of the Changeling's intense concentration to leap on him with the scalpel. But the shape-shifter was faster. He easily, fluidly eluded the assault, and Kaz fell to the floor. Even as he tried to scramble to his feet, he saw the Changeling approaching, grinning manically.

"I've been waiting for this for such a long time," "Chakotay" said.

Lyssa Campbell frowned at the flashing light on her console. It was a message from sickbay. As she touched a pad, a message began to flow across the screen:

After a thorough analysis of the data presented, the think tank has come to a consensus. The conclusion we have reached is that Captain Chakotay has been killed or abducted and is currently being impersonated by a

That was all there was, but that was all that was needed. A quick check confirmed that the message, sent to her from sickbay, had originally been transmitted by the think tank of which both Seven and the Doctor were members.

Suddenly everything made sense. Campbell realized what she needed to do.

"Red alert, all hands, red alert." Lyssa Campbell's melodic voice boomed throughout the ship.

The Changeling seized Kaz and wrapped arms that were stronger than iron bands around him, then paused to listen.

"Intruder alert. Captain Chakotay has been abducted. All crew are instructed to apprehend the intruder impersonating him. Use whatever force necessary."

The message repeated and the Changeling seethed. He wanted to snap Kaz's neck, but he needed the man now. Quickly he changed his form, and Kaz now stared wildly up at Harry Kim.

"I need to get off this ship," "Kim" said firmly. "And you're either going to help me or die. Do you understand?"

Kaz nodded. The Changeling hauled the Trill to his feet. "Come on."

As he and Kaz strode swiftly down the corridors, the red alert blaring, the Changeling went over his options. He could transport down, or he could take a shuttle. He decided on the latter. It wouldn't get him there quite as quickly, but he needed more than one ship to make good his escape with the creatures.

Kaz, wisely, said nothing. Nor did he appear to be planning to bolt. The Changeling approved of both courses of action.

He regarded the Trill intently as they stood in the turbolift, committing his image to memory in case he had to impersonate the doctor at any point. Kaz felt his gaze and gave him stare for stare. Despite himself, the Changeling grinned.

"Which Kaz is looking at me," he asked, "Jarem or Gradak?"

"Does it matter?"

"Kim" shrugged. "It might."

"How about both?"

"That's fine. You know, Doctor, the Trill were always the one species that I thought was most like our people."

Kaz looked skeptical. "We're not shape-shifters," he said.

"No, but you understand being more than any one individual. You've got the memories of a dozen people inside you by this point, right?"

Kaz's blue eyes narrowed. "How did you know that?"

The Changeling let Kim's face smile. "I make it my business to know things."

The turbolift came to a stop. The Changeling tightened his grip on Kaz's arm. "You've been behaving properly until now, Kaz. Don't do anything stupid, or, believe me, I will not hesitate to kill you or anyone else we run across."

"Just like you killed Ellis?"

"Figured that out, have you?" The doors hissed open. "I've killed a lot more than Ellis, Doctor. Many, many more than him."

Paris dropped out of warp close to Loran II. He had expected to be at least somewhat nervous now that the moment had arrived, but instead he found himself calm and focused. *Voyager* was on his viewscreen and he hailed the ship.

"*Delta Flyer* to *Voyager,* Tom Paris commanding. Request permission to dock, *Voyager.*"

As he watched, he noticed a shuttle leaving the ship and heading directly for the planet, and his calm demeanor slipped. *Please let that not be the shape-shifter,* he thought. He had still received no response from *Voyager,* and with each second that ticked past, his anxiety grew.

"This is the *Delta Flyer,* Tom Paris commanding, come in, *Voyager.*"

He wasn't sure exactly what he was expecting—the shape-shifter masquerading as Chakotay to respond, or maybe Kim. Instead, Lyssa Campbell's voice, strained and taut, replied.

"*Delta Flyer,* assist us in intercepting the shuttle. Repeat, intercept the shuttle! Our tractor beam is off-line."

She didn't know he knew, didn't have time to explain, but she trusted him to hear the urgency in her voice and respond.

He did.

He maneuvered the *Flyer* on an intercept course, forcing the shuttle, which presumably contained the shape-shifter, to veer sharply to starboard in order to avoid a collision.

"*Delta Flyer* to the *Carrington,* I have orders from Starfleet Command for you to surrender. Stand down immediately."

The response was a phaser blast that sent sparks flying on the console and almost knocked Paris out of his seat. Swearing, he began to lock his own phasers, when a voice chilled him to the bone.

"Paris, listen to me." It was Harry's voice. "I'm being kidnapped. There's a Changeling, he's pretending to be Kaz right now and—"

"Tom, don't listen to him." Kim again, sounding weaker, this time coming from *Voyager.* "He's pretending to be me and he's taken Kaz hostage."

"Got it," Paris replied shortly, and changed the target. If he could knock out the engines and weapons on the *Carrington,* they might have a chance at saving their friend. He'd never encountered a Changeling personally, except for Odo aboard Deep Space 9 very briefly, and had certainly never seen one in full-on shape-shifting mode. He'd always thought that if such a thing occurred, he'd be able to tell the real one from the fake one. But the voice that had come from the shuttle had sounded exactly like Harry, and he knew Kim almost better than anyone.

I've got to stop him. I've got to.

"Nice little ship you got there," the Changeling mused as he regarded the *Delta Flyer.* "Shame I'm going to have to blow it to bits."

"*Delta Flyer* to *Carrington,* stand down."

"Your record has lots of complaints about your attitude, Paris," said the Changeling mildly. "I'm starting to understand why."

* * *

Kaz intently watched the being who wore the face of Harry Kim, trying not be obvious. He was both tense and calm at the same time. Inside him, Gradak demanded to be in the forefront, and Jarem let him. A doctor was of no use in this scenario. A rebel fighter was.

"If you know my record, Changeling, then you know I'm also stubborn as hell," Tom's voice continued.

"That's gotten you into trouble before." The Changeling adjusted his features, and suddenly Kim's body wore Paris's face. In Paris's own voice he said, "And it's going to get you into trouble again, right now."

The moment had arrived. The Changeling was having fun, playing tricks, mind games, taunting Paris. His attention wasn't on Kaz anymore. Deliberately Jarem retreated. The Kaz that sprang, roaring, upon the startled Changeling was Gradak Kaz, not Jarem Kaz.

Taken by surprise, the Changeling, in his clumsy human body, toppled out of the chair. Kaz did not attempt to take control of the ship; he couldn't defeat the Changeling and he knew it. But he could hamper the bastard. He brought his elbow slamming down on the weapons controls. Sparks flew upward and he smelled smoke. Pain shuddered up his arm, and then, for a moment, it went numb.

The Changeling was up now and launched himself on Kaz. Fingers far more powerful than mere human hands closed on his throat. For a moment Kaz couldn't breathe. Slowly he felt the inhuman fingers contracting,

211

crushing him, and he let go. He surrendered to the inevitable. He had died in a good cause, attempting to save his friends. Both Gradak and Jarem agreed on that.

And then, suddenly, the pressure eased, and elation surged through Kaz. The Changeling needed him alive. Gasping for breath, he stared into the now-distorted face of Harry Kim and managed, "You need a living hostage, don't you, you bastard? You can't impersonate two people at the same ti—"

He felt pain explode across his head, and then knew no more.

The *Carrington* was almost to the planet. Paris didn't question the stroke of luck that had taken out the shuttle's weapons but was silently grateful for it. If only that piece of luck had extended to lowering the shuttle's shields, he might be able to get a lock on Kaz and the Changeling and—

He swore as the shuttle disappeared into the swirling storm on the planet. All at once, all traces of it vanished from his sensors.

"*Delta Flyer* to *Voyager.* The shuttle has disappeared into the storm system on the planet."

"I'm not surprised, unfortunately." Kim's voice, still weak.

"You okay, buddy?" Tom inquired.

"I'll tell you all about it once you're onboard. Dock the *Flyer* and then join me on the bridge as soon as you can."

* * *

Paris strode onto the bridge of the familiar vessel a few moments later. Red alert blared, and the bridge was bathed in a scarlet light. Kim sat in the captain's chair. Blood streamed down his face and a large lump was starting to rise, but otherwise he looked all right. Campbell gave him a quick, tremulous smile of greeting, but everyone was tense. As Paris entered, Kim rose from the chair and offered it to his old friend.

For a moment Paris just stared at it. He was the highest-ranking officer present, but it just felt strange for him to be in the captain's chair. His place was normally at the helm, and he stole a quick glance at his old position. The incredibly gorgeous woman seated there gave him a measuring glance, then returned her attention to her duties.

Cut it out, Tom. Focus.

With no more hesitation, he slipped into the captain's chair while Kim took the first officer's seat.

"Campbell, open the ship's channels," he said, his voice cool and in control. When she nodded to him, he spoke. "All hands, this is Lieutenant Commander Tom Paris. I have taken temporary command of this vessel under orders from Admiral Janeway. We now know that the man who appeared to be Captain Chakotay was in fact a Changeling. He has currently escaped with Dr. Kaz as a hostage and is now on the planet. We're going to find both of them. All crew prepare for landing on the planet surface."

"Landing?" Kim exclaimed. Tom was glad he'd at least waited until the channel was closed. "Tom, I don't know if you know this, but we're dealing with Sky Spirit stuff again. You remember what happened the last time we tried to take *Voyager* down in a storm like this."

Tom met Harry's brown eyes with his ice blue ones. "Chakotay's probably down on that planet, a prisoner. Kaz definitely is a hostage. What would you do?"

Kim opened his mouth, closed it, then, strangely, smiled.

"Take the ship down."

"Then let's do it. Pilot, what's your name?"

The incredibly gorgeous woman swiveled in her chair. "Lieutenant Akolo Tare, sir," she replied in a deep, melodious voice.

"Lieutenant Tare, I'm sure you perform your duties admirably, but I'm going to relieve you for right now."

She raised her ebony eyebrows in surprise and, Tom, thought, anger. "Sir?"

He rose from his chair and stepped down to the conn. "You heard me, Lieutenant. This used to be my position, and no one knows how to navigate this ship better than I do."

"Let him do it, Tare," Kim said.

Reluctantly Tare rose from her seat and stepped back. Paris sat down in the familiar seat and gave himself a fraction of a second to enjoy the sensation.

"Take her down, Mr. Paris," said Harry Kim.

Chapter 19

THE CHANGELING HAD TO ADMIT that Kaz had been right—for the moment, the Trill was safe. Not even a Changeling could be two people at the same time, and therefore, much as he might want to, the Changeling could ill afford to murder his only viable hostage. Chakotay and Sekaya were hostages, too, of course, but he wasn't about to give either of *them* up. He needed them far too much. He checked quickly to make sure the doctor was still alive, then returned to the helm, leaving his hostage unconscious on the floor.

"Ellis to Moset," he said, using the name that the Cardassian knew best. "I'm making an emergency landing. Get the storms up once I'm down." He let his face slip easily into the nondescript features of Ellis; it took less concentration to maintain that form than others, as he had held it for so many years.

"What's going on?" The normally self-assured, smooth voice was worried.

"Too much to go into now," he said. "They've figured it out and they've sent the *Delta Flyer* after me." He checked his readings and saw with a rush of annoyance that Moset had yet to comply. "I said, get those storms up now, and make them big. *Voyager*'s got the ability to land on a planet, you know."

"But what does this mean for me? For us?" the Cardassian wanted to know.

"We've got to leave at once."

"But I can't do that! I'm at a critical juncture in the experiments!"

"Once the Federation captures us, there will *be* no more experiments, don't you *understand*?" He was shrieking now, at the end of his supply of patience for the trying doctor. "Put Chakotay and Sekaya in stasis. Take my creatures and—"

"We don't have two spare stasis chambers. All but one are still occupied."

"Then kill one of the occupants!" Why did he have to explain the simplest things to the man?

"Which one would—"

"I don't care!"

He felt his features slip, reform into who knew what shape. When he lost his temper, he tended to lose control of his shape-shifting abilities as well. He didn't

216

care, though, not now. With an effort he forced himself to calm down.

"I have a few things I have to do before we depart," he said. "We'll escape in the cloaked ship." He'd hoped to be able to utilize the *Carrington* as well, but now that the jig was up, he would have to abandon it, and a few of the creatures as well. It would be too easy for *Voyager* to track one of its own shuttles.

A long pause. "I'll make the necessary preparations."

"See that you do." He stabbed a golden-hued finger down and terminated the conversation.

He had planned everything out meticulously. It ought to have gone without a hitch. Instead, everything was unraveling at a shocking speed.

But there was still time to escape. He'd have to destroy the lab, of course, and Moset would yelp over that. Frankly, he regretted the necessity of it as well. At least he and the scientist would be able to take the prime test subjects and one or two of the creatures with them, along with all the information on the years of Moset's research.

They could start over. It was something the Changeling was used to by now.

"You heard him," said Chakotay quietly. There was no need to bully the Cardassian now. He had almost completely capitulated, and now the Changeling himself had provided the last piece of proof.

"I heard him," said Moset quietly. He turned away from the two prisoners, so Chakotay couldn't see his face. "He said, 'Take *my* creatures.' Not 'your creatures' or even 'our creatures.' " Slowly he turned, and there was commingled pain and anger in his haughty face. "You were right, Chakotay. He doesn't intend for me to keep them. And I'm beginning to think he never did."

"What are you going to do about it?" Chakotay asked.

"I don't know. I just don't know." Abruptly he rose and stalked out of the room.

"What do you think he'll do?" Sekaya whispered.

"I've no idea," said Chakotay, "but it might somehow involve our release."

Moset was trembling as he went to the beings he had made. Had designed, created, with the same exquisite care and craftsmanship as an artist would employ to execute a painting, or an engineer would design a ship. He had analyzed them, blended their DNA with that of the Sky Spirits, changed direction to follow up on any and every new, startling development. The hours he had spent on them! The devotion. And yes, he named it: the love.

He was not a fool. He knew how the rest of the quadrant viewed him and his experiments. The "Butcher of Bajor," they had nicknamed him. They classified him with Kodos the Executioner, Colonel Green, Kesla, Beratis, T'sart, and Hent Tevren, and though he always responded with a cheerful shrug, he knew that this was how history was going to depict him.

But those who dared to judge him so mercilessly were wrong. They couldn't see the larger scope, couldn't understand the profundity of what he was doing. With the Sky Spirit creatures he had created from ordinary lumps of human flesh, he was going to prove them wrong. He was going to wrest his reputation away from those who would condemn so quickly, show them the heights to which a being could rise through the magnificence of so brilliant a mind as his.

But Ellis—Katal—the Changeling—he was going to take them away. Oh, Moset knew what the exiled Founder would do with such spectacular beings. He'd make his own little Dominion out of them; make them scrape and obey and mindlessly follow him and only him the way the Vorta and the Jem'Hadar had followed their creators. But at least the Founders had had the luxury of seeing the worship in the eyes of the things they had made. Moset would only stand by and watch his creations worship another; another who had no hand in their making.

If, he thought bitterly, he would even be *alive* to stand by and watch.

Moset regarded the ape-like creatures whose telepathic skills were beyond his imagining groom one another. He felt a deep, aching pain that was due to nothing physical.

He would do anything to keep these creatures; they were his rehabilitation in the eyes of the future.

And as far as he could reason it, there was only one way to do so.

219

When Moset returned to the lab, he found Ellis—looking like Lieutenant Kim—tossing the body of a Trill onto another bed. The Changeling glanced up as Moset entered.

"There you are," he said brusquely. "Help me with him."

Moset stared for a moment, and then moved to assist the Changeling. "Who is this and why have you brought him here?"

"Name's Kaz. He's the ship's doctor, and he's a valuable hostage." The Changeling yanked on the restraints, cinching them tight.

"Is he drugged?" Moset asked, slipping into scientific mode.

The Changeling smiled without mirth, twisting Kim's pleasant face. "Only as much as a good punch in the jaw will drug someone," he said. "I don't want him sedated; we may need him to talk to someone for us."

He glanced at Chakotay and Sekaya, who regarded him silently. "I thought I told you to put these two in stasis. Why are they still conscious?"

Moset bristled. "I told *you* I was at a critical stage," he replied testily.

"You idiot!" "Kim" bellowed. "We've got an *Intrepid*-class starship doing its damnedest to land on the planet! Stop whatever it is you're doing right now and start packing things up. I don't want to leave you behind, Moset, but I will if I have to. Don't push me."

How could I not have seen this in him? Moset

thought, almost with a brush of wonder. The Changeling had spoken this way before now, but somehow, Moset had always been deaf to it. Now, for perhaps the first time, he truly listened to what his companion was saying. More to the point, Moset was paying attention to *how* the Changeling was saying it. It had taken a human prisoner to open the Cardassian's eyes to the truth: He was at as much risk as Chakotay and Sekaya.

"Point taken," Moset said icily.

The Changeling appeared not to notice his ally's new demeanor. His eyes roamed over the occupied stasis chambers. "Kill anyone but him," he said, pointing to the humanoid that Moset knew was named Alamys. "I might need him. Finish up in here as quickly as you can. I'll be concluding some business of my own."

Attempting to look industrious, Moset began to gather up some vials and tools. As soon as "Kim" had disappeared down the corridor, however, he turned to the two imprisoned humans.

"Listen to me," he said quickly in a low voice. "And listen well."

Kaz returned to consciousness and searing pain. He felt the cool press of a hypospray against his throat, and the pain ebbed. He blinked, trying to focus, turned his head—and stared into the face of a Cardassian.

I know that face—

He tried bolting upright but was gently restrained by a strong hand. "It's all right, Kaz," came a familiar

221

voice. Kaz's head whipped around and he relaxed slightly as he saw Chakotay and—

"Sekaya!" Both siblings were standing beside him. Pleasure surged through him. "I thought you were dead. Chakotay—" He broke off in midsentence as more recent memories flooded him and turned again to regard the oddly familiar Cardassian.

Chakotay smiled. "It's really me," he said, "and this is really Sekaya."

Still, Kaz stared, not at Chakotay's face but at his shaved head and the blinking lights that had been inserted into his skull.

"What happened to you? Who's he? Where are we? Where's the Changeling?"

"It's a long story. Let's start with the introductions. Jarem Kaz, this is Crell Moset."

And suddenly, quietly, coldly, everything locked into place in Kaz's memory.

Crell Moset. The Butcher of Bajor. This was the man who had rounded up Bajorans like cattle, like lab animals, who had performed deadly and brutal experiments on them, blaspheming the name of "science."

Vallia. He killed my Vallia! The ones who survived told me that he gave her no relief from the pain, not even at the very end, when she was begging for death, for release from the torment—

Vallia's Revenge *was what Gradak had named his little ship; was what Gradak had vowed to achieve—*

222

The Cardassian's expression went from pleasant to wary as he regarded Kaz. "Have we met?" he asked.

Icy hatred seized Kaz's throat, closing it up. He wanted to scream, but he couldn't; wanted to cry out his fury, but remained silent.

"You might have," said Chakotay cautiously, "he's a joined Trill."

A joined Trill who had a Bajoran wife you murdered, *you son of a bitch—*

"You're dead," Kaz said, his voice as cold as death itself. "You were killed in a warp core breach accident years ago. It was the best news I'd heard in a long time."

"To quote one of Earth's more famous writers, 'Reports of my death have been greatly exaggerated,' " Moset replied mildly. The jauntiness of his attitude infuriated Kaz. He made an angry noise deep in his throat and tensed.

"Kaz. *Jarem.*" Chakotay's calm voice cut through the red haze. "Whatever's going on with your memories and Moset, you've got to put them aside. Right now I need you to focus." A gentle squeeze on Kaz's shoulder. Not knowing how he managed to do so, Kaz dragged his gaze away from the loathed visage of the Butcher of Bajor to the compassionate face of his friend. He took a deep, shuddering breath.

"I'm listening."

"Many years ago the Changeling who was impersonating me had his shape-shifting ability taken from him by the Founders as a punishment for going against orders.

223

He rescued Moset, and since then, Moset's been trying to figure out how to help Ellis get his powers back."

Kaz was puzzled. "Ellis?"

"He was impersonating Andrew Ellis when the Founders took away his powers," Moset put in, trying to be helpful. He drew back slightly at the look Kaz shot him.

"It might be best if he hears everything from me, Moset," Chakotay said quietly. The Cardassian nodded.

"So we never actually met the real Ellis?" Kaz was trying to follow the complicated story.

"That's right. The Changeling had kidnapped the real Ellis and kept his body in stasis."

It was all starting to make sense. Kaz recalled the autopsy and the mysteries it had yielded. "Go on."

"Over the years Moset had some success. Because of experiments with—with my people, he learned about our Sky Spirit DNA."

Kaz's blue eyes flicked to Sekaya's. She had her arms folded tightly across her chest and held her body in a defensive posture. Obviously Chakotay's sister, too, loathed the Cardassian.

"He was able to get some of the Changeling's abilities back. He can now shift into any humanoid male form, but that's it. Moset also crafted a way for him to lock into human form at will."

"So he could pass medical exams," said Kaz, looking over at Moset. Despite his loathing of the man, one couldn't help but admire his brilliance. "Very smart."

"Moset's also been experimenting on the colonists, crossing Sky Spirit DNA with human. The creatures who attacked the away team are the result. They've got incredible mental abilities, Jarem. They can control the weather, move things with their thoughts—all kinds of things."

"He told me they were my reward," Moset said, apparently unable to keep silent despite Chakotay's gentle warning. "But he lied. He plans to keep them for himself, to create a powerful race of devoted slaves. He's greedy and ambitious, and he wants to create his own personal Dominion. I won't let that happen. That's why I've decided to help you."

"As the old saying goes," said Chakotay, "the enemy of my enemy is my friend. And Moset is certainly Ellis's enemy now."

"Chakotay," said Kaz in a thick voice, "I don't know if I can work with him."

"Then you'd better know this," Chakotay said somberly. Kaz turned pained eyes upon his friend and saw Chakotay was deadly serious. "One of the people the Changeling pretended to be was someone we both knew." He paused, then said bluntly, "He was Arak Katal."

Kaz's mouth went dry. His throat worked, but no sound came out. Sekaya sat down on the bed beside him and slipped an arm around him. At any other time he'd enjoy the attention from the lovely human female, but now he was so stunned the gesture barely registered.

"Arak Katal?" he repeated. "We had Arak Katal *on our ship*?"

225

Chakotay nodded. "We've got to stop him."

"They're firing at us!" Ramma, only fourteen, his voice shrill with fear.

"Of course they're firing at us, they're trying to kill us," said Laskan to his twin, the harshness of his voice not quite hiding his own terror. They were so alike, but now reacted in completely different ways; Ramma terrified, Laskan, the elder by two minutes, trying so hard to look brave he only succeeded in looking angry. . . .

"Quiet, you two," snapped their mother. Tall, with piercing green eyes and a strong jaw to match her strong body, Tixari continued firing the weapons while Gradak desperately tried to find a clear path out of the hell that was exploding around them.

Gradak heard the soft whimper from the back even over the sounds of battle, and his heart ached. Kemi, only six years old. The blast had torn off her arm and her father had made an old-fashioned tourniquet from the fabric of his shirt. If nothing else, Gradak mused darkly, the Maquis had revived medical techniques that had been left behind two centuries ago. Sticks and fabric and water had been pressed into use when limited medical supplies ran out.

The ship rocked from another volley of phaser fire. A huge vessel passed within meters of them, and Gradak could swear he could almost see the occupants. Not Cardassian, not these ships. Bigger, faster, and deadlier, these were . . .

"Daddy," breathed Kemi, and Gradak had to blink hard to clear his eyes of angry tears. "Daddy, I can't feel my legs. . . ."

"Hang on, sweetie," the girl's father said in a broken voice. "Please hang on. We'll get you to help. Won't we, Kaz?"

"Yes, we will," Gradak Kaz rasped. "If it's the last thing I do."

He knew that it would, indeed, be the last thing he did. He did not tell them he, too, had been shot. He had told them that the blood was from Amgar and Rekkan, whose bodies now lay quietly in the back; that it was not his own. But even as he got the lie out, he knew that he could not hang on to consciousness much longer.

He had to get them to safety. Had to. From the depths of his brain, a tiny scrap of information floated up. There was a Federation ship stationed in this area of space. If he could just get to it—

"Jarem." The voice was soft, feminine. Vallia? No, Vallia was dead, had been killed by the Butcher of Bajor, along with so many others. "Jarem, I understand what you're feeling. Believe me, I do. But we need you now."

Kaz moaned softly and buried his face in his hands. Behind his closed lids, he saw Gradak, his jaw set, his eyes blazing.

Give me this body. I can take care of everything.

And oh, Jarem wanted to let him.

"No," Jarem said quietly, to the other Trill. But Chakotay misunderstood.

227

"There's a way to stop Katal—the Changeling. Moset thinks he can do it, but it's going to be risky, and I'd feel a hell of a lot better if you were working with him on this."

He sighed deeply. The two men he hated most in the universe were both on this planet. The question was, which did he hate more—the man who had killed Gradak's wife, or the man who had betrayed thousands, including children, to slaughter at the hands of the Cardassians?

The enemy of my enemy is my friend.

He gazed at Moset, who gave him back stare for stare.

"What do you need me to do?" he asked quietly.

Chapter 20

"I WILL NOT MAKE A DECISION until after I have spoken privately with Admiral Janeway," Amar Merin Kol said in her soft but stubborn voice. "She has treated me with consideration, concern, and respect. I owe her at least a hearing."

The Changeling couldn't believe his ears. When he'd last spoken with Kol, she'd all but capitulated to the "wisdom" he, posing as her adviser Alamys, had spoken. Now, even though she hadn't had a single private conversation with the woman, that damned Janeway was starting to make the amar change her mind.

"From what you have told me," "Alamys" said, "Janeway hasn't bothered to try to spend much time with you. Her Federation duties seem to keep pulling her away. How, then, do you come to the conclusion that you matter to her? That our humble little Kerovi matters?"

"I feel as though I've gotten to know the admiral during our conversations," Kol said, jutting her chin out a little. "If she says that she has something important going on, then I trust that to be the truth. She would not lie to me."

"How do you know that? How do you know anything like that about this human woman? She's a politician, a diplomat. How can you trust her?"

Suddenly Kol laughed, a bright sound. "I'm a politician, and a diplomat. And so are you. Do you mean to say you think we can't be trusted, either?"

The Changeling forced himself to chuckle. "I concede your point, Amar," he said graciously, inclining his head. He knew, of course, what she could not—that Janeway really did have important things that were drawing her away from conversing with the amar of Kerovi. Things like hunting down a Changeling. She had to have been the one to send Paris out after him. At least some good was coming from his being hunted—Janeway was too busy to talk to Kol.

"Nonetheless," he continued, "people always make time for what is important to them. I think, perhaps, you may be trusting her a bit much."

"It's not so much a matter of trust, as a matter of fairness. I feel I owe it to the admiral to listen to her and make up my mind then."

Then I must certainly hope that you don't get the chance to listen to her, the Changeling thought. Time to end this.

"I am going to be in a private conference for the next few days," he said. "I regret that contact will be infrequent, but I will manage what I can." He hesitated, then said in a softer voice, as if he was afraid of listening ears, "It is a most delicate stage, Amar. If you understand my meaning."

"I believe I do," she replied. "I shall wait to hear from you, then. Please come home as soon as possible. I have so much to discuss with you, my old friend."

He bowed deeply. "Time with you is an honor and a pleasure. Alamys out."

When her image vanished, so did the Changeling's smile. He adjusted the settings on the holoprogram to another room, similar to the first but with subtle differences. His features, too, adjusted. There were several more impersonations to perform, several more expectations to set. He had no idea how long he'd have to be away from such an elaborate setup, and each of his alter egos needed an explanation as to why they had dropped out of touch.

This was going to take time he didn't really have, but there was no alternative. The Changeling liked everything wrapped up neatly.

At first, as Moset began to explain the procedure they were about to perform, Kaz found himself not listening as attentively as he should. All he could think of was the last time he had seen Vallia, how they had made love with the same urgent desperation they had always made love, living with the knowledge that they led dangerous lives and that any moment one of them might be killed in the line of duty.

He would not have felt so helpless, so stricken, had Vallia died from a phaser blast. But to know she had ended her life at the hands of this . . . this . . .

Stop it, Jarem thought furiously. *I never knew Vallia. I'm sorry for her death, and I agree with you that this Cardassian makes the rest of his people look like innocent children, but I can't be in this place right now. I have to be alert, listen to what he's saying, or many more will die.*

"I'm sorry, Moset, could you repeat that last?" he said, flushing a little as he realized he'd missed a large chunk of important information.

"Of course," said Moset. "It's hard for non-Cardassian brains to grasp this sort of thing."

Kaz fought down the combined urges from Jarem and Gradak to strangle the arrogant bastard and concentrated on listening.

He was not a specialist in the field of genetics, and the sort of work Moset had been doing for the last three years was highly unethical and illegal, so he didn't quite grasp all the intricacies Moset was describing. He did understand enough so that his horror and disgust at the man's atrocities was mingled with admiration for Moset's brilliance and imagination. Some of the things

232

he had accomplished were truly amazing, and reluctantly Kaz found himself being drawn into Moset's realm of passion and enthusiasm for what he was doing.

Sekaya and Chakotay were listening as well, although Kaz could tell from their faces they grasped even less than he. It was enough, however, for Kaz to see awe, wonder, and fear flit over their faces, especially Sekaya's lovely, expressive one. Now and then she turned to her brother and regarded him with concern, for he was the one who would be subjected to Moset's latest experiment. Except this time the experiment would, they all hoped, save them instead of destroy them.

It was, to Kaz's surprise, Sekaya who spoke first after Moset had finished the explanation. "I think I know why your previous subjects had so much trouble," she said.

Moset looked at her with indulgent fondness, much as a doting owner might regard the antics of a kitten. "Really, my dear? Why is that?"

Despite the note of condescension in his voice, Sekaya regarded her tormenter evenly, calmly. Kaz felt a sudden rush of renewed pleasure that she was alive and, thus far, well.

"They had no *seklaar*," she said. "No roots, no anchor."

Moset looked puzzled, but Chakotay was nodding. "Pray continue, my dear," the Cardassian invited.

"You know a great deal about the aliens whose genes you have used on the colonists and on the

Changeling," Sekaya said. "But you don't know a lot about the Sky Spirits."

"I thought they were the same thing," said Kaz, wondering how confused he really was after all.

Sekaya turned to him. "Yes, and no. Moset knows about the scientific aspect of the aliens—the abilities of their minds. But forty-five thousand years ago, no one on Earth could even grasp such things. We knew these beings as the Sky Spirits, with the emphasis on *spirit*."

Moset sighed. "I don't really have time to get into a theological discussion right now, not when—"

"I'm not talking about theology," Sekaya said harshly. "I'm talking about spirit. The realm of the imagination. That's all wrapped up in the brain, too. I don't want to get into a discussion about the reality of our spiritual beliefs. What Chakotay feels, what I feel—that's our business. But what you're about to do requires knowledge of the spirit end of things, and you have no grasp of that."

"Native peoples used to use psychotropic drugs or extreme physical deprivation in order to achieve an altered mental state," Chakotay said. "It was in that state that we received visions. Now we use something called an *akoonah* to access that part of the brain. We call it spiritual; others call it mental."

"What you call it doesn't matter," Sekaya said. "But, Moset, you have failed to take this into account at all. Have you ever studied my people's beliefs?"

"I'm a scientist, not a cultural historian," Moset replied.

"Exactly. When we go on vision quests, or as my people call them, spirit walks, we usually don't journey alone. We meet the spirits of those who have gone before us, or animal spirits who befriend and advise us. We call these beings *seklaars*. They are the anchors that keep us sane." She shrugged her slim shoulders. "Maybe they really are separate entities. Maybe they're just part of our imaginations. I don't know and right now I don't care. What I do care about is, you have experimented on these people and done things to them they haven't been prepared for. They had no idea what they would experience, no way to call on *seklaars*. No wonder they went mad."

"Sekaya," said Kaz, very gently and very respectfully, "insanity doesn't turn men into monsters. Not literally, anyway."

She looked at him with her large, dark brown eyes and challenged him, "Doesn't it?"

Moset was now regarding Chakotay's sister with a new respect. "You could be on to something there," he said. "When you're dealing with mental powers at the level that the Sky Spirits possessed them, it isn't that hard to alter the physical reality."

" 'There are more things in heaven and earth, Horatio, than are dreamt of in your philosophy,' " Chakotay said. "Shakespeare wasn't a quantum theorist, but he knew what he was talking about."

Sekaya regarded her brother. "I don't want you to do this," she said.

"Sekky, I have to. The Changeling is much more

235

powerful than any of us, even if he can't shape-shift. The only way I have even a chance of stopping him is to take on the Sky Spirit powers myself. And I can't handle them unless I'm prepared, unless I undertake a spirit walk."

She held his gaze. "Then you aren't doing it alone."

Suddenly Kaz understood. "You're volunteering to be his *seklaar*," he said.

"Exactly. I'm not letting my brother go on such a dangerous spirit walk all by himself. Chakotay, I've been training. Deeply. This is something I know a great deal about. I've been the anchor for dozens of spirit walks. Let me do this for you."

"It could help," Moset said. "You'll need to keep your wits about you if you're going to be able to do this. If she really can perform this duty, then I say let's take her up on her offer."

"But she's my sister!" Chakotay protested.

"And Guillaume is Marius's brother," Sekaya responded. "He deserves to have his brother back."

As Chakotay hesitated, Moset added, "Time is running out, Chakotay. If we're to have any hope of success, we need to begin immediately. Ellis's business—"

"Quit calling him that," Chakotay snapped. "I know that's how you knew him first, but the real Andrew Ellis was a fine Starfleet officer who didn't deserve to be kidnapped, put in stasis, and cut to pieces with a scalpel."

Moset appeared to be slightly taken aback by

Chakotay's outburst, but Kaz understood exactly where the harsh words had originated.

"How shall I refer to him, then? It's awkward to just keep saying 'the Changeling.' "

Chakotay's eyes met Kaz's. "Katal," he said coldly. "We'll call our enemy Arak Katal."

Kaz smiled, slightly. A good choice. The face of a traitor who was responsible for the slaughter of thousands was a better one to hate than that of a Starfleet officer.

"We're arguing over semantics, but fine, we'll call him Katal. But by all means, gentlemen and lady, let's *get on with it.*"

Quickly Sckaya threw her arms around her brother and murmured something. Kaz didn't catch it and didn't want to; it was for Chakotay's ears alone. The captain nodded and held his sister tightly before releasing her. They returned to the beds and lay down.

Even though he knew that both Chakotay and Sekaya were willing participants, Kaz cringed inwardly as Moset bent over them and physically manipulated the inserts in their skulls. Sekaya hissed and tensed slightly as the Cardassian touched her with curiously gentle fingers, but forced herself to submit to his ministrations.

Satisfied, Moset looked up. "You'll be responsible for monitoring them, Doctor."

The Butcher of Bajor calmly giving him instructions, like they were colleagues. Kaz swallowed and nodded. Sekaya and Chakotay, and who knew how many others, were depending on the Trill to keep a cool head. He would not let them down.

Moset took a deep breath. "I know the situation is dire, but . . . this is so exciting! Now. We'll begin with Sekaya." He touched some controls and Sekaya's eyes closed. Quickly she sank to deep levels of unconsciousness, but Kaz could see that the right side of her cerebrum was highly active.

"Then Chakotay." He repeated the procedure, and the captain of the *U.S.S. Voyager* was soon as deeply unconscious as his sister. Kaz tensed; even now he suspected a trap. But Moset was engrossed in what he was doing.

The Cardassian nodded, satisfied, then stepped over to Chakotay.

"Dr. Kaz?"

Kaz looked at him. "Yes?"

"This is the tricky part. We'll need to pull them out quickly if something goes wrong."

"I understand."

Moset looked down at Chakotay's face almost hungrily. He pressed a hypo to the captain's neck.

"Here we go," said Moset.

Chapter 21

CHAKOTAY OPENED HIS EYES, unsure as to what to expect. He found himself not in his usually imagined place—the Central American rain forest—but in a forest of a more northernly sort. The sweet, powerful scent of pine filled his nostrils, and the cool moisture in the air felt good on his skin.

He sensed that he was not alone, and turned to regard his sister.

Here, in her purest aspect of spirit, she was even more beautiful than she was in her physical form. Tall, slim, her long black hair loose about her shoulders, her eyes sparkling like stars—

"Your spirit is so beautiful, my brother," she said

quietly, in tones of awe. Evidently, she saw in him what he saw in her.

They went to each other and clasped hands. "This is your place, isn't it?" Chakotay asked.

"Yes," she said. She looked over his shoulder and smiled. "Can you see Him?"

Chakotay turned and beheld a magnificent white-tailed buck regarding him with more than human intelligence. He felt a shiver. One never spoke the name of one's animal totem; that would anger it. But here, joined with his sister in a way that his people had never before attempted, he was being granted the privilege of sharing her visions.

Slowly he nodded to the great beast, Who inclined His own head in acknowledgment.

"Daughter of the Forest," said Stag in a musical voice, "you must be in great need to have brought Stone Keeper with you."

Sekaya's eyebrows rose as, for the first time, she heard her brother's spirit name.

"Yes," she replied. "Many are in danger. This was the only way we felt we could save them."

Stag nodded His comprehension. He turned His large, soft eyes on Chakotay.

"Then you must begin your journey. Each being that you encounter will give you strength to manage the burden you bear. Do not worry that it is taking too long; you must leave your impatience behind with your body. When you return, you will have been in this world for only a few moments, no matter how long it seems that

240

you have been away. Do you understand, Stone Keeper?"

"I do," Chakotay replied solemnly. "How do I begin?"

"Daughter of the Forest, you must release him."

Chakotay realized that his spirit-sister had been clutching his hands hard. She swallowed, then deliberately stepped back and loosened her grip. They both gasped to see a golden cord of light connecting them still.

"This is Sekaya's will," Stag said. "She will hold you and keep you safe on your journeying."

It was no small thing, and Chakotay worried about the toll it would take on her. He opened his mouth to voice his concerns, but Stag had read his thoughts.

"I and others will lend her our own energy to keep her safe. Have no fear, Stone Keeper. You must journey boldly, secure in the knowledge that all will be well. One bit of doubt, and you will falter. And if you falter, you will fail."

Stag walked on delicate legs to where Sekaya had settled herself against the trunk of a pine tree. Gracefully He knelt beside her and put His head in her lap. She reached to stroke His neck. There was an ease about the gesture that told Chakotay they had done this before.

"Go, my brother. I will keep you safe."

She closed her eyes and began to chant. Assured that she would be taken care of, Chakotay turned around.

"Heart rate dangerously low," said Kaz. "Blood pressure dropping. Abrupt cessation of activity in the medulla." He looked at Moset. "I'm worried she might be going into shock."

241

"The readings you gave me are all perfectly normal for humans at this stage," said Moset. *"Keep me notified, but I don't think we need to be concerned. Everything seems to be going fine."* He leaned closer and stroked Sekaya's cheek. *"Perfectly fine."*

"Took you long enough," Kolopak said, a twinkle in his eye and a slight smile belying the chastisement of the words.

"We've met before in this place, Father," Chakotay said.

"Not like this."

"What do you mean by that?"

"Look at you!" Kolopak said. He wore the battered old expedition hat that Chakotay remembered. A lump rose in his throat. If only he could be sure that this was real, that he really was speaking with his father, and not just imagining it, fantasizing about a forgiveness that could never truly come—

"Stop it!" Kolopak cried, seizing Chakotay by the arms and shaking him. "No fear! No doubt, or you will fail!"

"Looks like Sekaya inherited your confidence and optimism, Father," Chakotay said.

"My contrary son," Kolopak said affectionately. "Perhaps it took someone so willing to question things to embark on so important a journey."

"You know, then?"

"I do. You are accepting the burden of Sky Spirit

DNA," Kolopak said. "I see its powers beginning to settle in your mind. How does it feel?"

Chakotay considered the question. "I don't know yet. I don't feel any different."

"Here, all souls are equal in power and beauty," Kolopak said. "But when you return, then you will see what kind of an inheritance you have been given."

"The best possible one," said Chakotay, "with you as my father."

Kolopak softened and reached to embrace his son. Chakotay hugged him tightly. *I love you, Father. I'm sorry I couldn't be what you wanted me to be.*

Like a gentle breeze, he sensed Kolopak's thoughts: *You were always, ever what you were destined to be, Chakotay, even as you rebelled at the thought. I am proud of you, my son.*

He took the gift his father was giving him: reconciliation and love, a complete acceptance he had been denied while his father lived.

Tears leaked from Chakotay's closed lids. Sekaya's lips were curved in a half smile. Kaz regarded them with concern, then returned his attention to monitoring their vital signs. Whatever they were doing, it was intense.

"No sign of rejection. Preparing second infusion," Moset said.

Kolopak's image faded, then disappeared. Chakotay found himself on his back, staring up at a sky crowded

243

with stars. He sat up and discovered that he was lying on hard-baked earth, the only light and warmth emanating from a crackling, smoky fire.

Across from the fire sat Wolf. Her expression was kind and loving. Of all the companions he had had on his spirit walks, She was the gentlest. Her love was pure and demanded nothing in return, only that he accept it. His heart swelled with affection for Her.

Wolf was joined by Snake, who lay basking in the warmth from the fire. Her tongue flickered out lazily. And even Coyote was here, gazing mischievously at Chakotay.

"Only now can we all be together," Snake said. "Only now can your spirit hold us all. You have expanded since last we met, Stone Keeper."

"Is it the Sky Spirit DNA in me?" he asked.

"Possibly. Or maybe you've just evolved." Snake's tongue flickered in and out. Suddenly Wolf's ears pricked up and her tongue lolled.

"Welcome, Sister," Wolf said. Chakotay felt a prickling at the back of his neck and knew who he would see when he turned around.

She was not lolling on a sun-warmed rock, as She had been the last time he had beheld Her. This time Black Jaguar was all business. She stood, Her muscles tense beneath Her thick black pelt, the firelight glittering in Her golden eyes.

"Wolf gives you love," Black Jaguar said. "Snake makes you think. Coyote shakes things up when life becomes stale. I bring you the challenges that will make or break you. Are you afraid?"

He wasn't sure what answer She wanted. He was afraid, but he knew he wasn't supposed to be. He licked lips suddenly gone dry and said, "Yes, I am. But I will go forward despite my fear."

Her body relaxed slightly. As he rose, She stepped toward him on silent feet and rubbed the warm, long length of Her body against him.

"Only a fool is not afraid. And I have no time for fools. But you must trust in your heart that you are up to the task."

"I have that trust. Sekaya anchors me. Kaz makes sure my body is safe. Black Jaguar has come to challenge me. Such beings would not waste time on one who would not be worthy of such grace."

"A man is known by the company he keeps," Black Jaguar agreed. "Will you undertake this challenge?"

"I will walk with Black Jaguar," Chakotay said.

He rose and followed Her, walking away from the spirit animals by the warm fireside, walking into the darkness. Walking into the night sky as the ground beneath him disappeared and both he and the gigantic black cat trod on starlight.

"Quite remarkable," said Moset. "Not even a hint of rejection. This whole spirit angle is one definitely worth pursuing further. Preparing third infusion."

* * *

The golden cord spun into the distance. With every step that Chakotay took on his spirit walk, Sekaya felt him pulling a little bit of her essence with him. At first she could handle it easily. But now it was as if she were being forced to hold a rock that seemed light at first, but now was growing increasingly heavy. She saw that the cord had dulled slightly, from its rich golden tone to a pale, sickly yellow.

"Dear One, you are tiring," Stag said.

More pulling, tugging on her soul. Sekaya felt as if her very center was unraveling.

"Yes," she admitted. "Wherever he is going, it is becoming harder for me to follow him."

And suddenly it was as if Chakotay had yanked on her heart. She gasped in pain. "Stag . . . I don't know if I can keep this up much longer. . . ."

Agony blossomed and she screamed.

"Her heart is slowing even further," Kaz said, starting to become alarmed despite Moset's dismissal. "Brain activity—damn it, she's flatlining!"

Sekaya couldn't feel the earth beneath her feet. She was drifting; she, the anchor, suddenly had no anchor of her own. Misery flooded her. She and her brother would be lost, wandering aimlessly, mindlessly, in the world of spirit. They would become like the colonists, mad things who had one foot in each world and a soul in neither.

246

A soft sound penetrated her haze of terror. She knew that sound; sweet, haunting, clear. A flute. She gasped and drew breath into her lungs even as a gentle touch on her hand guided her back into herself.

She opened her eyes. Stag was gone. Instead, a man regarded her with a dark, intent gaze. As she blinked, reorienting herself, he smiled.

"Hello, Sky," said Blue Water Dreamer.

"What did you do?" Moset cried.

"Nothing," said Kaz, as baffled by the sudden development as Moset. They had lost Sekaya for a moment. She had died. But she'd been gone for only an instant. There hadn't been any time to perform any emergency revival procedures before her heart had begun to beat again. It was a stronger heartbeat now, too—slow, yes, but steady. Her brain activity had stabilized as well.

"Well," said Moset, "I guess we just count our blessings, then."

Sekaya dragged her eyes away from Blue Water Dreamer's and saw the cord stretching off into the distance. It was a vibrant gold again, not the pale, almost translucent yellow it had become.

"Thank you," she said.

"You're welcome."

She drank in the sight of him. In a thick voice she said, "I didn't think I'd ever see you again."

He smiled his sweet, soft smile. "I have been in love

247

CHRISTIE GOLDEN

with you all my life, Sky. Of course I would come when
you needed me."

She wanted to ask him so many things. What had really happened to him? Was he real? Could she see him
every time she spirit-walked if she wanted to?

Her heart lifted at that last. There was so much between them that was unfinished. *A whole life,* she
thought, with a stab of pain. *A whole life together,
taken from us by Crell Moset.*

He frowned a little. "I wouldn't do that, Sekaya.
Look at the cord."

She obeyed and saw that the cord was turning a dull
bronze shade.

"Its purity is fading because of your hatred," he said.
"You have to keep your spirit pure, or else you'll taint
the cord that binds you to your brother."

"I can't help it," she said. "I do hate Moset for what
he did to us—to you. I miss you so much. I would give
anything to be with you."

He had been sitting across from her, his legs crossed
in the so-called "Indian style." Now he rose and settled
down beside her.

"Then be with me," he said. He opened his arms and
she leaned into him, feeling the cord brighten and
strengthen as their lips met.

Pure.

There had been a moment of terror, but it had faded
quickly, and now Chakotay soared in delight. He raced

248

through the cosmos, no longer a fragile physical being but a mighty thing of spirit, like Black Jaguar who flew beside him. He had always loved the colors of space; now it was as if he saw them with fresh eyes, and their beauty was almost too much to bear.

"This is what it means to be like us," said a voice beside him. After what had happened to him thus far, Chakotay was not surprised to see that Black Jaguar had disappeared. Soaring beside him now was a Sky Spirit alien, a sweet smile on his chalky white face.

"The colonists were like you," Chakotay said, "but they didn't know *how* to be like you."

"Well said," the Sky Spirit replied. "And even now you are not able to grasp all of what it means. We possess tremendous mental powers, developed and honed through millennia. We have telekinesis, telepathy. We can control the weather, change matter at will, and we have an awareness of everything that's happening over vast distances."

The alien flipped around and placed his hand on Chakotay's chest. "The genetic code is the pathway to accessing these powers. Your sister understands. The mutated colonists have some of these powers, but they have no idea how to control them. They see themselves as monsters, and so monsters they have become. They are lost in this spirit world, as you would be without your sister."

Chakotay looked behind him and saw the golden cord, strong and radiant, trailing behind him.

249

When he turned around, his companion had changed again. This time it was a young man who seemed vaguely familiar. He had light brown hair and large eyes.

"My name," said the young man, "is Wesley Crusher."

"Report," snapped Moset. Barely two minutes had elapsed since Chakotay and Sekaya had been sedated. Kaz felt as if it had been hours.

"No change in Sekaya," Kaz said. "Chakotay's condition is actually improving." He touched a pad. "His immune system is .87 percent stronger than before. Seems like this Sky Spirit stuff is suiting him."

"Any sign of . . . of rejection of the DNA?"

Kaz knew what he meant. "None," the Trill replied. "He's still a man, not a monster."

"Then I'm going to increase the dosage. We need him as powerful as he can possibly be."

"Crusher," said Chakotay, reaching for the name. "That sounds familiar."

The young man smiled. "I'm Jack and Beverly Crusher's son. But what's important now is that I'm studying with a being called the Traveler. My first school, as it were, was your planet."

Now Chakotay knew where he had heard the name. "You probably know my sister, then. Were—were you there when the Cardassians began their experiments?"

Wesley shook his head. "The Traveler and I had gone on to . . . other things by that point. But I learned about the Sky Spirits from your people. The Traveler is similar to them in many ways, so he thought that was a good place for me to start my education. This was a world in which humans had been given a genetic bonding as a gift, and could embrace that gift and become something more. I did it. You are doing it right now."

"Can anyone do this?"

Wesley smiled. "I'm afraid I'm not allowed to tell."

Chakotay returned the smile. "I guess some things just have to remain mysteries."

"I'm curious," Wesley continued. "You've been . . . well . . . I don't mean to be rude, but . . . you've been awfully passive. You've followed where you were led willingly enough, and that's important. But why haven't you tried to test your powers?"

"I didn't know I was supposed to. I thought someone would come and tell me when it was time to . . ."

Wesley looked meaningfully at him.

Chakotay laughed. "So, what do I do?"

"What do you most want to do?"

And Chakotay knew what he wanted to do. There was someone who, he knew, was worried about him. Someone he cared deeply for, someone he wanted to reassure that he was all right, more than all right.

And just that quickly, he was there.

The warmth, deep affection, and worry he experienced flowing from the mind of Admiral Kathryn Janeway was almost overwhelming and humbling in its power. He sensed everything: her concern for him and the colonists, her desire to keep the Federation together, her irritability that she was stuck in a conference and couldn't go do something about the problem herself.

Chakotay chuckled. That was Kathryn, all right. He opened his mind further and there was another presence, physically closer, also deeply concerned. To his surprise, Chakotay realized he was sensing Tom Paris's mind.

Paris had taken the *Flyer* to *Voyager* and had apparently kicked out the actual pilot and taken the helm himself. Because Moset was currently in charge of the colonists—Chakotay was starting to think of them that way, rather than as "creatures" or "monsters," now that he understood the poignancy of their ordeal—the storms were not as bad as the Changeling wanted them to be. Paris was having a tough time getting *Voyager* onto the planet, but he was doing it.

Chakotay, you damn well better be all right, Tom was thinking. *You've just got to be.*

Janeway's thoughts: *I think I'd know if you were dead. Hang on, Chakotay. Hang on, we're coming for you.*

Chakotay realized that this powerful communication was largely one way. He could sense their thoughts, but they could not sense him.

There was one more person he needed to check on— his friend Kaz. He brushed the mind of the Trill and for a moment was bombarded with thoughts—the thoughts of every one of Kaz's hosts. But he focused, and it was easy enough to concentrate and home in on Jarem.

Chakotay and Sekaya seem to be all right, Kaz was

thinking. *I just hope they have time to do whatever they need to do.*

"I've got to let them know I'm okay," Chakotay said to Wesley.

"Then do it. This is all so much easier than you think, Chakotay. You're making it much harder than it has to be."

The young Traveler was right. Chakotay felt the re-assurance, the calmness, and knew that his friends had received it.

"It's time," he said, not knowing how he knew, but knowing that it was urgent.

Wesley smiled. "Good luck, Chakotay. Maybe I'll see you around."

Chakotay closed his eyes. He was ready now; each encounter had given him a gift of love, confidence, or understanding, and he knew he was, finally, mentally prepared to claim his heritage fully. He opened himself to the powers that came with the Sky Spirit DNA. He felt them flooding him, warming him, lending him strength and clarity and a power that came from a pure, strong, sweet source.

He felt himself falling, but knew no fear; he was falling into his body. And when he bolted upright in Crell Moset's lab, seeing the Cardassian and Kaz star-ing at him with open mouths, he realized he had not re-turned from his spirit walk alone.

Beside him on the bed, body taut and alert, was an enormous black jaguar.

Chapter 22

AKOLO TARE HAD STARTED to move toward the conn when the storms first hit. She stumbled and clutched the railing. Tom cursed, but realized if it were him, he'd be doing the exact same thing. He'd want to get close to the conn, close to the pilot navigating the ship.

"Hang on!" he cried, nodding his head in the direction of the chair. She surged forward and grasped the back of his chair. *Probably better this way,* he thought. *If I bash my head against the conn, she'll be able to take over.*

The storms were vicious. Kim had briefly filled him in about the Sky Spirit connection, and Paris had no trouble recalling the storm that had threatened to make them all stains on the back wall. They'd come very close to death that day, everyone on the ship. But at the last minute

254

Chakotay had been able to convince the Sky Spirits that humans were peaceable creatures, that *Voyager* came on a friendly mission, not to terrorize and conquer. That was a legacy of the past, not the present or the future.

But down on the planet were no peaceful aliens thinking they were simply defending themselves. On Loran II was a Changeling who had demonstrated that he was quite capable of cold-blooded murder, and who had no compunctions about using his technology against *Voyager.*

Still, in the back of his mind, Tom thought that the storms weren't quite as bad as he remembered. He was actually able to get through them, which was little short of a miracle. Bad, yes; manning the helm and navigating the vessel at the moment was hardly a walk in the park. But it wasn't impossible.

"Almost there," he called to Kim. "Brace yourselves." And indeed, it was quite likely the bumpiest landing he had ever made. *Voyager* thudded heavily onto the soil, rocking violently as she settled into position. Paris heard a thump beside him and saw that Tare had landed in a heap on the floor. She'd cut her head and blood matted her thick, dark hair.

"You okay?" he asked, reaching down to help her up. Something flashed in her eyes and she recoiled—there was no other word for it—from his touch.

"Yes, sir. Thank you sir, I'm all right." Unsteadily she got to her feet.

"Status report," Paris ordered Campbell.

"Damage reports coming in—there's damage on decks four, eight, and two," Campbell said. "Engineering reports the warp engine is off-line. Twenty-three injuries, four severe. They're transporting to sickbay."

"Activate the Doctor," Kim ordered. "Tell him to prepare to receive injured."

Tom had a brief disconnect. He was about to say, "The Doc doesn't need to be activated anymore," but realized that the new holodoctor was a slim, attractive African male with a gentle bedside manner, not the cranky, arrogant, balding, and beloved Doc he'd gotten to know.

The thought fled before the more pressing need. "Lieutenant, I'm going to lead an away team. You're to assume command of this ship until we get back."

Tom saw in his eyes that Kim wanted to lead the team. He was, after all, chief of security. But Paris outranked him right now, and he wanted Kim right where he was in case something happened out there. Kim, ever the good Starfleet officer, nodded. "Aye, sir," he said.

It didn't take long for the team to assemble in the docking bay. Since Kaylar and Niemann had been part of the original away team, Paris asked them to join him. They'd know the layout of the place the best. Along with Ashton, the third-shift doctor, he figured that would be sufficient.

He briefed them while they checked their phasers and equipment one last time. Tom had requested they all don special raingear and helmets equipped with goggles that provided infrared vision. The storms were

256

still fierce, and their task was going to be hard enough without squinting in the rain. Ashton went a little pale at the mention of a Changeling, but her hands were steady as she checked her medikit.

"Our primary mission is to get Kaz and Chakotay, if he's still alive." *Which you'd better be, you . . .* "It's likely we'll encounter resistance from the creatures. Phasers on stun; remember, these things were once human and hopefully will be again. We're going to try to lock on to human and/or Trill life signs and head straight for them. Failing that, Niemann and Kaylar will take point position and lead us to the settlement where we'll regroup and assess the situation. Any questions?"

They shook their heads.

"Let's go."

The docking bay doors opened to gale-force winds. Tom lowered his head and pushed forward, trying to stay on his feet despite the buffeting and the torrential downpour. He was grateful for the protective gear.

He was even more grateful for it when something loomed up ahead of him. Something big, and red, and moving really, really fast.

Paris fired, and the creature fell to the ground. All around him, his team was emulating him. Still the things kept coming, and Tom started to taste fear in the back of his throat. Between the storms and the horribly mutated colonists attacking them, progress would be slow. How much time did Chakotay have?

* * *

Kaz didn't dare breathe as he stared at the big cat. It graced him with a quick glance, its lambent yellow eyes seeming to see right through him.

Moset, too, stood stock still. Chakotay smiled. He seemed . . . different, somehow, to Kaz.

"Don't worry," Chakotay said. "She's with me." He glanced over at Sekaya, lying still on the bed. "How is she?"

"She's fine," Kaz said. "We've been monitoring her."

"What did you . . . how did you . . ." Moset, ever curious, began. Suddenly the black panther was on its feet, its hackles raised, its ears flattened against its head. A low rumble issued from its throat. It stared directly at the door, and both Kaz and Moset shook off their shock and refocused. Their eyes met and Moset nodded.

"We've worked out a plan," Kaz said, quickly telling Chakotay. Chakotay nodded. He turned to the beast that he had somehow brought back with him and their eyes met. Graciously, the big cat inclined its head. Silent as a shadow, it melted into the darkness behind a jumble of discarded equipment. Kaz and Chakotay lay back down on the beds and closed their eyes.

This has to work, thought Kaz.

Moset was excruciatingly nervous. He liked to operate openly, honestly. His work was never for nefarious purposes, but for the good of all. Now it was all going to hinge on how well he could fool his former friend.

The big cat had heard the approach of Katal before

any of the humanoids. Or maybe it'd sensed it, who knew. Regardless, now Moset himself could hear the sound of footsteps coming down the corridor. He realized his hands were shaking as he filled the hypospray with the medicine that would be their hope; his hands, which had operated on countless thousands—

"Moset!" The Changeling wore the face of Andrew Ellis again. Moset knew the Changeling despised that face, yet he always reverted to it when tired; it took the least energy for him to maintain. "What are you doing? I thought you'd have everything ready by now. I brought some help."

Moset's heart sank as he saw three of the creatures standing at attention behind Ellis. They obeyed *him,* they served *him* . . . they loved *him.* The Cardassian's first thought was worry, that they might get caught in what was about to happen, but now he steeled himself against the wave of paternal affection that washed through him.

They were made to be the Changeling's creatures, not the Cardassian's. Moset would simply have to regard them as casualties of war.

He cleared his throat. "I know it doesn't look like it, but I have been preparing for our departure. First, pick a form and let's stabilize you in case we run afoul of anyone."

Frowning, the Changeling waved the hypospray away. "Get that thing out of my face," he growled. "I need to be able to change, I've got a few more people to talk to." He turned to the creatures. "Start taking equipment to the ship," he told them. Obediently they lumbered to a corner.

Ellis sighed. "Look, I know you hate closing shop like this, but it's necessary. Let's put these three in stasis and . . ."

Moset followed the Changeling's gaze and his innards clenched in horror.

"Why are their restraints undone?" On the alert, the Changeling plucked his phaser from his belt. At the same time the creatures were acting strangely, hooting softly and staring at the corner.

With a cry that really *was* almost sufficiently chilling to freeze blood, the spirit cat leaped from hiding.

Chakotay felt like a toddler learning how to walk. The knowledge of so many things was now encoded in his body. All he had to do, he knew, was understand that code and use it. At the sound of Black Jaguar's cry, he bolted upright. All of a sudden he was bombarded with power akin to his own—power that, he knew, came from beings who, like he, had Sky Spirit DNA.

But this was as far a cry from the uplifting, invigorating, yet calming energy he had experienced on his spirit walk as could be imagined. For a moment Chakotay was paralyzed, gasping like a fish out of water as his mind struggled to make sense of the cloying, dark tendrils of insanity that closed upon him and threatened to drag him down.

This, then, was what it was like to be "gifted" with

Sky Spirit DNA when the receiver had no idea what it was all about. The colonists—for it was indeed they whom Chakotay was sensing—were lost indeed, and their powers were base and primal and all linked with the simplest of needs—survival.

Fight it, Stone Keeper! came the voice of Black Jaguar in his mind, slicing through the haze of terror and confusion like a laser. *Remember what you learned on your spirit walk!*

With an enormous effort Chakotay wrested himself free, at least for the moment, and saw clearly what was going on. Black Jaguar, manifested in this physical world as a physical being, was locked in battle with the three creatures who had once been human. He saw her muscles ripple under her glossy black pelt, saw her trying to fight and yet not wound, for she knew, as he knew, that they were not the real enemy, but tragic beings lost to darkness, perhaps forever. All four combatants had an aura about them that was quite clearly visible to him. Black Jaguar's was a rich indigo hue, vibrant and clean. All three of the colonists emitted auras that were various shades of sickly yellow and muddy brown, shot through with angry red.

I can see their souls, Chakotay thought with a rush of wonder.

Slowly, as if he were moving through water, he turned and saw Moset dive for the Changeling, frantically trying to press a hypospray to Ellis's throat. Chakotay knew that if Moset were successful, the Changeling would be locked for a time in true human form. And if he was human, he could be hurt. Moset's aura was a color that ranged from a healthy, forest green to a putrid, rotting hue. Even the Changeling had one—inky black with hints of rust.

Moset has done evil things, but he isn't an evil person. But the Changeling is almost lost. Chakotay was surprised how much this mattered to him.

Snarling, the Changeling blocked Moset's clumsy attack with ease. He shoved the Cardassian back forcefully. Moset stumbled and his head struck the side of one of the beds. At once his aura shifted hues. *Unconscious, not dead,* Chakotay thought, somehow knowing that if Moset had been killed, the aura would have vanished.

Out of the corner of his eye he saw Sekaya lying on the bed, not moving, but enveloped in a warm golden color that told him she was all right. Kaz, his aura shifting from blue-green to rust-orange and back, lunged for Ellis, wielding Moset's chair. But the Changeling saw the Trill coming and darted out of the way in time. Kaz slammed into the table. Vials and other pieces of equipment went crashing to the floor.

I've got to help them! Chakotay thought. He tried to summon the powers he knew lay within him. But there were so many clamoring to be used . . . and how did one grasp them . . . ?

Yes. This was how he was to use it. Just when he thought he'd captured one of the slippery things, the Changeling cried out, "To her!"

Like creatures of a single mind, which in a sense they were, the colonists abandoned their attack on Black Jaguar and raced toward Sekaya.

"No!" screamed Chakotay, reaching out with his powers in shock and desperation. He was too slow, too late to stop them. The mental blast he fired sent the huge creatures flying through the air, but not before one of them had leaped onto Sekaya's bed and slashed her body with both powerful forepaws.

The lovely golden aura that had swaddled his sister disappeared. Chakotay stared at the grisly sight of several gaping wounds across Sekaya's torso.

"Sekaya!" he cried. He jolted stubborn, sluggish limbs into action, tried to move toward her. Surely there was something he could do. But before he could reach her, Arak Katal was upon him.

And it truly was Katal now, the familiar face from years past filled with hatred and a cruel amusement. Alerted by his heightened senses, Chakotay turned in time to meet the threat, roaring in fury. But even as Chakotay closed his hands over the throat of someone he had called "friend," he realized his error.

Katal wasn't a full Changeling with all its attendant abilities, but he wasn't a human, either. Chakotay couldn't hurt him, hard as he tried.

Only your thoughts and your spirit can cripple him. Black Jaguar lurked in the doorway, tail lashing, her eyes fastened on Chakotay. *Yours, and that of those he has so cruelly abused.*

263

It was hard to detach from the heat of grief and fury; hard to cease trying to physically subdue his enemy and instead back off and try another tactic. But it was the only option Chakotay had.

Still holding on to Katal, as much to protect himself, Kaz, and the still-unconscious Moset as anything, Chakotay gathered his thoughts. He leaped backward and issued a mental command. It was obeyed. Every item in the place that was not securely fastened down was lifted and brought crashing down on Katal. Cursing, the Changeling went down under the barrage of chairs, equipment, tools, and cabinets.

But it would not hold him for long. Chakotay retreated into himself, ignoring the part of him that wanted to panic, wanted to somehow avenge the murder of his sister. He reached out instead to the chaotic minds and spirits of the colonists.

This time he knew what to expect, and he walked inside their minds with no fear, but with a deep compassion. In the swirl of emotions and thoughts given shape and color, he stretched out his thoughts and sent a message of calm.

It's all right. It's all right. Remember who you were, who you still are. See yourselves as you once were. This isn't a curse, it's a gift, but it's one you can refuse if you don't want it.

The swirls shifted hue. Curiosity, hope. Chakotay continued to urge them on. He changed his focus from Katal, trying to dig himself out as Kaz kept pummeling him with broken pieces of equipment, to the creatures who now stared raptly at him.

"Attack them!" cried Katal. The creatures ignored him. They were engrossed by Chakotay's thoughts, by the bright possibility he dangled before them.

"Chakotay, look out!" Kaz's voice pierced Chakotay's deep state. He turned, again feeling as if he were moving through water, and saw that Katal had managed to find his phaser. His teeth were bared in a grimace of pure hatred. He lifted the phaser and fired.

Everything slowed down. He saw Katal's finger tighten, saw the yellow beam of phaser fire crawl from the opening. It crept toward him. Sudden, swift knowledge filled Chakotay. He didn't have to obey the laws of the physical world if he didn't want to. This phaser blast, this lethal stream of energy—it was nothing to him. Time and matter were his friends; they would obey his whims now. Chakotay did not move out of the way of the blast. Instead, he understood, really understood, that the only way this would harm him would be if he let it. He stood and watched as the phaser blast reached his chest, passed harmlessly through him, and blasted a hole in the wall on the other side.

Kaz now moved to grab Katal's hand, and Chakotay shook his head dazedly. He suddenly felt terribly weak. The colonist's thoughts had changed from tentative queries to a bombardment. Without Sekaya to keep him anchored, he was beginning to succumb to the burden of Sky Spirit DNA as the colonists had done.

He fell hard to his knees. If a second before he had been master of matter and time, now he was their slave; he was no longer outside the boundaries of physics. Through suddenly blurred vision he saw Katal strike Kaz, hard. The doctor fell to the floor as Katal scrambled up from the pile of debris and fled. Even as Black Jaguar leaped to block his path, she disappeared. He couldn't focus enough to keep her here, Chakotay realized.

This is your enemy, Chakotay thought to the colonists even as his eyes closed. *The Changeling ordered these things done to you. Do what you will with him.* The last thing he saw was the creatures that Katal had ordered brought into being running down the corridor, eager to exact revenge.

How could it all have crumbled to pieces like this?

The Changeling ran with all his might, cursing his limited abilities that now, perhaps, would never evolve. If he could turn into a bird, or a long-legged *jatham,* he might escape. But the things he had ordered Moset to make, the things that he had thought would be his new army, were turning on him, and they were fast.

He heard their gibbering howls. They were getting closer. Panic closed in on him, lending him fresh speed. The exit was just up ahead, through that door—

He slammed his shoulder into the door, bursting through. No time to close and lock it behind him, only time to run across the grassy field into the small vessel, leap into it—

The door shut behind him as they tumbled out of the earth, red-brown furry things that were all teeth and claws and hatred. Frantically the Changeling punched in the commands as they threw their hairy bodies against the unyielding metal. He glanced up to see one of them plastered to the viewscreen, clawing futilely, trying to rip his face off through the transparent barrier.

He was safe, and he allowed himself a grin. "Hang on, if you like!" he shouted at the creature. "Going to be quite the ride!"

Chapter 23

FOR THE SECOND TIME in three hours, Kaz awoke to pain. Hissing, he sat up and gingerly touched the knot on his head. His hand came away covered with blood, but he knew he was all right for the time being.

Beside him on the debris-littered floor of the lab lay Chakotay. Kaz glanced around for a medical tricorder. There was none to be found; everything in the lab had been smashed. He felt for a pulse; solid and strong. No immediate injuries. With luck, Chakotay would recover.

He looked around for Moset, who had fallen in the first few moments of the fight. But at some point the Cardassian had obviously recovered and fled.

Go after him, Gradak urged. And Kaz wanted to, badly. But his first duty was to his patients. He suddenly remembered something that had happened in the heat of the fray and stumbled to his feet.

"Oh, Sekaya . . ." Kaz said softly.

Sekaya lay on the bed, her eyes still shut. Several enormous slashes lacerated her abdomen. She had never regained consciousness.

Sekaya frowned, vague discontent creeping into her awareness even as she leaned against the warmth of Blue Water Dreamer.

"Something's wrong," she said, although it still felt as though everything was perfect with the universe. Reluctantly she lifted her head and saw with a shock that the cord had disappeared.

She bolted upright, crying, "Chakotay!"

Blue Water Dreamer's hand on her shoulder tried to soothe her. "He is fine," her beloved said. "Chakotay has returned to his body. He will be tired, but he will be all right."

Sekaya turned to stare at him, and then dawning realization swept over her. "If we are no longer connected by the cord," she said slowly, "and he's all right, . . . that means that I'm . . ."

"Dead, as you understand the word," said Blue Water Dreamer with infinite tenderness. He stroked her cheek. "That's why I came for you. I wanted to be the one to be with you. So that you wouldn't be afraid."

"I'm not afraid," Sekaya replied, and realized with

269

mild surprise that she spoke the truth. But there was a strange resistance.

He rose and extended a hand to help her up. "Look there," he said, pointing to the north. "See the pine forest? That's the barrier, according to the traditions of the Lakota. That's the Land North Beyond the Pines."

He turned to her and his heart was in his eyes. She felt herself tremble. "Come with me, Sekaya, my Sky. Walk along the Star Road with me. You'll still be able to visit Chakotay from time to time, when he needs you. Every time he looks at the stars, he'll see those of us walking the Star Road."

It sounded so beautiful, so perfect. And yet, she hesitated. Seeing her doubt, Blue Water Dreamer said quietly, "I came to you first in your spirit walk, when you wanted to know if you should reveal everything to Chakotay. I came to you a second time in your dream, where you relived our first kiss." He ran his fingers through her hair. "And now I come to you a third time. Among our people, if one who has passed into the Land North Beyond the Pines appears three times to someone still living, that person must come back with him."

Again Sekaya looked toward the waiting Land, and knew what she needed to do.

"I am not of your tribe, Blue Water Dreamer," she said.

He laughed softly, so close that his breath stirred her hair. "That ever was the problem between us, Sky."

She let him fold her close, hugging him in return.

"When the true time comes . . . will you come for me?"

"Of course I will, if you want me to."

Sekaya closed her eyes and inhaled the scent of him. "Then I will never be afraid to die."

At last he let her go and stepped back. Spreading his fingers, he gently placed them on her belly.

"Here is where the wound is," Blue Water Dreamer said. "I will hold it so that you suffer no more harm, until your doctor can heal you himself."

Sorrowfully Kaz went to the body of the beautiful young woman. He pressed his fingers to her throat, confirming what his eyes told him: There was no heartbeat. Sekaya was dead.

As he regarded the body, something seemed . . . off about it. When he realized what it was, he was utterly confused. The blood should have spilled all over the place. Instead, it never seemed to have flowed at all. Again he leaned beside Sekaya and touched the blood; it was warm and wet, but somehow it wasn't flowing—

As if time were standing still.

No, more like . . . somehow, Sekaya was *outside* of time.

His scientific brain raged against what he beheld, but he shoved the complete impossibility of it all aside. He had a chance to save Sekaya, and it didn't matter one damn bit if he understood how.

He touched his combadge.

* * *

The away team's experience had taken on the quality of a nightmare. Firing at the creatures who kept charging, slogging through mud, turning shoulders to the winds, and pushing steadily forward. And forward to where? The storms continued to wreak havoc with their sensors. At one point Paris waved to Kaylar, and she nodded, understanding his command. She turned and began to lead them to the settlement.

All of a sudden, as if someone had touched a control pad, the brutal storms stopped.

Tom removed his helmet just in time to see the clouds turn from blackish gray to white and fluffy, and then zip away altogether. A bright, cheerful sun now beamed down on them from a blue sky.

"What just happened?" Niemann said, voicing the question everyone was thinking. The rest of them began to remove their helmets.

And then Tom was suddenly hit with a very strong sensation that everything was going to be all right. It was as if someone had touched his brain and said so in as many words. He *knew* it in his bones, knew past all logic and understanding. The joy that washed through him was so powerful he stumbled. Grinning like an idiot, he looked around at his team.

"It's going to be okay," he said as they stared at him. "Everything is going to be fine."

At that moment his combadge chirped.

"Kaz to *Voyager* and any away teams. Requesting emergency medical beam out *now*."

*   *   *

Kim met them in sickbay. "What happened? Are they okay?"

Kaz threw him a brief glance. "I don't know and I can't talk. Out of my sickbay now."

Kim seemed a bit taken aback, but Paris nodded. "Come on, Harry," he said. "Let's give the doctors some room."

As they went to the bridge, Tom filled Harry in. "I didn't get a lot out of Kaz, he wants to operate immediately, of course. But I did get a few things. You remember that hologram of a Cardassian scientist the Doc created when B'Elanna was attached to that thing?"

"The mass murderer?"

"Crell Moset. The Butcher of Bajor, they called him," Tom affirmed. "Turns out he was working with the Changeling. Kaz didn't give me all the details, but once we learn everything, it's going to be a hell of a story."

"Wow," said Kim. "But I notice that you haven't come back with a shape-shifter."

"Yeah," Tom said. "He was able to escape. Had a cloaked ship and apparently made it out just in time— his own creations were hard on his heels, Kaz said."

"That's too bad," Harry said. "He's not someone I want running around loose in this quadrant."

"Well, at least he's not our problem anymore. Moset escaped as well—I guess they left together. Kaz said there are some people still in stasis down there. I'll take a team and get them back."

"What about the colonists?"

"We're to beam them up and hold them until the think tank can figure out how to change them back."

"You think they can?"

Tom shrugged. "They've got Seven and the Doctor working on it. What do you think?"

For the first time in a long while, Harry Kim laughed.

Kaz was glad that they were gone, not just because he certainly didn't need any distractions right now, but because he wasn't sure he wanted them to see what he saw.

"Computer, activate EMH," he snapped as he ran his hands under sanitizing light and gathered his tools.

"Please state the nature of the medical emergency," said the slim, elegant holodoctor.

"Check him out, then assist me in surgery," Kaz told him. The hologram tended swiftly and efficiently to Chakotay while Kaz frantically worked on Sekaya.

It was the strangest surgery he had performed in his entire life. Sekaya seemed to be frozen in time, the damage that ought to have inevitably killed her halted so that he could repair it before the body could react. He thought he'd have one hell of a paper to present on the power of mind over body when this was all done.

He didn't know how long . . . whatever was happening would continue to happen, so he worked quickly. At one point the EMH stepped quietly in to assist him.

At last they were done. Kaz stepped back and then wondered what he should do next. He glanced over at Chakotay.

"How's he doing?" Kaz asked the EMH.

"Better than well," said the hologram in a puzzled tone of voice. "He's in perfect health. Better than he was when you performed his physical. I can't explain it, Doctor."

"Don't try," Kaz said, "just accept."

Following a hunch, he turned back to Sekaya and leaned down to whisper in her ear.

"Sekaya," he said softly, "I don't know if you can hear me, but it's all right now. You're healed. Your body's whole, it's safe to return to it. You can let go now."

Nothing. Then, suddenly, Sekaya's chest heaved as she took in air. Her pulse began to beat and her brain waves to register again. Quickly Kaz glanced at her vital signs and shook his head. Just like her brother, Sekaya was completely healthy.

"Kim to Kaz."

"Go ahead."

"Paris has returned to the planet and has prepared the stasis chambers for transport."

"Excellent. Beam them directly here. I'll revive them once we've finished surgery."

The EMH looked at him quizzically, but Kaz shook his head and put his finger to his lips. "When will we be leaving Loran II?" Kaz asked.

"I'll send an away team down in the morning to conduct a final investigation on Moset's lab. We'll have to see if we can find anything useful, anything that might help the colonists."

"Good idea," said Kaz. "It's late and we've all been through a lot."

"My thoughts exactly. How is the surgery coming?"

"Well, but I need to get back to it."

"Of course. Kim out."

"Doctor, why did you lie to Lieutenant Kim?" the EMH asked.

"Long story," Kaz said, realizing he had already chosen his path. He had fulfilled his obligations. Everyone in his charge was safe now. It was time to fulfill another obligation, one from years past.

"I'm going to keep you activated in case anything goes wrong," he told the EMH. "There will be four stasis chambers materializing here momentarily. Everyone will be all right until I return."

"Where are you going, Doctor?" the EMH inquired.

Over his shoulder Kaz replied, "To tie up some loose ends."

Kaz sat alone in the dark, in the wreckage of the laboratory. He was exhausted, but he was not about to let physical weariness stand in the way of what he was planning to do.

The driving need to get Chakotay and Sekaya proper medical attention had outstripped all others, but now that need had been met. Both were safe. He could return before the away team beamed down in the morning, and do what he had come to do.

Moset wasn't gone, and Kaz knew it.

It was easy for Paris to leap to the conclusion that the two former allies had escaped together, and Kaz had opted not to disabuse the lieutenant commander of the notion. The Changeling—Katal—might have had the good luck to evade the wrath of his own creations and flee in a cloaked vessel, but Moset would hardly be welcome on that ship after turning on his partner. And Moset would want to get to the creatures before *Voyager* did, in order to continue his work.

Kaz was surprised at how calm he was. His heart wasn't racing, his palms weren't wet; he was focused and intent.

He stayed that way for a long time, the phaser that Katal had dropped held in his hand. How long, he didn't know; time had no meaning here. Only revenge had meaning.

He heard the sound of footsteps coming down the hall; slow, careful. Cautious. Wary of a trap.

Kaz closed his eyes and saw himself by the ocean again.

"So here we are," Gradak said.

"Yes," Jarem Kaz replied. "Here we are."

"Why are you doing this?"

Jarem regarded Gradak evenly. "Because you lost

your wife to Moset, and your people to Katal. And neither of them is going to pay the price they should."

"You sure about this?"

Jarem nodded. "I've never been more certain about anything. This is for you to do."

Kaz's eyes snapped open. And Gradak Kaz saw out of them.

A faint light, bobbing in the darkness. The crunching sounds of glass under feet. The light shone about, narrowly missing the corner in which Gradak Kaz crouched, ready to spring.

A sigh. "What a mess. Lights," called Crell Moset.

Kaz leaped. It was pathetically easy, almost an anticlimax after the years of dreaming of this, both as a living being and as a collection of memories contained in a symbiont. Moset was a scientist, not trained in combat, and he went down far too easily for the moment to be satisfying.

"Dr. Kaz," he gasped.

"Not Doctor," Gradak hissed, his face within a centimeter of the alarmed Cardassian's. He pressed the coolness of the phaser to Moset's throat. "Gradak Kaz."

"I—I'm sorry, I don't recognize that name." The Butcher's voice had crawled higher in fear. It was sweet to hear.

"Of course you don't," drawled Gradak. "Nor would you know the name Vallia Kaz. Bajoran. Beautiful. Dead."

"Oh, dear," said Moset.

"Yes, now you're starting to understand," Gradak said. He ran the muzzle of the phaser along the curves of the Butcher's brow ridges, along the thick tendons that stood out from his neck. Almost a lover's touch. And indeed, there was rapture and delight for Kaz in the gesture. He was enjoying this with a savage pleasure that thrilled him.

"You experimented on Vallia, and killed her. You killed hundreds. There's a reason you were dubbed the Butcher of Bajor."

"It was necessary for my research," Moset began. "Research that would benefit millions."

Gradak uttered a blistering oath and shoved the phaser under Moset's chin and tightened his finger. Moset whimpered—actually whimpered—like an animal.

"The thing that makes this frustrating," said Kaz in an almost conversational tone, "is that you really believe that. You don't exult in your evil. You hang on to this ludicrous notion that somehow what you did was all right. That the end truly justified the means. That finding a cure for a disease made it all right to murder hundreds in the attempt. That turning innocent people into monsters and foisting powers onto them that they couldn't possibly handle was a good thing. You wanted your own little group of sycophants, didn't you?"

"No! I wanted to show that we can change, can evolve—"

"You named the littlest one after your father, Moset. The most malleable, the most impressionable, the easiest to teach to love you. What do you think that means?"

"I—I—"

"You're not stupid, I'll give you that, but you are blind. Can't you see? You can't change how history will judge you!" He was screaming now, spittle flying off his lips to splatter in Moset's face. "You can't make it all right! But on some level you know what you've done, and that's why you're so hungry for acceptance and approval. You know you've committed atrocities and you want to atone, but you won't really let yourself see it. So around and around you go, Moset, like a dog chasing its tail, craving a pat on the head, but until you can really comprehend what you've done you can't do anything but go in circles."

Something flickered in Moset's eyes, something haunted and unspeakably sad. Elation shuddered through Kaz.

"I really was trying to save lives," Moset whispered. Suddenly his face crumpled and he began to sob. "I'm a healer . . . I'm not a butcher . . . I want to make things better for everyone. . . ."

Kaz pressed the phaser in more firmly and tightened the trigger.

"Do it," gasped Moset, tears streaming from his eyes down into his ears. "I don't want to look inside any- more . . . I don't want to see this. . . ."

Jarem Kaz braced for the inevitable. He had known what he was doing when he surrendered the Kaz body

280

to Gradak; had known that the man was out for re-
venge—Moset's life for Vallia's. That Jarem would
have to live with the consequences. He'd accepted that,
and waited for the sound of phaser fire.

It didn't come.

Gradak Kaz spat in Moset's face and rocked back on
his heels, still keeping the phaser trained on the Cardassian. Moset blinked and tried to focus.

"You're—you're not going to kill me?" he whispered.

Grinning, Kaz shook his head. "I came for revenge,"
he said, "and I got it. I held up a mirror and you finally
caught a glimpse of the monster that you are. And now
you're going to get to live with that, Crell Moset. No,
I'm not going to kill you in cold blood. That would
make me like you, and there's nothing I can think of
that would dishonor my wife's memory more than that."

Suddenly frantic, Moset made a grab for the phaser.
"No, please—"

Kaz fired and Moset collapsed, unconscious. Gradak
had never set the phaser to kill, only to stun.

Take the body back, boy, Gradak told a shocked
Jarem Kaz. *I've done what I wanted to do.*

You didn't kill him. You never intended to kill him.

I did something better, and Gradak's joy was fierce. *I*
broke him.

Chapter 24

B'ELANNA COULDN'T SLEEP. Her dreams were painted in good Klingon shades of red and black, fraught with the sounds of shouting and the clash of *bat'leths*. She awoke feeling exhausted, as if she had no sleep at all.

She had just reached for Miral, who was squalling her hunger to the world, when a slight movement caught her eye.

Someone had slipped a piece of parchment under her door.

Moving quickly, cradling her daughter in one arm, B'Elanna leaped from the skins on the floor and tugged the heavy door open. She glanced left, then right. Nothing, not even the sound of echoing footsteps. Frowning, she closed the door and picked up the paper, awkwardly opening it with one hand.

She went cold as she read the words.

You and the Kuvah'Magh *are in danger.*

That was all; no sense of where the danger might lurk, what form it might take. *How very cryptic,* she thought, focusing on her annoyance in an attempt to diminish the fear that rushed through her.

She thought about contacting Tom, but decided against it. This was Klingon business, taking place on a Klingon world. She would get to the bottom of this alone, and as she angrily crumpled the paper and held her daughter protectively to her breast, she made a vow:

"No one will hurt you, Miral Paris. I will keep you safe. By the human and Klingon blood that flows through both our veins, by the love of the man who is father and husband, by every ounce of strength I have in my body—*I will keep you safe!*"

Sekaya opened her eyes to see Jarem Kaz smiling down at her. "Welcome back," he said. "Looks like you had quite the journey." He tapped his combadge. "Kaz to Chakotay. Someone's awake and would like to see you."

"On my way," Chakotay replied.

Memories of her spirit walk flooded back to Sekaya. She reached for her stomach, but Kaz caught her wrist gently.

"It's healed, but you shouldn't touch it right now. Let your body recover a bit."

"What happened?"

Kaz filled her in on the fight and the injury she received. "You should have died, Sekaya."

Though she was still drained, her lips curved in a smile. "You sound disappointed."

"No doctor is disappointed when a patient that should have been a corpse is alive and well," he replied, "but we do get puzzled when it goes against everything we know to be true."

Sekaya thought of Blue Water Dreamer. She would see him again one day, she knew; he kept his promises. But she also knew that she was willing to wait for that ultimate meeting.

"It's a long story," she said. "Maybe later."

Chakotay strode swiftly into sickbay and reached for her hand. "Well, hey there," he said.

"I'll be in my office if you need me," Kaz said.

The two siblings nodded, but their eyes were for each other.

"You were amazing," Chakotay said.

"No, it is you who are amazing," Sekaya said. "Telepathy, telekinesis, phasing in and out of time— can you still do it?"

He shook his head. "Even I, prepared as I was, couldn't hold it without you supporting me. It's going to be some time before humans can safely handle that kind of mental power."

"So they all faded? Your abilities?"

He hesitated. "Well, there is one thing. I don't need

to use the *akoonah* to spirit-walk anymore. I can just close my eyes and I'm there."

"Maybe the rest will come back to you. When you're ready for it."

He shrugged. "Right now I don't care about Sky Spirit powers. I'm just glad that my sister and I are all right."

"Kaz said you brought back Black Jaguar. How did that happen?"

"I'm not sure, but I think that part of my powers permitted me to manifest help. She exists in the spirit world, in my mind. I wanted Her there with me, physically, and She came."

"What about Moset and Katal?"

"We've got Moset. He's in the brig right now. Something happened to him—he's a wreck. Astall is trying to talk to him, but he's just babbling incoherently and crying."

Sekaya felt shamefully pleased. "I know it's not kind, but I'm glad. He killed so many, Chakotay, on Bajor, on our world, on Betazed. He should suffer for it." She smiled a little. "But I understand Astall. She tries to see the good in everyone." She paused. "You said you got Moset. What about Katal?"

Chakotay grimaced. "Unfortunately, he escaped. We think he had a cloaked vessel, as we detected nothing. We've transported the colonists aboard *Voyager*, and my friends Seven and the Doctor already have some ideas for how to help them." He hesitated. "I was able to reach them, Sekky. I was able to touch their minds, to remind them that they're human. They can't communicate verbally, and of course I don't have the ability anymore to understand them mentally, but they seem . . . different. More rational."

Sekaya's flesh erupted in goose bumps. "Then they're halfway home," she said softly. "Once they begin to see themselves as people again, most of the hard work will be done. It will just be a question of physically disentangling the DNA."

Chakotay laughed a little. "Yes, just that," he said.

She punched him playfully, but weakly. "You know what I mean."

He sobered. "Yes," he said, "I do know." He bent and kissed her forehead, on the tattoo that they both wore. "Get some rest. Everything is all right now.

As she drifted into slumber, Sekaya heard a gentle voice saying, *Yes, everything is all right now.*

Marius Fortier stared at the large, red-furred creatures who had once been his friends and family. Tears filled his eyes. "May I . . . can I have some privacy?" he asked of the security guard.

"Certainly," the guard said quickly. "I'll be right outside."

The animals behind the forcefield had become aware of his presence. They turned to look at him steadily. Marius's skin prickled when he saw intelligence in their black eyes. They were no longer monsters; they were people, trapped in this form.

"We'll get you back," he said softly. "I don't know how, but we'll get you back. I swear."

One of them lumbered forward, stopping just shy of the forcefield. It looked over at the controls, and then back at Marius. Knowing he shouldn't be doing this, but also knowing at a deep level that it was all right, Fortier lowered the forcefield.

Slowly the big creature stepped forward. Clinging to it was a smaller one, a younger one.

"Guillaume?" Marius whispered. "Paul?"

They nodded, and reached to embrace him. Marius Fortier began to weep as he held his brother, who shuddered and clung tightly to him. He couldn't understand Guillaume's thoughts, but the feelings that washed over Marius were clear: Guillaume was in torment, and had no desire to return to the place where such atrocities had been performed.

"I understand, my brother," Marius murmured, awed and humbled that he did. "We will make you whole, and then we will make a new beginning."

Two weeks later the old friends were back in Sandrine's on a quiet Thursday evening, shooting pool, downing drinks, and soaking up the atmosphere. Janeway couldn't help but reflect how much had changed since she was last here with Kaz and Chakotay. Then they had been discussing Chakotay's first mission as captain, the upcoming conference, and what a shame it was that Tom Paris couldn't have been first officer.

Now, while the bar itself was almost exactly the same, and the drinks in their hands were similar, and Janeway continued to beat the pants off of everyone at pool, nearly everything else had been turned on its ear.

"I heard from Seven and the Doctor today," Janeway said. "The progress they are making with the colonists is extraordinary. The documentation you retrieved from Moset's lab was key, as was Sekaya's willingness to work with them. She's a remarkable woman, Chakotay. I'm sorry I didn't get a chance to meet her."

The ball obediently went into the side pocket.

"You'll get a chance one day," Chakotay said. "We're definitely going to be better about staying in touch."

"Will she still be working with the colonists?"

"Yes, for a time. Since Fortier has decided that they won't be returning to Loran II, Sekaya will stay with them until they select a new site."

"Understandable. The Federation will help them find another world. They can make a fresh start." Janeway called her shot, then sank the ball. "How are you doing, Jarem?"

"Counselor Astall has pronounced me fit for duty, and my thoughts are my own again," Kaz replied. "Gradak finally seems to be appeased with Moset's capture and breakdown."

Janeway shot him a penetrating look. Kaz had acted on his own initiative in transporting down to Loran II and taking Moset prisoner by himself. Moset had displayed no signs of rough treatment, and heaven knew that he'd piled up enough dark deeds to finally collapse under the weight of them, but something about the doctor's explanation didn't add up. Still, a mass murderer was in custody, Kaz was himself again, and the colonists were going to be all right. Janeway decided not to probe further.

"I spoke with Deirdre Ellis today," Chakotay said rather solemnly. Janeway paused to regard him.

"How did that go?"

"As well as could be expected. They divorced several years ago. She said that although she was shocked to learn that Ellis had been impersonated by a Changeling all these years, she wasn't actually surprised. Said he had returned from a mission drastically changed. Not like himself at all. She told me that she felt he had died a long time ago but it was only now that she could really mourn him."

"I suppose we should have caught on, all of us, long before," said Kaz. "That whole cookie-dough bit was just too over the top."

"Actually," Chakotay said, smiling again, "the real Ellis *did* love to eat raw cookie dough. Cake batter, too. Deirdre said Andy was a stickler for the rules—that was what the Changeling latched on to—but he was a loving husband and father and a lot of fun."

"Andy, huh?" mused Kaz. "I like that nickname a lot better than Priggy. Wish we'd known the real Ellis."

"We don't have to have known him to grieve him," Janeway said quietly. For a moment they were all

289

silent. Janeway moved to the other side of the table, lined up the shot, sank the ball, and heard Tom Paris, new first officer aboard the *U.S.S. Voyager,* sigh heavily. Smothering a grin and grateful for the change of topic, she asked, "How did B'Elanna take the good news?"

"She was very happy for me. Told me to keep an eye on Vorik for her." He hesitated. "She seemed a little distracted, though."

"See what you've done, Tom?" Janeway teased. "You've set her off on that whole *Kuvah'Magh* path. There'll be no stopping her now."

"It's going to be great to serve with you again, Tom," Chakotay said, clapping Tom on the shoulder.

Paris grinned. "Likewise," he said. "Somebody's got to keep you guys in line."

Sandrine stepped up beside Janeway. "Pardon, Madame Admiral," she said, "but there is a message for you. Would you like to receive it, or shall I say that you are far too busy to be interrupted?"

"Don't tell me you told Starfleet where you were tonight," Chakotay chastised.

"Actually, no, I didn't, and I'm wondering who had the tenacity to track me down. Apparently, Starfleet simply cannot function for an evening without me." Janeway sighed and handed the cue to Chakotay. "I'd better take it," she said. "I'll make it quick. Play nice, gentlemen."

She stepped into a private room. As the door closed, the sound of singing and laughter from the bar disappeared. Admiral Montgomery's craggy face appeared on the viewscreen.

"Well, hello, Ken," Janeway said. "I might have known you'd be the one to hunt me down on my evening off. If you wanted to come play pool with us, all you had to do was ask."

"I wish it were about pool, Janeway. And you know I'd normally let you be. But I thought you'd want to take this one." He hesitated. "It's Amar Kol. Kerovi is withdrawing from the Federation."

"Damn. I had so hoped . . . you were right, I do want to take it. Put her through." Janeway felt a pang as Merin Kol's pleasant face appeared on the viewscreen.

"Amar Kol," she said. "From what I understand, this is perhaps the last time we will talk."

"Officially, yes," said Kol. In a voice laced with regret, she added, "Most likely unofficially as well, I'm afraid. Despite my personal fondness for you, Admiral, I cannot in good conscience allow my people to continue to be a part of the Federation."

"We'll miss you," Janeway said. "Kerovi has always been a highly regarded member."

Kol's wide mouth stretched in a sad smile. "This is truly the best thing for us, Admiral. I hope you can respect that decision."

"Of course I respect it, and I respect you. I only wish things had turned out differently."

"As do I. I wanted to say a special thank you for your crew's assistance in safely recovering my friend and adviser, Alamys. I had no idea that he was being imper- sonated by a Changeling for so long. It's a frightening thought. Too bad you weren't able to capture him."

"Indeed," said Janeway. "But at least we're aware of him, and we know that he's only able to impersonate humanoid males. That limits the damage he can do."

Kol shuddered. "I earnestly hope so. Farewell, Ad- miral Janeway. Getting to know you has been one of the few bright spots in a difficult time for my world. The decision wasn't made lightly, as you must know."

"I do know that, Amar. I wish you and Kerovi all the best. I hope your decision is indeed the right one. And don't forget," she added, "you can always rejoin. We'd love to have you back."

"Thank you, Admiral. But that won't be happening."

"Good-bye, Amar."

Janeway tried not to feel a sense of failure as Kol's image was replaced by the Starfleet insignia on the screen. She didn't succeed.

Amar Merin Kol sighed, tossed long red hair, and let it- self change back into the form it was most comfortable with—Andrew Ellis.

Wearing the face of a dead man, the Changeling re- flected that it was an unfortunate thing that Moset had turned out to be so untrustworthy.

The Cardassian's research was really starting to get somewhere.

About the Author

Award-winning author CHRISTIE GOLDEN has written twenty-four novels and sixteen short stories in the fields of science fiction, fantasy, and horror.

She is best known for her tie-in work, although she has written several original novels. Among her credits are the first book in the *Ravenloft* line, *Vampire of the Mists;* a *Star Trek* Original Series hardcover, *The Last Roundup;* several *Voyager* novels, including the recent bestselling relaunch of the series, *Homecoming* and *The Farther Shore;* and short stories for *Buffy the Vampire Slayer* and *Angel* anthologies. Sales were so good for *Homecoming* and *The Farther Shore* that they went back for a second printing within six weeks of *Homecoming*'s publication.

In 1999 Golden's novel *A.D. 999,* written under the pen name of Jadrien Bell, won the Colorado Author's League Top Hand Award for Best Genre Novel. Golden has just launched a brand-new fantasy series entitled *The Final Dance* through LUNA Books, a major new fantasy imprint. The first book in the series is entitled *On Fire's Wings* and was published in trade paperback in July of 2004. Look for the second in the series, *In Stone's Clasp,* in 2005.

Golden invites readers to visit her Web site at www.christiegolden.com.